Murder at the Con

A Jackson Winters Novel

By Ron Francis

Acknowledgements

I'd like to thank God for giving me the time and ability to write this book. I would also like to thank my family for their encouragement and my incredible beta readers for their assistance. Finally, I would like to thank Mike Brennan of Mike Brennan Design for an awesome cover.

Chapter 1

Alone in a hotel room, he sat on his bed. Even though the convention was paying for his lodgings, he still felt somehow ripped off. *Four hundred dollars a night doesn't get you much anymore*, he thought bitterly as he stared at the mahogany bureau. On the right side of the dresser sat a small lamp, and perched on the left, closer to the door, stood a large flat screen television.

Outside, the gray sky cast a dull almost lifeless hue, like a fisherman's net, over the Manhattan skyline. Building after cement building ran together becoming an indistinguishable mass of glass and concrete. He had always hated coming to this city, and he hated it even more now. Forcing himself up, he plodded over to the window and took one more disdainful look at the city below before closing the curtains. An alert popped up on his phone drawing his attention. Finding the on switch for the lamp, he sat at the dark mahogany desk to dig through his bag for his glasses. The message brought ill tidings, and his mood was further darkened as he slumped in his chair. *Not only did he screw me over, now I'll have to see his smug face all weekend*, he mused. The anger boiled up inside him as he thought about this upstart who had now become his nemesis.

"How could he do this to me? Me!" he growled as he began pacing the room. "Who the hell does he think he is? He's going to regret the day he ever met me." Pausing, he threw his arms in the air and said, "Great. Now I'm talking to myself. What's next?"

Passing by the mirror mounted over the center of the dresser, he hardly recognized the person he saw. *I've worked so hard to get to this point. At last, I have fans, money, everything I've always dreamed of, and this no talent hack is going to ruin it all for me.* Sweating with anger, he plucked the TV remote off the bed and hurled it into the mirror, no longer liking what he saw. The cracked reflection seemed far more fitting to his mood.

Right there he vowed not to let that happen. Both his pace and his pulse quickened as he felt tiny rivulets of perspiration rolling down his neck. The striped wallpaper passed in his peripheral vision, thick stripe, thin stripe, thin stripe, over and over, first on the left, then on the right as he continued the angry stalking.

Stopping his trek, he decided to try one more time. *Maybe this can still be salvaged. Maybe things can be worked out.* Calling the number, he waited for the ring, but it went straight to voicemail. Frantically, he tried again then again before realizing he was being ignored. *He's going to find out real soon that it is not a good idea to ignore me.*

"I'm gonna meet with him in the morning whether he wants to or not," he mumbled. His Comic Con routines were well known to all, and if he persisted in his betrayal, he would have to die.

Chapter 2

Jackson Winters strode down Thirty-Fifth Street towards a three-story, window-laden building. The cool air invigorated him as he walked to the rhythm of the streets. Gleaming blue letters labeled the building as MIDTOWN PRECINCT SOUTH, and after being laid up for almost eleven weeks, it was a sight for sore eyes. With a steaming cup of black coffee and file folder in one hand, and a buttered egg bagel and folded up newspaper in the other, he took a moment to catch his breath. Because he left his parking tag home, he couldn't find a spot anywhere near the precinct and had to hurry so he wouldn't be late on his first day back. At least the sun is out, he thought.

As he looked up and down the car-lined block, he watched a car pull out of its spot right in front of him. He could almost smell the exhaust as it merged into the endless stream of cars waiting to leave the busy street. "Just my luck," he mumbled as another car instantly appeared in the vacant space.

A Hispanic woman stepped out of the black Ford Explorer and placed her coffee on the roof as she began to don her jacket. Flashing him a sweet smile, she said, "That was lucky. I never thought I'd get to park so close." Flipping her pony tail over the collar of her blue blazer, she slipped a tan hand through the arm of her jacket, straightened her lapel, and picked her coffee up. Several men gave her curvy body a double take as they entered the building

He would have liked to have given her another once over as well but made sure to hold eye contact as he replied with a hint of mischief crossing his face, "Yeah, I just had to walk two blocks, so don't mind me if I'm a little bitter."

"No hard feelings," she said offering him her hand in a friendly manner.

Looking down at her outstretched hand and glancing at his two full hands, he shrugged. "Hands are kind of full, but no hard feelings."

Batting thick dark eyelashes at him, her lips curled up once again as she said, "Why thank you so much."

Was that flirting or mocking? he wondered. Taking a sip of his coffee, he turned to enter the building. She walked next to him with a bounce in her step and he said, "If I didn't know any better, I'd say you actually look happy to be here."

Stopping in front of the elevator, she leaned towards him and half whispered, "Don't tell anyone, but I've just been transferred here, and I've wanted this position for a long time, so I'm kind of excited." Suspicion colored her dark eyes as she added, "You don't exactly look like someone dreading to be here either."

The door to the elevator opened, and several people spilled out into the lobby. They stepped into the metal box with three other people. A chunky officer pressed the button for the second floor, and as she was reaching out to press the button for the third, Jackson noticed there was no wedding ring on her finger. Allowing himself a moment to ponder that development, he said, "I've been out of action for a while and I'm excited just to be out of the house." After another slurp of his caffeine fix, he added, "I'm Jackson by the way."

The elevator stopped, and the three passengers stepped out only to be replaced by four more. They were now standing a little closer together than he had planned as she replied, "I'm Diaz, nice to meet you."

"Anyway, I was climbing the damn walls after a week, so coming back to work is like going to freaking Disneyland."

"I'll bet." The door opened, and they filed out into a bright corridor. Turning left, she added, "Nice to meet you." With a final glance at him, she sauntered down the corridor in the opposite direction. This time he let his gaze linger for a moment.

That was a damn fine way to start the morning, he thought as he watched her walk away. Stopping in front of a door labeled Captain Wilson, he held his coffee cup in his mouth with his teeth and rapped on the window three times before turning the knob and peeking in. To his disappointment, his boss was nowhere to be seen. In fact, the office had been cleared out, so he strolled past the elevators and into the familiar chaos of the homicide squad room.

Giving the room a once over, it was almost exactly as he remembered it. To the left sat four desks back to back, followed by a medium-sized conference table and another two sets of four desks. A small kitchenette sat in the dim far corner of the room, and along the right wall were a series of storage rooms. His eyes stopped when he saw a glass door in the center of where two storage rooms had once been. On the new door was written: Captain Daryl Wilson. Jackson gave the change an approving nod as he looked over to his unit. The first thing he noticed was Detective Richie Lucco ogling his new friend Diaz.

"Why don't you take a picture?" Diaz said as she put her bag down on Boyd's desk.

"Busted," Chang said with a laugh as he stepped in front of his gaping partner and offered his hand. "I'm Detective Peter Chang, nice to meet you." Pointing to Boyd's desk, he asked, "Are you Buddy's replacement?"

"Detective Boyd?"

"Yeah, we all called him Buddy."

"Yeah, I guess I am," she replied, apprehension halting her movements. "Sorry for your loss."

Suddenly, Richie snapped out of his funk and offered his hand. "I'm Detective Richie Lucco, it's nice to meet you."

"Smooth, Richie," Chang said.

"I'm Detective, Julia Diaz, it's nice to meet you both. Are you partners?"

"Yeah," Lucco said, but then his eyes widened and he added, "On the force I mean, not like—"

As Diaz tilted her head, unsure of what to say, Chang shot him an incredulous look and said, "What the hell is wrong with you?" Turning back to Diaz, he said, "Never mind him. He's a moron."

"Still as smooth as ever, huh, Looch," Jackson said as he drifted across the room.

"Jackson, my man!" Lucco shouted as he stepped out from behind his desk and wrapped him in an embrace. "We missed you, brother. I was starting to think you up and retired on us. Three quarters, tax free. I'm sure the thought crossed your mind."

"Looch, you were at my house like three times a week, so was Pete, and so was Cap. Even McGinnis and Rivera were regular visitors. Not to mention all of the phone calls and meals. You didn't leave me alone enough to miss me," he said with a hearty chuckle

"I know, but you weren't here where we need you."

"I get it, brother. It's good to see you, too."

"Hey, Winters, it's good to see you back on your feet. You had us all real worried," Chang said. With his hands up, he added, "I know we saw you regularly, but it's not the same as sitting across a desk from you every day."

"I get it. I'm loved," Jackson replied with a laugh. "You guys weren't the only ones who were worried, though. Raina and Jacob cried when I left the house this morning. They're really scared I might get hurt again."

Diaz watched the exchange, and it seemed as if a light had turned on in her mind when Chang called him Winters. He realized she probably thought Jackson was his last name, not his first.

"This is Detective Julia Diaz," Chang said.

"Yeah, we met downstairs. Would've walked in together, but no one told me Wilson's office moved in here. All those visits for the last three months and no one thought to mention it," he said with a laugh. Diaz nodded at him and he raised his coffee cup in her direction as he put his folder and paper on his desk and went to work on his bagel. "So, what's new? What did I miss?" he asked between bites of his breakfast. Some of the butter had leaked onto his hands and he searched around his desk for some napkins.

Chang offered him a paper towel as he replied, "It's been pretty busy with just me and Looch, but we've actually hit a lull these last few days."

"Even got most of our paperwork done," Lucco said.

"Not too shabby," Jackson said, impressed with his teammates. Looking at Diaz, he added, "Last time Looch had most of his paperwork done I think Bush was still in office."

With a shrug, Lucco replied, "I was a rookie Bush's last year in office."

"Jackson's right. You haven't really done any paperwork since," Chang added.

Diaz' lip curled upward. "I was hoping to join this kind of team."

"You may not like it as much tomorrow," Jackson said. "So, what new nicknames have you come up with to torment your partner, Looch?" he asked before popping his last bit of bagel in his mouth and wiping his hands.

"I got a good one this time, Jax."

"Oh no," Jackson said.

"Oh no, what?" Diaz asked with a smile.

"Wait for it," Jackson said smiling in anticipation.

"Chick Flick Chang," he replied with a gratified grin at his partner's discomfort.

"I hate you so much," Chang mumbled while his head hung ever so slightly.

"Why Chick Flick Chang?" Diaz asked, her smile growing wider.

"I found out he makes his wife watch chick flicks with him," Lucco replied making an aww face.

"Has anyone seen the captain?" Jackson asked, admitting to himself he had missed these exchanges.

"He'll be up in five. I think Alvarez is ripping him a new one for no reason again," Chang said with a grimace

"Hate that guy," Lucco added. "Just go be a politician already and leave the real cops alone."

Jackson nodded his agreement. "I wonder what it would be like to have a Chief of Detectives who actually cared about detectives."

"We all wonder that same thing, Winters," Captain Wilson said as he paraded into the room with bright white teeth lighting up his dark face.

"Captain," Jackson said with a grin engulfing his face and his arms stretched wide. After they embraced, he patted the captain's bicep and said, "You been working out, Cap?" Standing six foot one, Jackson had him by an inch, but Wilson had him by twenty-five not so solid pounds.

Looking at the smirk on his detective's face, he shook his head and mumbled, "Wiseass. You saw me on Sunday." Waving them towards the conference table he added, "I see you've met your new partner."

"Julia and I met outside, but I'm pretty sure Looch is hoping she's his new partner," Jackson replied.

As Diaz and Chang started cracking up, Captain Wilson glanced over to Lucco then back at Diaz and said, "I'm sure he is."

"I'm hoping she's his new partner, too," Chang quipped to another round of chuckles.

"Do I get a say?" Diaz said as she sat down at the table.

"No," Captain Wilson replied as he took his seat as well. "Can we get started please?" Glancing over to their newest member, he said, "Detective Diaz, since you're new, I'll go over the basics with you. The homicide unit at Midtown South is a prestigious unit that is not only responsible for homicide investigations in our precinct, but also the Tenth, Thirteenth, Seventeenth, and Times Square precincts. If they catch a high-profile case, a case they can't handle, or anything the mayor or commissioner think we need to be involved in, we take the lead. Are you sure you're ready for that kind of responsibility and scrutiny?"

With a confident smile, she replied, "Yes, sir."

"Good. Let's get started then."

Chapter 3

After a thirty-minute state-of-affairs meeting to catch him and Diaz up, Jackson met privately with Captain Wilson. Looking at the generous size of the captain's office, he couldn't believe that three months ago it was two storage rooms. All of the furniture in the room was light wood and matte gray colors, and from the personal touches he knew that Belinda had been there because she had much better taste than her husband. "Office looks good, Cap."

"Yeah, the department gave me all this stuff, but it was my wife's feng shui skills and little additions that made it somewhat homey." Sitting heavy in his chair, he let out a sigh and said, "So what did you want to ask me?"

Glancing around the office, he looked at a framed picture of the captain and Buddy on the wall. His heart wrenched when he thought about his mentor and friend, and it took a moment to compose himself. Gathering his thoughts, he remembered why his conscience had driven him to follow Captain Wilson into the office.

As he sat in one of the two plush chairs in front of the captain's desk, he took a deep breath and said, "The commendations, Cap. We both know that Buddy deserves them, not me."

Another sigh escaped Wilson's lips that said he was expecting this but hoping to avoid it. Looking at his detective, he said, "I know Boyd deserves a lot more credit than the commissioner's giving him, but stop selling yourself short. You found the diner receipt that put Buddy onto Hodges in the first place, and you killed the sick bastard."

Putting his face in his hands, Jackson wiped at his eyes remembering the nightmare. Every moment of that night up until he lost consciousness was burned into his memory. The broken streetlights had left the alley in a perpetual gloom, the dumpsters wreaked of spoiled food which barely managed to cover the stench of vomit and urine, and he was on the ground with his blood pooling around his body. All he could think about was getting home to Raina and Jacob, but it didn't look like that would be possible. He remembered wondering if Emma would actually take them in or leave them parentless.

Shaking his head clear, he said, "Cap, I was already shot three times in that alley. I was fumbling around on the ground for my weapon and Hodges was smiling at my futility. God, I'll never forget that sadistic bastard's smile. Buddy came around the corner and fired, but Hodges was wearing a vest. Still, it was enough of a distraction for me to find my gun. As I was stabilizing my hand to fire, Hodges shot Buddy in the head. I got caught out in the open, and Buddy gave up his life for me. I don't deserve any awards."

"Well the brass happens to disagree, and I'm with them on this. Sure, Buddy deserves more than they've given, but you deserve to be honored as well. And, if I recall, it was Buddy's idea to split up, so it's not your fault."

His look was as stern as Jackson could ever remember, and he was right. It was Buddy's call, and he made the wrong one, but it wasn't entirely his fault. Hodges had managed to get the drop on him, but that was in the past. Right now, Captain Wilson's face told Jackson he was one hundred percent behind him.

"Cap, I —"

"Don't 'Cap' me, Jackson. Buddy was one of my best friends. I know what's up, and I appreciate you wanting to give all the accolades to him. I really do. Truth is, it's been a bad couple years for the NYPD, and this city needs a hero. You killed the serial killer, so you're it. Like it or not. End of story."

Standing, he walked over to his file cabinet and withdrew Detective Diaz's file. "Now, about your new partner. Julia Diaz is as sharp as they come."

"I knew you'd never let her in the unit if she weren't, Cap."

"I let Lucco in, didn't I?" he said and they both laughed.

"He's from Staten Island. It's not his fault," Jackson replied to another chuckle from the boss. "So, what's her background?"

Raising an eyebrow, he opened the folder. "Graduated magna cum laude from St, John's with a criminal justice degree. Seriously, she was like third in line for valedictorian. She's been on the force for eleven years, last five with vice. She's the officer who took down Tony Dobbs."

Now it was Jackson's turn to raise an eyebrow. "Wow, that's an impressive pedigree."

"Nothing but the best for you, Winters, and in case there was any doubt in your mind, you are the lead detective for the unit."

Leaning back to test the chair's balance, he replied, "Are you sure that's a good idea? Alvarez has it in for me, and he wanted his guy in here. That's like putting a bull's-eye on both of our backs. I can take the backseat if it's easier for you."

"Like I told Diaz, this is prestigious homicide unit. You need to be in the front seat. Let me worry about Alvarez. The commissioner has our back, and that's enough for me. Now, get out of here and go catch some killers."

A smirk played across his face as he stood, "Yes, sir." On his way out he stopped and turned. "Poker at my place tonight?"

"I already told Belinda I'd be home late."

"Is it okay if I invite Diaz?"

"Yeah, it'll be a good bonding opportunity for her. It'll also be good to see Buddy's chair filled again."

Jackson walked back out into the squad room and over to his desk. Three faces turned to him, and Chang said, "Well?"

"Cap put me in charge of the unit, Julia is my new partner, and poker is at my place tonight. Bring your kids if you want, Raina and Amanda will be there to watch them."

"Excellent, Junie loves Raina. She'll be very excited," Chang said.

"I'm in," Lucco said. "It's on the way back to Staten Island anyway."

Jackson looked at Diaz and said, "You're invited, too."

Diaz fidgeted while she cast a nervous glance at Jackson and said, "Are you sure? I have a seven-year-old, and he's very energetic."

"Absolutely. I have an energetic eight-year-old. They'll be fast friends. This will be a great chance to get to know your new team, but if it's too short a notice we understand."

"Who are Raina and Amanda?"

"Raina is my daughter, and Amanda is my niece. They're both sixteen, and I've already paid them to watch Jacob and Junie. Amanda's father is my best friend, and he'll be there tonight as well."

A smile tugged at the corner of her lips as she said, "Count me in."

Chapter 4

Jackson was carrying a bowl of pretzels out to the poker table he had set up in the living room when the doorbell rang. Their last player had arrived. Raina practically knocked him over to get to the door first, her braided brown hair smacking off her shoulder as she moved. Opening the door all the way, she saw Diaz and said, "Hi, you must be my dad's new partner."

"You can call me Julia. You must be Raina." A look of surprise crossed her face when the teenager gave her a big hug.

"She really likes people," Jackson said in greeting. "Glad you could make it."

A little boy peeked out from behind Julia, and Raina's green eyes lit up as she knelt down and said, "And you must be Hector. My brother is so excited to meet you." She took him by the hand and led him up the stairs.

Watching with an awe-struck look on her face as her son left with the enthusiastic teen, Julia said, "She's really good with kids." After she stepped in to the inviting home, Jackson closed the door behind her. She took off her jacket and hung it on one of the nearby hooks. A vanilla candle burning in the room scented the air as she walked into the living room and said, "Hi, Captain Wilson."

Wilson stood and put his hand straight out. "Let me stop you right there, Julia. Our main rule at poker night is first names only. None of this captain this and detective that. Here it's just Daryl, Peter, Richie, and Jackson." A light cough alerted him that he forgot the last member of the game. Jerking his thumb over his shoulder, he said, "Oh yeah, this clown in the Yankees hat is Jackson's friend Martin. I'm not sure why we let him play."

"Thanks, Daryl," Martin replied, hoisting a beer in his direction.

Julia sat next to Richie and looked around the living room. Jackson watched her eyes move from the black leather couch to the off-white recliner, but they settled on a landscape painting over a short bookcase. "That's a beautiful painting."

"That's a Winters original," Peter said.

Julia's eyes grew a little bigger as she said, "I had no Idea you were so talented, Jackson."

The room erupted in laughter, and Julia's face grew flush as Jackson said, "Don't worry. They're not laughing at you. They're laughing at the thought of me painting. I wish it were a Jackson Winters original, but it's actually a Jacob Winters original as in my Father. I think the talent skipped a generation because Raina is also very creative. Me on the other hand, I'm doing well if I find matching socks."

"Got that right," Richie said.

"Enough yammering, let's play some cards. It's a ten dollar buy in, and the winner buys lunch for the unit on Monday," Daryl said.

"Ahem," Martin said.

"Right. Unless the winner is him," Daryl replied. "If he wins, he gets to buy the pizza for the next poker night."

"And pay the girls to watch the kids," Richie added.

An hour later, the pizza arrived from Joey's Pizzeria, and the game was put on hold while the kids came down to eat. Junie showed Peter a bracelet she had made for her mom with Raina's help, and Amanda was playing the quiet game with Jacob and Hector while they ate. Every time Amanda turned away, the boys looked at each other and started to giggle until she would swing her head back in their direction trying to hold a stern look, but failing. Jackson gave Julia a tour of the house while Richie brought out another six-pack of Brooklyn Lager.

As the kids were heading back upstairs for some more fun and games, Jackson caught up with Martin in the kitchen. Martin was huddled in the corner speaking in hushed but gruff tones. "We can't afford to mess this up, Vince. Just get it done!"

"Is everything okay, brother?" Jackson said. His question startled Martin. Best friends since elementary school, they knew each other well enough for Jackson to know something was wrong.

Averting his eyes briefly, he replied, "Nothing major, just a deal we're working on. If Vince messes it up, it could have some serious ramifications for the firm. I'm just a little tense about it is all."

Jackson caught his hesitance, but decided when his friend wanted him to know what was going on, he would tell him, and instead he said, "Well you know the rules. No business at poker night." Grabbing a new bag of pretzels off the oak table, he refilled the bowl and strolled out of the room. Five minutes later, Martin was back at the poker table, smile fixed firmly in place.

As the evening came to a close, the moon was three quarters full and hung low in the clear sky. An early October chill was in the night air as Jackson's guests began to leave. Martin was the first to leave, which was unusual. Peter said his goodbyes and carried a sleeping Junie out of the house. Richie followed him out, and Daryl gave Raina and Amanda each a hug before he took off. Jackson carried a sleeping Hector out to Julia's Explorer and placed him in the car seat. As Julia strapped her tired son in, Jackson said, "Thanks for coming. I hope you had a good time getting to know our crazy team."

Still leaning inside the car, she replied, "Thanks, I did. You have a beautiful home and beautiful children."

"Thanks. Hector there is a keeper, too."

Backing out of the car, she gently shut the door and faced Jackson. "I love him more than anything." Glancing around at the ground, it seemed like she had something to ask but couldn't find the words.

"What's on your mind?"

"Can I be blunt?"

"Sure," he replied, with a suspicious squint and a slight tilt of the head.

"I've worked really hard to get here, and this is a dream come true for me."

"But?" he said, wary of where she might be going with this.

"Is there anything I should know about you or the team that might give me pause? Fitzgerald is retiring from Midtown North in three months, and I can still go there, but I have to decide now."

He was taken aback but replied, "Honestly, Chang and Lucco are as solid as they come, and I think I do a good job as well."

"What about personally?"

"I can only give you my history there, but I'm not sure what you want to know. My wife left about six years ago, and I have almost no contact with her, but when I do, it's never good. Is that the sort of thing you're looking for?"

"Not exactly, I'm sorry, is this awkward?"

"It's getting there."

"I meant personally with respect to the job."

"I love the job. There's nothing else I want to do. I give a good effort every day, and I'm proud of the work our team has accomplished. I will always have my partner's back no matter what, and when you join this unit, you're joining a family. I'm not really sure what else to say. Do you want references? A dating history? What?"

Julia's cheeks flushed, or it could have been the cool breeze, but she looked a little embarrassed. "I'm sorry. This team seems like right where I want to be, and I just wanted to make sure. I didn't mean to come across as flakey. Can we pretend this conversation never happened?"

"What conversation?" he said. She opened her door to get in the car, and as she sat down, he added, "You really are going to like it with us. Don't worry." She gave a half wave and closed the door. A few beats later, she was driving away, and he still wasn't sure what it was she had wanted to know.

Jackson stood outside for a few minutes savoring the cool breeze. Fall had always been his favorite season, and clear cool nights like this were why. Raina came out to join him, "So, is she going to stay in the unit with you guys? I hope so. She seems really cool, and Hector is adorable."

"Eavesdropping again? You know that's frowned upon in most circles, right?"

"You know I can't help myself. I'm nosey," she replied with a laugh as she wrapped her arms around his waist and leaned into his chest. "I love this weather, dad."

Leaning down, he kissed her forehead and enjoyed the moment. "Me, too, Peanut."

Chapter 5

Colin Stone, star of the fledgling HERO Network's hit show *Blue Fire* found himself fired up as he jogged though Central Park. Wearing a pair of navy-blue Nike sweats and a white Hard Rock Cafe tee, he hoped he looked low key enough to get through his exercise without too many people recognizing him. The cool October air felt great on his face as sweat dripped from his jet-black hair. When he started the run, the sun had just begun its assent into the morning sky, but now it was out and millions of people with it. Central Park was about as close to nature as you could get in the Empire City, and the scent of the freshly cut grass filled his nostrils with every breath he took.

Taking a longer run than usual, he wanted to burn off all of the negative energy his argument with Garrison had caused before he met with his fans at Comic Con.

"I swear that guy is gonna bring down the whole network if he doesn't get his head out of his ass," he mumbled as he ran.

Colin would hate himself if his frustration with Garrison caused any of his fans to have a bad experience at the con, so he poured on the speed hoping his exertion would cancel out Garrison's stupidity. *A hundred thousand dollars! What the hell is wrong with him?*

Legs pumped faster, and calves burned as he descended the wide grey stairs towards the tunnel that opened into the famous Bethesda Fountain. Approaching the fountain, the Angel of the Waters statue seemed to hover above the flowing water, and he immediately understood why so many movies shot scenes here. Galloping over the red bricks, he touched the fountain and turned back towards the elaborate stairs, this time foregoing the tunnel and racing up the outer steps. Upon reaching the top, a Rocky moment flashed through his mind, but he realized he was in the wrong city just in time to avoid the embarrassing faux pas.

His run ended near the Metropolitan Museum of Art, and he strode to the curb by the south corner of the famous museum raising his hand to hail a cab. Several cabs ignored him until a young blonde stepped up to the curb and said, "You gotta do it like this." Sticking two fingers in her mouth, she let out an impressive whistle. A moment later, a taxi pulled up to the curb. Colin tried to decide if it was the whistle or the body that drew the cabbie's attention. Either way, he was thankful for it.

"Thanks a lot," he said as the young lady began walking away.

Turning back to him, her eyes widened in recognition and she shrieked, "Oh my God, you're Colin Stone. I just hailed a cab for Colin freakin Stone. Maryanne is gonna be sooo jealous." Sauntering over to him, she took out her phone and said, "Mind if I get a quick selfie with you?"

"Ay, you coming or what, pal?" The cabbie yelled in a thick Brooklyn accent from inside the car.

Colin leaned in and said, "Yeah, just give me a second." Looking at the blonde, the driver nodded a grudging affirmative. Turning back to the woman, Colin said, "You sure you want to get a picture of me? I'm kinda nasty from my run."

"I don't care," she replied as she leaned into him and snapped off a few pictures in burst mode. "This is the best day ever," she said with a grin that covered her face.

"Thanks for the cab," Colin said as he stepped in and waved. Turning back to the driver he said, "Marriott, West Fortieth Street please."

"You got it," the accent replied. Tires screeched as he peeled away from the curb into the normal heavy traffic of Midtown. "You're the guy from that show, right? Colin something? You shoot fire out of your hands, right?"

"That's me," he replied, trying not to laugh at the cabbie's less than eloquent query.

Merging within inches of another cab at thirty miles an hour, he glanced in the rearview mirror and asked, "Mind if I get a shot for my daughter? She's in love with you." The cab swerved as he took his phone out of his pocket.

Seeing his life flash before his brown eyes, Colin white-knuckled the grip handle on the passenger side door and stuttered, "N, no problem, but how about we wait until the car is stopped."

The driver's wry smile and ensuing wink suggested that the man enjoyed putting the fear of God into tourists as he turned onto West Fortieth Street. Three blocks later, the car stopped in front of the hotel, and Colin gave the man a megawatt smile as he took a picture for his daughter.

"That'll be twenty-seven even," the driver said.

Colin reached into the pocket of his sweat pants and took out two twenties. Handing them to the driver, he said, "Keep the change." As the cab pulled away, Colin hurried into the hotel to ready himself for a day of fan-filled fun, feeling much better until he saw a clearly nervous Garrison Williams pacing in front of his room.

The star of his show's spinoff stood a solid six-two with platinum blonde hair and icy blue eyes. Wearing a pair of distressed Lucky jeans, and a Battlestar tee, his aviators hung from the neckline of his shirt. His show, *Tough Justice* was actually doing better ratings than *Blue Fire* was, and Garrison had been eager to let everyone know about it. The network was already unhappy with him over his ongoing shenanigans, and if his current situation made its way to the press, it might be the breaking point.

"You have it?" Garrison said, glancing up and down the hallway.

"Are you crazy coming here like this? What's the matter with you?" he growled as he slid the key card in the door to his room. The light on the door handle flashed green, and he pushed the door open to his penthouse suite. The living room of his suite looked like a home decor magazine cover, but he ignored the lavish furnishings as Garrison followed him into the room.

As soon as the door closed, Colin rounded on him. "You can't be asking me for a hundred grand in the hallway of a hotel. What if a fan were to see that? Or worse, the paparazzi? It's not like I have that kind of money lying around the room, Gar. I told you last night I'd have it by the end of the con and I will. Don't ask me about it again."

With all of the good energy built up from his run gone, he let out an angry breath and said, "If I'm pissy with the fans today, it's gonna be your fault." Garrison's shoulders slumped, and Colin decided now wasn't the time to pour it on. After all, they were still friends. With a lighter tone, he said, "What do you even need the money for anyway?"

"I lost big at the Tropicana in Atlantic City. Now I owe a guy. It's no big deal. I'll move some assets around and get it back to you next month."

"Gar, if you have a gambling problem, you need to get it under control. Gigs like ours don't come around every day. We're role models like it or not, and the network can fire you if they find out."

"They won't. No one at the casino recognized me, and as long as I get this guy his money this weekend, it'll be fine."

"My agent assures me it'll be here by tomorrow night, but I'm letting you know. This is a onetime bailout. This doesn't happen again, got it?" The tenor of his voice and stern set of his eyes conveyed his seriousness.

Raising his hands in surrender, Garrison said, "Yeah, I got it."

"Alright, now get out of here. I need to get ready for the con." As his fellow celebrity exited the suite, Colin was suddenly thankful for the penthouse suite's bathroom spa tub. Hopefully a few minutes of soaking in the hot water would relax him for the fans. He always strove to give them the best experience possible in the few seconds they had together. Spontaneously showing up at local pubs or restaurants where the fans would be dining after the con hours helped his image as well, but he wasn't interested in just an image. He really wanted to live up to that ideal, and Garrison was making that a difficult task at the moment.

Melting into the steaming water felt good, and ten minutes later, he was reaching for a protein bar and a bottle of water in a better frame of mind for the weekend to come.

Chapter 6

Jackson held the New York Post sports section up in front of him as he strolled into his kitchen to make coffee. Having just put Jacob on the school bus, he had a few extra minutes before he needed to leave for work. The words, "C'mon, Amanda, just do it already," uttered by his daughter, made him lower his paper and stop in his tracks wondering why they weren't in school.

"Hi, daddy," Raina said as Amanda was zipping up the back of a black spandex Batgirl costume he wasn't sure she should be wearing. One look at Amanda's Supergirl outfit told him his best friend had not seen his daughter before she left the house.

Casting a suspicious glance at the teens, he said, "Halloween isn't for another few weeks. Is your school having some sort of costume party early?" Glancing at Amanda, he added, "And isn't there some sort of dress code?"

Exhibiting a patience that was certainly not a product of his DNA, Raina replied with a sigh, "Dad, today is the first day of the Manhattan Comic Expo. You bought us the tickets for my sweet sixteen and said we could skip school to go, remember?"

"We made this deal while I was still in the hospital, didn't we?"

"Yeah, but we had to get the VIP tickets before they sold out."

Turning up the mock indignation, he gasped, "You bilked me for VIP passes while I was on morphine?" Seeing the guilty look on Raina's face he added, "Well played, Peanut."

"You wanted to throw me a huge expensive party for my sweet sixteen, but I just wanted to go to Comic Con with Amanda. Even the VIP passes are way cheaper than the party would have been. Besides, we didn't even go yesterday because it was only half a day. All the stars start showing up today."

"Okay, fine, but we need to talk about these costumes. Isn't that Batgirl get-up a little… tight?" He desperately wanted to be upset but found he couldn't. Green eyes lit up, and rosy cheeks peeked out from under the edge of the mask. Her brown locks escaped the back of the cowl just like on the old TV show. It was a great costume, even if the dad in him would rather she wear a burlap sack.

"It's fine, Dad. My entire body except part of my face is covered. Relax."

Relax? Easy for her to say. He decided to let it go as he looked to his niece, wondering if she got her costume in the naughty nurse aisle. The skirt was short, but the problem was the shirt barely covered anything and looked more like Victoria Secret's superhero line, which he sincerely hoped wasn't a real thing. "Amanda, correct me if I'm wrong, but doesn't Supergirl actually wear a shirt on that TV show you guys watch every week?"

Putting on what he imagined was her most convincing smile, she said, "This is one of the comic book versions, Uncle Jax."

With a sigh, he pulled out his phone and replied, "Okay, picture time." Before they could reply, he snapped a couple pictures and added, "Amanda, are you sure your dad okayed this costume?"

"Of course. He bought it for me." Her blonde hair shook as she nodded her head up and down in earnest, but her blue eyes said she was trying to get one over on him.

Jackson seriously doubted Martin would buy his sixteen-year-old daughter an outfit like that, so he played a dad hunch. "You guys look great. Martin is going to love these pictures." Pressing a few buttons, he added, "I'm sending them now."

Amanda's eyes widened as Raina whispered, "Busted."

Jackson was actually deleting the photos instead of sending them, but a defeated Amanda yelled, "Wait, don't. Could you delete those, please, Uncle Jax. I'll go change into the shirt that came with the costume." She hurried out of the room and came back a couple minutes later wearing the Supergirl outfit he knew Martin would buy.

"Okay, now let's get some pictures before you go off to nerd con," he said with a smirk.

Instead of posing, Raina put her hands on her hips in indignation. "Don't make fun, Dad. Comic Con is for everyone, and it's all in good fun."

"You're right, Peanut, I'm sorry," he said, proud of his little girl because he knew she meant it. Still, he knew he would be unable to stop himself from making more con related wisecracks. "Okay, pictures," he said. Holding his phone up, he waited for the girls to strike their best superhero poses and snapped a few shots. He couldn't wait to show Captain Wilson and the unit, because the girls looked adorable, although he admitted to himself that he was probably a little bit biased.

"Dad, can you send those to our phones? They might be the only pictures we get together all day, and these costumes are amazing."

"Okay, and be careful if you do let someone take a picture with your phone. Some of these weirdoes haven't been out of their parent's basements in thirty years, and you might be the first real girl they've ever seen."

Amanda stifled a laugh as Raina yelled, "Dad!"

Wrapping them both in a hug, he said "Okay, girls, I have to go to work. Have fun at the comic thing." Turning to leave, a thought hit him. "Do you want a ride to the Javits Center, or is riding the subway dressed as superheroes part of the experience?"

"We wouldn't say no to a ride, Uncle Jax. We can always ride the subway home," Amanda said while Raina nodded her agreement.

"Okay then, let's go. And, Amanda, you can leave the um, Supergirl bra here." With a frown, she dug the almost shirt she had previously been wearing out of her bag and dropped it on one of the kitchen chairs as they left. Jackson allowed himself a smile at thwarting his niece's nefarious plan. As they walked to the car, he took out his wallet and said, "Do you guys have enough money for snacks and souvenirs?"

"Yeah, we've got plenty," Raina said as Amanda whacked her arm. Rubbing at her forearm, she said, "Ow, Amanda."

"Raina, never turn down free money," she whispered in her outdoor voice.

"She's right," Jackson said as he handed them each a twenty-dollar bill and got in the car.

"Thanks, Dad."

"Thanks, Uncle Jax."

"I'd say don't spend it all in one place, but that'll probably only get you three fries at the Javits Center."

"Yeah, the food there is super expensive, but we're planning to walk to a pizza place for lunch," Raina said as she dropped the twenty in her Batgirl-themed pocketbook.

"That's a good idea. I see my fantastic parenting is finally paying off." Theatrically, he took one of his hands off the steering wheel and made a show of patting himself on the back.

"And he calls Comic Con people nerds," Amanda whispered and they both started cracking up. Looking in the rearview mirror, it reminded him of the hundreds of times he had driven the two of them places over the years. Always the whispering, always the giggling, and at that moment, they were six years old again. His content smile lasted all the way over the Brooklyn Bridge.

Chapter 7

An hour before the first people were due to be let into the convention center for day two of the Manhattan Comic Expo, he scoured the area waiting for Garrison to arrive. Knowing from previous cons that Garrison was borderline OCD, he knew the actor would be by to make sure his autograph and photo-op areas were stocked with hand sanitizer, wet wipes, the proper flavor of Vitamin Water, and the correct assortment of Sharpies. Most celebrities left that sort of thing up to their agent, but not Garrison; he was a bit of a micromanager.

Prowling back and forth between the two areas in costume, he noticed someone go into the curtained off photo area. Glancing in every direction, he saw vendors hard at work setting up their booths, volunteers milling about, and security guards at each entrance keeping the hordes of rabid fans at bay. No one seemed to notice him as he slipped in behind the curtain to see a distracted Garrison Williams hunched over with his hands on a table facing the back wall.

Heavy black curtains almost eight feet high formed the makeshift room. The front curtain was pulled back just enough to form an entryway of sorts, and a folding table for people to place their belongings while their picture was taken sat next to the opening. A professional background dominated one of the walls next to the exit. The egress of the enclosure stood partially open and he could see the back wall of the conference center was lined with tables standing a few feet in front of a bank of printers. Between the booth and the printers stood a maze of stations which herded the people to the proper printer for their photos. The area was dim now, but in another hour or so the lights would be on, and a photographer would be sitting on a stool taking hundreds of pictures of the stars with their fans.

Standing there for a few minutes, the actor was still unaware of his presence. *I can end him right now*, he thought. *But he's worth more alive at the moment.* Anger at his betrayal and dismissal still filled his mind. Pacing the industrial gray carpeting, he gathered his nerve. He knew it was now or never. Another opportunity to catch Garrison Williams alone was not likely to arrive, and business needed to be taken care of. Taking off his mask, he placed it on the hilt of his plastic replica broad sword and called out in an angry voice, "Garrison. Did you think you could ignore me forever?"

The sound of his voice seemed to startle the actor, but he regained his composure as he spun around, and said, "What are you talking about?"

"I called you eight times last night, and you ignored every call. Eight times! I will not be ignored. Do you understand me?"

With a healthy amount of celebrity attitude, he said, "First of all, I don't report to you. I can ignore whoever the hell I want whenever the hell I want." Seeing the anger in the man's eyes, he added, "But I wasn't avoiding you. I left my phone somewhere, and I haven't been able to find it."

He felt some of the anger melt away. That was a good sign, perhaps things were looking up. If he wasn't actively avoiding the calls, maybe he would be inclined to rethink the proposal. Blowing out a steadying breath, and trying to sound casual, he said, "I suppose there're worse things that could happen."

Lowering his guard a bit, Garrison smiled and said, "I suppose." Sitting on the edge of the table, he added, "What are you doing here anyway? Shouldn't you be getting ready for the weekend? It's a big year for you. It's a big year for all of us."

This is cordial, no time like the present to ask, he thought. "You know why I'm here."

Expression hardening, he said, "Dude, I told you I can't right now. I've got some serious network issues I'm dealing with."

No, this couldn't be happening. It was cordial, and it was going well. How could the answer still be the same? Feeling his calm melt, he lowered his voice and said, "This could ruin me, Garrison."

"I never agreed to anything, so you'd have no one to blame but yourself if this blows up on you."

Throwing his hands up in frustration, he said, "What the hell is that supposed to mean?"

"It means I got problems of my own and I don't need to be having this conversation with you right now, so leave." Shoving the man towards the door, he turned to leave through the other exit.

Rage finally getting the better of him, he ran back towards Garrison and spun him around to face him. "You won't ruin me, you, arrogant prick," he growled as he landed a hard right to the actor's eye.

Garrison looked at him in disbelief and yelled, "Are you crazy? Now you're gonna lose all your money AND get your ass kicked." He shoved him and the man stumbled backwards. Marching towards him, he added, "No one hits me."

Before Garrison could throw a punch, the plastic sword was out of the sheath and ripping into his neck. It may have been plastic, but it was hard and sharp and more than he needed to end the star's life. Surprise filled Garrison's eyes and blood gurgled in his throat as he grasped at his neck with both hands. The shock turned to terror as he fell to the floor, gasping for air, blood dripping on the industrial gray carpet.

Wiping his sword on Garrison's leg, he placed his mask back on and leaned over the dying actor. "You should never have betrayed me, Garrison," he whispered as the light left his victim's eyes.

Leaving through the opening in the curtain, he glanced around to make sure no one was watching. As the fear of what he had done began to overtake him, he picked up his pace and made a beeline for the exit. He still had to get changed and ready himself for the con. If he were to be missing when Garrison Williams' body was discovered, it would reflect badly. Going through his mental checklist, he remembered wiping his prints from the replica plastic sword last night, and the gloves he wore had kept the sword clean. As far as the mask was concerned, there could be hundreds of people with the same mask, but he still had to dispose of the sword without being seen.

Leaving the Javits Center, the bright sun betrayed the way he felt inside. He felt like he was trapped in a bubble of darkness as he worked his way to his car. Halfway there, he lifted his mask leaned over and threw up. "What have I done?" he muttered. "I've taken a life over what? Money?" *What's done is done*, the thought interrupted his panic. *Now, focus on not getting caught.*

Leaning on a car for balance, he took a moment before he started walking again. He let the cool October air wash over him as some of the color returned to his face. Walking past a half-full, green dumpster a couple blocks from the Convention Center, he started to toss the sword in but noticed a piece had broken off. *Oh no*, he thought as he tossed it in the dumpster and hurried to his car.

Chapter 8

Jackson stepped into the squad room after dropping Raina and Amanda off near the craziness that had descended on the Javits Center. Carrying his coffee and a bag of bagels in his left hand, he fired off a crisp salute with his right when he saw Captain Wilson. The captain shook his head, chuckled, and waved him off as he stepped into his office. Jackson followed him in taking out his phone as he went. He couldn't wait to show everyone these pictures. His daughter and niece looked so good and so happy, and as a parent, those smiles were treasured and he wanted to share the joy with his team starting with the captain.

"What's up, Jackson?" he said.

The bags under his eyes suggested he had not slept as long as he was accustomed to, and he was paying the price for his late night now. Daryl was the type of guy who was usually in bed by nine and any deviation from that routine took a toll the following day. To his credit, he still came out to play poker every month.

"There's the big winner," he said.

"That's right, sixty dollars richer until Monday."

"I'll take a brat with sauerkraut and mustard."

"Same as always," he replied with a smile. "So, what's up?"

Scrolling through the pictures on his phone, he came to his costumed daughter and niece. Lifting the phone into Wilson's view, he smiled the smile of a doting parent. "Raina and Amanda went to Comic Con today. Apparently, it was my sweet sixteen gift to her. I think she pulled one over on me while I was still in the hospital."

Looking at the girls in their costumes, Wilson's face morphed into a toothy grin. He was surrogate grandfather of sorts to Raina, and it was clear he missed having kids this age as he said, "That's adorable, and they can use the costumes again in a few weeks for Halloween."

"That's what I told them, but apparently that wouldn't be cool."

"Kid's today," Wilson replied with a dismissive wave.

"I just dropped the girls off at the Javits Center, and it's a madhouse, but I'm sure they'll have a great time."

"Yeah. They'll do all right."

Patting the captain on the back, he turned to leave, saying, "I'm gonna show these pictures to the squad."

"Close the door on the way out, would ya?" he said as he plopped into his chair and picked up what appeared to be a half-gallon-sized, truck stop coffee mug and two aspirin. Yeah, he was paying for his win last night.

"Sure thing, Cap."

Jackson was sitting on his desk showing Lucco and Chang the pictures as Diaz breezed into the bustling squad room. Lucco looked up and waved her over. "Julia, Jackson's daughter went to Comic Con in full costume. Come check it out."

Diaz' face brightened as she hurried over. "Cool. I went last year. I wanted to go this year, but I didn't think it would be a good idea to put off a new position for a few days to dress up as a Viper Pilot."

"A what?" Jackson replied both eyebrows arched as Diaz beamed at the enthusiastic teen heroes.

"A Colonial Viper Pilot from Battlestar Galactica." The look on his face must have communicated his lack of knowledge because she threw her hands up and said, "Seriously? You've never heard of Battlestar Galactica?"

"No!" Jackson replied with a laugh. "Are you really into all of this costume stuff?"

"Absolutely," she replied with a smirk. "I also cosplay Wonder Woman, and Catwoman," she added with a sly wink in Lucco's direction.

Lucco was now very interested in the exchange. It was almost as if Christmas had just come early for him. His eyes brightened and he rubbed his hands together as he smiled and said, "Really? I need to see those pics immediately."

"We know you have them," Chang added with a laugh.

"What's cosplay?" Jackson said, confused by the whole thing.

Pursing her lips as if she were about to explain something simple to a three-year-old, Diaz looked at her new partner and said, "Cosplay is when you dress up as a fictional character. It stands for costume player. It's a whole sub-culture. People do it professionally. There are stores, websites,

33

and contests. There's probably going to be a cosplay contest at some point this weekend. It's pretty big business."

"So, dressing up and pretending to be someone you're not is the thing to do these days?"

"Looch has been pretending to be a cop for years," Chang deadpanned.

"I got a badge and everything," he added, raising his gold detective shield over his head with a look-at-me expression on his face.

Jackson smiled. One of the things he had missed most during his extended recovery was the camaraderie. Yes, he did see his team fairly often, and he was more than thankful for it, but they were focused on him and what had been lost in that alley. They were taking care of him and his kids, and they helped his whole family get through it. Unfortunately, easy exchanges like this were for the most part absent, and he missed them. Fortunately, things were back to normal, and Diaz seemed like she was going to fit right in.

Captain Wilson ended the discussion when his door opened and he signaled them over. As they approached, a solemn look crossed his face and Jackson knew they had a new case. "We got a dead body at the Javits Center."

All eyes turned to Jackson, and his brow furrowed as a frown spread across his face. About the quickest way to kill a good mood was for a dead body to turn up at the same location you just dropped your daughter off. In reality, the likelihood of it being Raina or Amanda hovered near zero, but in his mind at that moment, it was beyond frightening.

Taking a deep breath, he said, "Do we know who it is?"

Leaning in, Wilson dropped his voice to a conspiratorial whisper as he said, "Garrison Williams."

Diaz gasped as her hand involuntarily moved to her mouth. "No," she whispered.

"I don't have to tell you how sensitive this is, do I? No press, and no leaks. This Comic Expo is big business for the city, and the mayor wants this handled quietly."

"No press might be tough, Captain. Local news would already be on the scene for the convention, not to mention social media. Depending on who discovered the body, the info could already be out there," Diaz said.

"Do your best to keep it under wraps. If the local media is already there, ask them as a favor to the mayor if they'll hold off for at least a couple hours until Williams' family has been notified."

"We're on our way, Cap," Jackson said as they hurried to their desks to retrieve their side arms.

"I think Diaz needs to get her Wonder Woman costume and go under cover," Lucco said.

Smacking his arm, she shook her head in disappointment and said, "You're a mess."

Sliding into the driver's seat of his immaculate black Challenger, Jackson inhaled the lemon scent of the air freshener as he looked over to Diaz and said, "Okay, I didn't ask upstairs, because this is hush, hush, but who is Garrison Williams?"

A surprised grimace played across her face and she replied, "Wow, you really don't know anything about this world, do you?"

"Not much," he admitted. "Ask me about my Mets, and I'll tell you anything you want to know, but this sci-fi stuff is foreign to me."

"Mookie Wilson eighty-six stats," Diaz said with a challenge implied in her face.

"What?"

"You said to ask you anything about the Mets," she replied with an, *I'm waiting,* gesture.

Pulling out into the street, he turned on the lights and siren and started over to the Javits Center. His first case in almost three months, and it was a big one. Famous people being murdered in your city were near the top of the things no mayor or police chief ever wanted to see happen, so this was going to be a closely watched investigation by both the public and the brass. For a brief moment, he had a strong desire to go home and crawl back into bed, but he got over it quick. This was far better than being stuck in bed, and as an added bonus, he had the opportunity to school his new partner on his favorite Met.

"Wilson batted .289 with nine homers, forty-five RBI's and twenty-five stolen bases in eighty-six." Swinging around a truck unloading food for a deli, he scoffed and added, "At least make it challenging. Now, who is this Garrison Williams character?"

"Williams is the star of a new superhero show called *Tough Justice*. His character is the hero Justice. *Tough Justice* is a spinoff show of the popular *Blue Fire*. There's news of another spinoff coming soon to the HERO Network as Bad Cow attempts to get the Elite-verse up and running on TV like the Marvel and DC expanded universes."

Confusion worked its way through Jackson's eyes as he turned onto West Thirty-Fourth Street "All I got out of that is that some bad cows want to infect the universe," he said with a shake of the head.

Taking a deep breath, she started over. "Bad Cow is a comic book company, and HERO TV is a fairly new cable network and streaming service they own. The Elite are what they call their superheroes, and the Elite-verse is their attempt to get all of their best characters on TV or in the movies like Marvel and DC are doing."

"Okay, now that I understood. Do you think it's possible someone might not want to see that happen?" Honking his horn, he leaned out the window and yelled, "Get out of the way, jackass. Do you not see the lights?"

"Road rage much?" she said with a chuckle. Contemplating his question, she pursed her lips in concentration. "I suppose it's possible, but it's unlikely. Garrison hasn't been the best role model, and it would probably be easier to let him implode and take the network with him."

"So, it's likely personal."

"That would be my guess."

"I don't know anything about this guy or his show. Off hand, do you know of anyone who might have a beef with him?"

"Well, his show is doing better than *Blue Fire*, and Williams wasn't shy about letting everyone know. Word on the comic blogs is that *Colin Stone*, the star of Blue Fire, was getting pretty ticked at Williams. There's also the Silver Asp."

"The what?" he said as he swung around a double-parked van.

"Jasmine Connelly. She's Colin's co-star on *Blue Fire*, but she's Garrison's on again off again in real life."

"And I take it they're both in town for this convention?" he said as he leaned on his horn.

"Yeah. They're both here for the con, and you're a really aggressive driver."

"It's New York. You have to be."

Chapter 9

Pulling up to the Javits Center, they could see thousands of people, many of them in interesting attire, milling around as people wearing lanyards with plastic passes attached entered and exited the building. The interest level of the crowd was barely nudged by his unit's arrival as there were already several police cruisers on the scene. Lucco and Chang pulled in right beside them, and as they exited their cars, they were met by Sergeant Molly McGinnis. As Irish as they come, her strawberry blonde hair and green eyes stood out from her blue uniform, and her smile could power a city block. She carried a few extra pounds, but that never stopped men from hitting on her.

"Hey, Jackson, it's good to see you back on your feet," she said in greeting.

"Thanks Molly. It's good to be back." As Diaz approached on his right, he pointed to her and said, "This is my new partner, Detective Julia Diaz. Diaz, this is Sergeant Molly McGinnis. She's one of the best, and we'll be seeing see her on a lot of our cases."

"Nice to meet you," Diaz replied, shaking her hand.

"You as well."

"Okay, where are we headed?" he said.

"The body is by the photo-op area. It's a long way," she replied, turning to begin their trek.

"Yeah, this place is huge," he mumbled as he fell into step alongside her. Diaz, Chang and Lucco followed through the colorful crowd. His mind could barely even comprehend the sheer amount of outlandish costumes he saw. Giant Robots, furry mascots, Storm Troopers, zombies, vampires, superheroes, Wookies, scantily clad women of all shapes and sizes, and enough soldiers to field an untrained battalion were passing them in both directions.

Leaning towards McGinnis, he said, "So is the naughty nurse aisle the only place these girls are allowed to shop for Comic Con? You should have seen the costume I made my sixteen-year-old niece change out of before I let her and Raina come here."

Shaking her head, she replied, "I don't get any of this, but I see what you mean about the costumes." She eyed a girl wearing knee high boots, a bikini bottom and pasties. White makeup adorned her face, and she wielded a giant inflatable mallet. A line of men waited to take a picture with her, many of them old enough to be her father, and she was eating it up.

"And they let her in the building dressed like that?" Jackson asked, barely able to keep the shock off his face.

"Yep," she replied with a sad shake of the head.

"Look, that's a great Psylocke," Diaz said, pointing to a brunette in a purple bathing suit with long purple boots and elbow length purple gloves

"Checkout Grimwolf," Chang said, pointing to a bald Nordic style warrior with a goatee, no shirt, and two double-bladed axes sitting in crisscrossing leather sheaths on his muscular back. Light brown fur-lined boots almost reached his knees, and a knife hung from his belt, halfway down the thigh of his dark brown pants.

"I love that video game," Lucco said, head spinning in every direction like a kid in a candy store.

"He can't possibly be allowed to bring those weapons inside," Jackson said as they walked past a Slave Leia with her tongue down a Storm Trooper's throat.

"That wasn't in the movie," Lucco quipped.

"The weapons are likely plastic replicas. Still look pretty real, though. They're checked before they're allowed in," McGinnis said as they entered the building. Jackson immediately saw what she was talking about. There was a heavy security presence at all the entrances and exits. Convention security had tables where they were checking bags and weapons. Replica weapons that passed inspection were given an orange tag that would need to stay on the prop at all times or it would be confiscated. Passing a group of soldiers, he noticed an orange tag on each of their P90s.

"Looks like SG-1 is here," Chang said, pointing to a patch on one of the men's arms. "And Lucco, look to your right."

"Black Widow. Very nice. I may need to question her before we leave," he replied.

Jackson shook his head as they continued to move through the costumed crowd, hoping his team would tune out the distractions once it came time to work the case. They were all very good at their job, so he had faith they would, although he was fairly certain he'd have to yell at Lucco at least once. Stepping into an enormous hall, he was hit by the buzz of activity. The din of thousands of conversations happening at once created a comfortable background static as faithful fans moved about, unaware that one of their heroes was dead.

There must have been several hundred vendors selling all kinds of merchandise from booths as small as a six-foot plastic table to booths with elaborate temporary walls that gave the illusion of being in a store among the indoor flea market of fandom. A man in a Green Lantern shirt bought several action figures from an overweight man. Three teen girls wearing tee shirts emblazoned with anime characters were bartering with a hipster on the other side of the table to get three stickers for ten dollars instead of twelve. A middle-aged Batman held up two Star Wars hats to a middle-aged Catwoman who nodded enthusiastically as he plunked down two twenties.

Seeing a larger booth with a sign that read Midtown Comics, he nodded, realizing he recognized the name of that store. Toys, hats, tee shirts, elaborate costumes, mugs, replica weapons, comics, and anything else fandom related were on sale somewhere in this room. This cavern of capitalism was any fan's dream, and there was a ton of money exchanging hands around him. There was also a whole section of artists selling detailed pictures of characters he had never seen before, but were obviously very popular. Many were ready to draw a picture of attendees dressed as their favorite sci-fi or fantasy characters.

As he continued to survey the room, one costume seemed to appear more than all the others. Nudging McGinnis, he asked, "Who's the guy in the red and black?"

Looking at him as if he had just told a bad joke at a funeral, she said," Seriously? That's Deadpool. Where have you been?"

"In the hospital almost dead from being shot three times," he replied with a straight face.

Covering her mouth, her eyes widened as she said. "Oh my God, that was so stupid. I'm sorry, Jackson."

With a chuckle he replied, "Don't be. I said that for the shock value."

After a quick elbow to his stomach, she pointed towards the far end of the room to a curtained off area with yellow crime scene tape around it and said, "Crime scene is over here."

As they approached the area, he said, "Did they put the curtains up to hide the body?"

"No. This is one of the photo-op areas where fans can pay to get professional pictures taken with the celebrities." Stopping by the tape, she added, "I'm needed outside, so this is where I leave you. Give me a call if you need anything." Spinning on her heel, she turned and marched back into the crowd.

"Will do. Thanks, McGinnis." Jackson flashed his badge as he stepped under the yellow tape, and his team followed him in.

As they worked their way around the curtains, Diaz fixed Jackson with a playful stare and said, "What's the story with McGinnis?"

"Like I said, we see her at a lot of crime scenes." Knowing what she was really asking, he decided to make her work harder for the info.

"Anything else?"

Lucco leaned in between them and said, "They've never dated if that's what you're asking."

"I was gonna draw it out a bit before I let her know that," Jackson said as they passed the final uniform before they saw the dead body of Garrison Williams.

Chapter 10

Garrison Williams lay on his side in a pool of his own blood. His hands were fixed around his throat in a futile attempt to stop the bleeding. A slight bruise around his left eye highlighted the icy blue color of his dead eyes. Three techs from the crime scene unit buzzed about taking pictures and searching for any clues to process. "Anyone touch the body?" Jackson called out.

A young tech named Luis Rivera looked up and said, "No, Detective. We only arrived a few minutes ago, and we wanted to work the scene around the body before too many people arrived."

"Good call, Rivera," he replied as he pulled on his baby blue, latex crime scene gloves. He preferred the black gloves, but he was pretty sure Lucco was hoarding them because there were never any extra-large ones around. A distraught young woman sat in the corner, and Jackson motioned Diaz to go talk to her while he looked at Lucco and Chang and said, "Canvas the closest vendors and see if any of them noticed anything strange when they were setting up this morning." As they turned to leave, he bent over the body and took a long look.

"We've already photographed him, so you can move him if you need to," Rivera called over to him.

Nodding at the young tech, he said, "Can I see his phone?"

"Sorry, there was no phone here when we arrived."

"Maybe the killer took the phone with him," Jackson mumbled as he rolled the body a few inches and looked under the back. Something caught his eye and he called out, "Hey, Rivera, can you get a shot of this?"

Taking out his camera and leaning in close, he said, "Let me take a couple shots and then roll him further." Jackson did as instructed and after the pictures had been taken, he reached down and picked up a bloody piece of plastic. Droplets of blood splashed to the industrial gray carpet as he turned the piece over in his hand and studied it. Rivera held an evidence bag out, and Jackson deposited the broken plastic shard inside. Rivera sealed the bag and said, "You think it might be part of the murder weapon?"

"I do," he replied as he looked at the blood on the star's Lucky jeans, musing at the irony of the name. "Looks like the killer wiped off the murder weapon on the vic's leg. Can you get a close up on that, Rivera?"

"Already did, Detective. Looks like the edge of a sword or something."

"You think Williams' neck was sliced open with a plastic sword?"

"It's possible. Some plastics are easily hard and sharp enough, and a lot of these sci-fi enthusiasts love for their replicas to be as realistic as possible."

"I guess so," he replied as he walked over to Diaz and the young woman. She sat on the floor holding her knees tight to her chest as she rocked back and forth. Mascara had been smeared around her dark eyes beneath her glasses as tears had left trails down her rosy cheeks. Her brown hair was pulled into a ponytail and thread through the back of her *Tough Justice* ball cap. Diaz knelt next to her comforting her.

Jackson leaned over with a hand on Diaz's back, and in a whisper said, "Is she okay to answer some questions?"

"Yeah. I think she can handle it." Diaz stood and helped the young woman to her feet.

"Let's sit in the next booth," Jackson said as he held the curtain open for them. Seeing there were no chairs, he called over to the officer by the crime scene. "Hey, Jones. You think you can score us a couple chairs?"

"Sure thing."

Jackson followed Diaz into the next booth. A moment later, Jones was setting out three chairs. Without a word, he turned to leave, and Jackson called behind him, "Thanks, Jones."

As he sat down, Diaz said, "This is Jen Webber. She was supposed to be the photographer for Garrison Williams this morning."

"Hi, Jen. I'm sorry you had to walk in this morning and see all of this. If you wouldn't mind, do you think you could walk me through it?" Jackson leaned back and waited while Jen tried to find the words.

"I came in to set up about nine-thirty, and he was just lying...." Putting her head in her hands, she started bawling. "I'm sorry," she said between heaving sobs.

With a concerned look in her eye, Diaz put a hand on her back and said, "It's okay, Jen, just take your time."

"It's just that he was my favorite, and I was so happy I was going to meet him, and now he's dead and I feel so selfish right now." Diaz handed her a tissue, and she wiped at her nose with a sniff.

Using the voice he would use to sooth Raina when she was younger, Jackson said, "Did you see anyone enter or leave the photo area this morning? Maybe someone who didn't belong?"

"No. I'm sorry. I wish I could be more useful," she replied, holding back the next wave of tears.

"You're doing great, Jen," Diaz said in a light, encouraging voice. "Is there anything you can think of that might be helpful? Anything at all, even if it wasn't this morning?"

Sitting up a little straighter, it looked as though a light bulb just went on behind her eyes as she said, "I overheard my boss on the phone saying that he heard Garrison having a huge argument with someone last night. Is that helpful?"

"Very helpful," Jackson said. "Did you hear who he might have had the argument with?"

"No. I'm sorry, but my boss is named Barry Habershaw."

Leaning towards his shaken witness, Jackson said, "Jen, Garrison's phone was missing when our crime scene unit arrived, and it might have some insight into who did this. You didn't happen to see Garrison's phone when you arrived, did you?"

"I'm sorry. No."

"No problem, Jen. We'll be in touch if we have any further questions," Diaz said.

Standing, Jackson pointed to a uniformed officer and said, "This is Officer Tomlin. If you'll follow him, he's going to take your statement." She started to follow the officer and Jackson added, "One more thing, Jen. It's very important that this stay secret. At least for now. We'd like a chance to notify his family before the media frenzy. Do you think you could hold off on telling anyone about this for a while?"

"I suppose."

"Thanks, Jen." A moment after she exited, Chang and Lucco walked in. Chang was shaking his head, and it seemed like Lucco had just won the lottery. "Anything, fellas?"

With a quick shake of the head, Chang replied, "No one saw anything. They were too busy getting all of their stuff ready for the crowds."

"Why's Looch so happy?"

"He handed out business cards to a few dozen young ladies. You know, just in case they remember anything." With a wry grin he added, "I'm not sure why he took their numbers down, though."

Everyone turned towards Lucco and his face darkened a shade. With a shrug, he said, "What? Those women, those costumes... What do you think it is I'm praying for in Mass every week?"

A disappointed sigh escaped Jackson's lips, and he looked at Lucco and said, "We're here to solve a murder, not get lucky. Get your head out of your ass, got it?" Lucco's head dropped and he nodded as Jackson said, "Okay, I need you two to go find the guy in charge of these photography booths. His name is Barry Habershaw, and our witness thinks he may know something about an argument Garrison had with someone last night." Looking at Lucco again he added, "Think you can do that without collecting any more phone numbers?"

"I'm on it," he replied as he turned and walked out of the booth.

"Keep an eye on him, Peter."

"On it," Chang replied, hurrying after his partner.

"You think Richie is going to call any of those numbers?" Diaz said as she watched them go.

"Probably all of them."

"Bad news," Diaz said as she looked at her phone. "#Whodiedatcomiccon is already trending."

"I thought it was called comic expo?"

"Same difference. Comic Con is generic for every show like this regardless of the actual name."

Jackson nodded his head in understanding. "Now, we should probably go ask our friends in the press to do us a favor and hold off on naming names for a little while."

"Think they'll go for it?"

"Probably not, but we have to try."

Chapter 11

Edgar sat outside the Collingsworth Hotel on West Thirty-Fifth Street in the back of his stolen, white Chevy van. Grey bricks and gleaming windows shooting up into the blue morning sky sat before him. Having rented one of those rooms for the weekend, he watched thousands of people rush back and forth like rats trapped in a maze unaware of his presence. Two uniformed patrolmen sauntered past the van, but he was unafraid. The owners would be in Puerto Rico for another three weeks before they came home to find their vehicle missing, and he would be long gone by then. After this score, he would spend the next few years relaxing on a beach far away from the traffic, the noise, and the snow that would fall in a couple short months.

With four marks already on the hook for a hundred grand apiece, he was a few minutes away from making it an even half a million. It never ceased to amaze him how quick most men were to fall for a pretty smile. His next mark, a chubby, balding, upper-middle-aged man in a Star Trek sweat shirt and slacks walked into the hotel with not one, but two beautiful blonde Harley Quinn cosplayers in tow. The first Harley was dressed in the traditional red and black onesie made popular by Batman the Animated Series, and she carried an over-sized mallet. Imitating the Suicide Squad version of Harley, the second young woman was wearing tight blue and red shorts that couldn't have been more than six inches long, a tiny white half tee with the inscription: Daddy's Little Monster, and knee-high boots. Instead of a mallet, she opted to carry a baseball bat.

Edgar sat peering at the Sony flat screen mounted to the van wall. As soon as they reached their hotel room, the motion activated cameras he had planted would start rolling again and another hundred grand blackmail payment would be his. He had chosen eleven targets for the weekend, and all of them were men who could afford the payment but not the scandal. He had only picked men he knew would fall for his assistants and their doe-eyed, college girl routine.

While these girls were college age, they had never seen the inside of a university. They were high-priced escorts that he was paying twenty thousand each to use their services for four days, and they had no idea he was blackmailing the men they were having sex with. He had told them these men were prospective business partners, and he was using them to sweeten the deal. Neither one of them seemed to care anyway since he had given them half of their payment up front.

The screen flared to life as red Harley was first to enter the room. She was leading the mark, who was actually the influential Judge Hastings, by the hand while white Harley was draped over the happy man's shoulders. They led him to the queen-sized bed, and red Harley pushed him back onto the mattress, while white Harley sat down on his left leg and began kissing his neck. His eyes slid shut as his hands moved up and down her back. Red Harley unzipped her onesie and stepped out of it wearing some heart-stopping red lingerie.

Edgar was starting to feel warm watching the action. "Damn these girls are good," he mumbled while to took off his Deadpool mask and began fanning himself with his sombrero. To fit in with the crowds at the Comic Expo, and keep an eye on his investment, he was cosplaying Mexican Deadpool. The costume included bandoliers and everything. Last night he had gotten dressed up as Chef Deadpool. He thought it a fitting costume for this sort of endeavor since the anti-hero was always engaged in his own shenanigans. *A Deadpool and two Harley Quinns causing trouble at the con? Who would believe it?* he mused as his lip curled into a smile.

With the push of a button one of his cameras zoomed in on the action. Lingerie Harley was now on the bed behind the judge, while the man's hands were now at the edge of the other Harley's tiny shirt. "That's it, keep going." The judge's hands moved back down to her midriff as both women were now kissing him.

"No. You're going the wrong way, amigo. Why do you think her shirt is so small?" he muttered. All he needed was for the man to lift the shirt a couple inches for the money shot and Judge Pervs-a-lot would be on the hook for a hundred grand. It didn't take very long for the shirt to come up. "Cha-ching," Edgar exclaimed in victory. He had seen enough. The cameras would continue rolling, but he no longer needed to watch. He knew he already had what he needed to get the judge's money.

Stepping out of the van grinning from ear to ear, he fed the meter. Hurrying back to the con, he hoped to have found his next lucky victim by the time the Harleys returned from their current assignment. *Best Comic Con ever*, he thought. As he walked, the mood hit and he even started to whistle. Next on his list was Congressman Vasserman. The thought of the loudmouth who always bashed the family values guys when they were caught, wrapped in his own scandal, almost made him want to forego the blackmail and leak the footage to CNN and Fox News. Almost!

Chapter 12

Chang and Lucco brought Barry Habershaw into the Javits Center security office to talk to Diaz and Jackson. The captain had called with instructions directly from the mayor to do all interviews on site. City Hall instructed them to cause as little disturbance to the flow of the convention as possible. They were also gently reminded that the press was off limits. To that end, all witness and suspect interviews were to be conducted in the security office in the convention center. Jackson understood that an event drawing a few hundred thousand people over four days every year was not a part of the economy you should mess with, but the restrictions would undoubtedly make his job more difficult.

Jackson held up his finger for them to hold on for a moment while he was on his phone. He was trying to explain that the news had broke on Williams' murder before his team had even arrived on the scene. "Cap, the press was already all over this by the time we got here, and the homicide unit being on the scene basically confirmed their suspicions. Urbanich from the Times said a confidential informant inside the department had already confirmed the victim was Garrison Williams. At that point, all I could really do was ask for their discretion, but I'm sure it's already running on all the networks."

"Mayor's not gonna be happy about that."

"Probably not, but he couldn't really expect anything different."

"You're right. Let me know as soon as anything drops."

"Will do, Cap."

After ending the call, Jackson stepped across the bright office and extended his hand towards the man with Lucco and Chang. "Hi, Mr. Habershaw, I'm Detective Jackson Winters, and this is my partner, Detective Julia Diaz. Thanks for coming in to talk to us."

There was a hint of frustration hiding in his dark eyes as he looked at Lucco and Chang and said in a condescending whine, "I wasn't given much of a choice, Winters, was I?" Pausing for a moment, his eyes lit up and he pointed at Jackson. "Winters? You're not the Detective Winters who killed that serial killer are you?"

Jackson's first impression was that Barry was famous adjacent. He seemed like the type of guy that hung around famous people, dressed and talked like famous people, and did whatever he could in hopes of their fame rubbing off on him. He was cursed with an eternal desire to remain relevant even if he became a caricature of himself in the process. As if proving the initial impression, Barry's dark tan suggested a recurring appointment at the spa. Dressed to the nines in his Gucci horsebit suede loafers, Givenchy jeans and black Vuitton tee, his casual outfit may have cost more than Jackson's entire wardrobe. He was trying too hard.

Jackson picked up the hint of excitement in the man's voice as he replied, "One and the same." Placing his hand on Barry's back, he directed him over to a chair and added, "I know you're really busy, so I'll try to be as brief as possible."

The vibe he was catching from Habershaw told him it would be better to have Diaz do the questioning. Looking over to his partner, he saw that she had caught it, too. With a slight nod of her head, she agreed to ask the questions.

As he sat across from the detectives, he held eye contact with Jackson and said, "I'd appreciate that. Jen is in no shape to work now, and that's going to make navigating the event challenging until her replacement can get here from Brooklyn."

"Barry, can you tell me the routine for you and your employees here this weekend?" Diaz asked while Barry continued looking at Jackson. After a long pause, she added, "Mr. Habershaw?"

Snapping back to the present, he said, "Sorry. I was just thinking about how many people would line up to take a picture with your partner." Spreading his hands in a theatrical manner, he added, "The man who killed Tanner Hodges. I know I'd pay to snap a shot with him." Crossing his legs, he placed both hands on his knee.

"That's very kind of you, but I think I'll pass," Jackson said with a chuckle.

"Your loss," Barry mumbled as he looked at his fingernails.

"The routine, Mr. Habershaw," Diaz prodded.

"Right, your partner is very distracting," he said with a wink. "We set up the curtains and the backdrops the night before the event, and then we show up about a half hour before the shoot starts in the morning to set up the lights and flash. The Comic Con volunteers start letting the people line up and we all wait for the celebrity to show up. Most of them are good about keeping to the schedule."

"Sounds like a simple enough routine," she said. "Does it pay well?"

Dark eyes lit up and Habershaw waved his arm as he said, "Sweetie, you have no idea. I used to do the runway circuit, but this has the potential to pay even better and it's easier, and you almost never have to deal with a tantrum, which alone would make the move worth it."

Diaz eyebrow shot up. "So, this business is that lucrative?"

Leaning forward, he looked in her eyes and said, "You know, you have striking features, Detective, and a body that won't quit. You ever thought about modeling?"

"Not at all, but thanks," she replied, flashing a wide smile.

The truth was this wasn't the first time someone had mentioned modeling to her. It wasn't even the tenth, but she had never been interested in that lifestyle because she liked both food and freedom too much. She wanted to be able to go out for burgers and beers with the guys. She wanted to be free to play football with her cousins without worrying that the paparazzi might catch a photo of her with a bruise and turn it into a thing. Protecting people as a cop appealed to her way more than walking a runway or sitting in front of a camera.

With a sigh she said, "Let's get back to it, shall we?"

"Right, sorry. I skipped my Ritalin this morning. These shows are very lucrative. Even after I pay my people, I'll clear a couple hundred grand, and I do all the big shows. San Diego, London, Toronto. I'll clear two million working less than fifteen weekends this year."

"Wow, that's not a bad deal." After a short pause, she said, "Mr. Habershaw, Jen told us she overheard you on the phone telling someone you heard Garrison Williams in an argument last night. Do you know who he was arguing with and what the disagreement was about?"

Glancing around the room, he leaned in even though it was just the three of them. Looking back and forth between them, he whispered, "He was arguing with Colin Stone, but I'm not sure what it was about. Colin kept saying 'I'm not gonna let your stupidity destroy this network, but Colin is the sweetest guy ever. He would never hurt Garrison."

"You're probably right, but he may know who did," Diaz said.

Jackson stood and opened the door to the office. After calling Chang over, he asked, "Do you know where Colin Stone is right now?"

"According to the convention schedule, he's taking photographs for the next half hour before he takes a short break."

"As soon as his photos are finished, bring him down here."

"You got it." Chang walked away and Lucco joined him as Jackson closed the door.

Chapter 13

The door to the security office opened, and Detective Chang peered in. Glancing at Jackson, he said, "You ready for the next interview?"

"Yeah. Send him in," Jackson replied.

Diaz straightened her shirt, still unable to believe that she was going to meet Colin Stone, even if it was just for a case. This was shaping up to be a memorable day. She took out her notepad as the star entered the room with a look on his face that suggested he had been gut-punched. Even in his distressed state, he had a presence that drew in the room. Star quality emanated from him even in his casual attire. He was an impressive person to stand in front of.

"Mr. Stone, thank you for speaking with us," she said, but Stone just plopped down on the empty seat.

"This is real? This is really happening?" he mumbled as his head sunk into his hands. "Is Garrison really dead?"

"I'm afraid so, Mr. Stone," Jackson replied.

His countenance fell further as he looked back and forth between the detectives. A look of helplessness crossed his face, and she wanted nothing more than to run to him and comfort him, but that would have been unprofessional.

"Who killed him?"

"That's what we're trying to figure out," Diaz said

"Can you tell us about the last time you saw him?" Jackson said, while Diaz watched Colin's face for any cues or hesitation.

"I guess it was around eight this morning. He was waiting for me outside my hotel room when I got back from my run."

"So, he was alive at eight o'clock this morning," Diaz said in confirmation as she wrote on her pad.

"Yeah. We talked for about five minutes and he left."

Diaz canted her head to the left and said, "When did you leave your room?"

"Quarter 'til ten," he replied. Suddenly a look crossed his face and he shot up in indignation. "Wait a second. You think I'm a suspect, don't you?" He started pacing as his grief began to turn into anger. Turning glistening eyes in her direction, he said, "I didn't have anything to do with this."

"We're just trying to establish a timeline," she replied.

"He was my friend, damn it. Why are you questioning me?"

Standing, Jackson motioned to the seat and said, "Please have a seat, Mr. Stone." Waiting until the actor sat, he continued, "What was the nature of your argument with Mr. Williams last night?"

"My what?"

"We have eyewitness testimony that says you were on a phone call arguing with Garrison Williams last night. What was the nature of that argument?"

Leaning back in his chair and crossing his legs, Colin looked up towards the office lights and said, "I don't know. Just stuff. Friends argue sometimes. It doesn't mean I killed him."

"I'm not gonna let your stupidity destroy this network. That's what the witness heard you say several times. That sounds like more than just stuff," Jackson said.

Confusion hit Colin's face and with a dismissive wave he said, "That? That's what this is all about? That was nothing. He's been pushing for a comedy based on a throw away character. An alien reptile that acts like a parrot named Zonk. The writers at Bad Cow use him for occasional comic relief. Zonk is the type of character you might give a few minutes of screen time to if you want to please the diehard fans, not the type of character you give an entire show. It was a terrible idea."

"Mr. Stone, we know that you've got a lot of money invested in the network. If Mr. Williams was doing something to jeopardize that, it could be seen as motive, which is why we need to ask these questions," Jackson said.

Letting out a tired sigh, Colin leaned forward and said, "It's fine, I get it. I used to do a cop drama, so I understand why you have to ask, but please, move on to someone else. Garrison was my friend, and I'd like to see his killer caught." Pausing for a moment, he added, "There are cameras in the hallways of the hotel. You should be able to see what time

I left my room. If it was after Garrison was killed, that should eliminate me as a suspect."

With her notepad still opened, Diaz replied, "We'll check that out, Mr. Stone. Thank you."

Jackson stood, signifying the interview was coming to a close and said, "Do you know of any problems Garrison may have been having with anyone?"

Standing, Colin said, "No. Sorry. Not off hand."

"We have yet to recover his phone, is it possible he left it in your hotel room?"

"It's possible. I didn't notice it, but I wasn't looking for it either. I can check."

"We'd appreciate that, Mr. Stone," Diaz said as she stood.

"No problem, just please, catch whoever did this."

"That's the goal," Jackson said as he opened the door.

Colin passed through the door without a word, and Jackson closed it behind him. "What do you think, Diaz?"

"I think he's telling the truth." Seeing the wry look cross her partner's face, she laughed. "And not just because he's the hottest man on the planet. Oh my God, did you see the way that tee shirt hung on his body?" she mumbled as she licked her lips.

"No. I hadn't noticed," he replied in a teasing tone.

"I'm sure you'll be more observant when we interview Jasmine Connelly," she quipped.

"Fair enough. Speaking of which, we need to get her in here." Turning towards the door, Jackson looked at his watch then turned back to Diaz. "For the record, I don't think he murdered Williams, but I do think he's hiding something. They're always hiding something."

"That's just the jaded detective in you. Colin Stone is a nice guy. He's always raising money for charities —"

"And he's the hottest guy on the planet, right?" he finished with a grin.

"Fine. You may be right, but I'd be really surprised." Standing, she looked over to Jackson and said, "I'm going to go find a cup of coffee. You want one?"

"Yeah. Black no sugar please."

"Got it." Passing through the door, she made her way back out into the craziness of the convention. She found a coffee kiosk and thought about badging her way to the front of the line but instead opted to wait on line and engage in some people watching. Maybe she couldn't be a part of the con this year, but she could at least take in the ambiance and get some costume ideas for the next one.

A twenty-foot Lego Star Destroyer display caught her eye while she inched up the coffee line and she wondered how long it took Lego to put that thing together. It was massive, and it dominated the center of the room. While she continued to wait, she thought it odd she had missed it before and wondered if she should risk going over and getting a picture of herself in front of it.

Tapping her foot impatiently, she looked to the front of the line and saw a man departing cradling six cups. A moment later the line began to move. Continuing to look around the Convention Center, she noticed a man dressed as Grimwolf and did a double take. It was Grimwolf, or at least Steve Jenkins, the creator of the game and star of all of the commercials. She moved forward and was now only two people away from getting her caffeine fix as she glanced back to where Grimwolf had been standing. He was still there, and she shot him a friendly wave. Returning the gesture, she noticed him still checking her out and mumbled, "You like what you see, don't you?"

Stepping up to the kiosk, she glanced back toward Grimwolf one last time before she ordered a cappuccino and a black coffee. A few ticks later, she was on her way back to the security office still thinking about Grimwolf looking at her the way men usually look at her. Too bad Colin had failed to look at her that way, and too bad she was working a case or she might have introduced herself to Grimwolf. That was interesting, she thought as she entered the security office with a smile on her face.

Chapter 14

Detective Chang escorted Jasmine Connelly and a faint scent of white orchids into the security office they were using for an interview room, and Jackson immediately found himself sitting up straighter. Standing before him was a truly beautiful and very distraught woman. Dried tears were evident in her emerald eyes, and her blonde hair had been pulled back into a ponytail. Wearing light blue jeans and a black tee, she grasped her clutch tight and her head hung as she moved. Several people had accompanied her to the room, and they waited outside for the interview to be finished. Jackson had heard that she usually travelled with an entourage, and now he knew that rumor to be true.

"Miss Connelly, thank you for coming down," he said as he guided her over to her chair. "I know the timing is terrible, but we have a few questions for you."

"I understand. I'll do my best to help you catch whoever did this," she replied, hands trembling and voice shaky.

"Thank you, Miss Connelly, and we're terribly sorry for your loss," Diaz said as she handed the starlet a tissue.

Jasmine reached for the whole box and held it in her lap as if it were a precious gift. Taking another one, she wiped at her nose. It took her a few moments to gather herself, and she reached into that tissue box a few more times before looking up.

"Can you tell us the last time you saw Garrison?" Jackson asked in as gentle a tone as he could while omitting the word alive. Jasmine was a mess, and he wasn't sure what might trigger another round of sobs.

"He um, left my room about quarter to eight this morning." Pausing, she wiped at her eyes with the tissue and added, "He must have had a lot on his mind because he usually stays and has breakfast with me. I went into the bathroom and he was gone when I came back out. I was really mad that he didn't even say goodbye, and now he's dead." A fresh glisten started to coat her eyes.

Giving her a moment to collect herself, Jackson said, "Do you know where he was going?"

With a voice growing smaller by the second, she replied, "I think he was going to see Colin Stone. Colin was helping him out with something, but he didn't say what."

"If you had to guess, what would you think it was about?" Diaz said in a sympathetic tone.

Jasmine dug into the box and retrieved another tissue. "No idea. We didn't really talk about that kind of stuff."

Jackson gave her a moment before he said, "Do you know of anyone Garrison was having trouble with?"

Scoffing, she replied, "Who wasn't he having problems with?"

Holding up her hand, she began ticking off numbers with her fingers as she found her voice. Sticking the first finger up she said, "I was pissed at him because I think he was cheating on me, although I don't know he was for sure. I know that probably makes me a suspect, but if he was cheating, you probably would have found that out anyway, so I might as well tell you now."

She held up a second and third finger next to the first and added, "The network was angry with him because his off-screen shenanigans were costing them money, and Steve was mad at him, too, but I'm not sure why." Holding up a fourth finger, she said, "Even Colin was starting to get fed up with him, and they've been friends for years. Garrison just didn't realize how good he had it, and he was doing everything in his power to blow it all."

Jackson and Diaz took in everything she had just told them. She had just given them four clear suspects including herself. They now had a starting point for the investigation. It could be none of those people, but more often than not, people were murdered by someone they knew.

"Thank you for your honesty, Miss Connelly," Jackson said. "Can you tell me who Steve is?"

Jasmine stared at him with a confused look on her face. "How do you not know who Steve is? Everyone knows who Steve is." With shock still evident on her face, she spoke a little louder as if that would make a difference, "Steve."

Diaz leaned over and whispered, "My partner here is sci-fi impaired. Assume he needs everything related to this convention explained to him."

Looking to Diaz as if pleading, she asked, "But you know who Steve is, right?"

"Who's Steve?" Jackson called into the conversation that suddenly seemed private.

"She's referring to Steve Jenkins, the creator of the video game; Grimwolf," Diaz replied.

"It's like the best game out right now, and Steve modeled the title character after himself, so he's in all of the commercials." Realizing she had implicated her friend, she quickly added, "But Steve is a really nice guy. I don't think he could ever hurt a fly."

"We'll still talk to him. Maybe he knows something that can help us find Garrison's killer." Pausing for a moment, he added, "One more thing. Mr. Williams' phone was not found with him. Is there any chance he might have left it in your room?"

"I doubt it. He never leaves it anywhere, but I'll check."

"Thank you, Miss Connelly. It could be very helpful to the investigation to find his phone."

Standing, Jackson motioned towards the door, held out a business card, and said, "We're finished for now, but if you think of anything else, please let us know."

She stood to accept the card, and the white orchid scent was a little more noticeable as she took the card from Jackson's hand. "I will."

Standing next to Jackson a moment longer, she brought another tissue up to her eyes and said, "And thanks for not being mean like the cops on TV. I'm having a really crappy day. I think I'm going to go lay down until I have to sign autographs at three."

Impressed, Diaz said, "You're still going to sign autographs? That's very kind of you."

"There are a lot of fans who spent a lot of money and came all the way to New York to meet me, and if I'm not still bawling like a baby, I'm gonna try and be there for them. Who knows? It might even cheer me up a little?"

Jackson couldn't believe she was going through with the weekend in light of what happened. Jasmine was being a real trooper, and he was rooting for her to make it through this weekend without any public breakdowns. His first reaction would have been to cancel the whole convention but tens of millions of dollars were in play, so he understood that wasn't an option. He also realized that if the killer was among the suspects Jasmine listed, canceling the conference would send them all far away from New York before he caught the killer. Still, this case was shaping up to be a pain in the ass. Why couldn't he catch an easy one for his first case back?

He held the door open and said, "I can have a couple officers escort you to your room if you'd like."

Pointing to a group of people in the hallway, she replied, "Thanks but I have my entourage for that." Drying her eyes one last time, she hefted a wave and padded out the door.

As the door closed, Diaz looked at Jackson, smiled, and said, "I don't remember you offering Colin any officers to escort him to his room."

"Okay, you were right. I observed Jasmine a lot more closely than I observed Colin."

Diaz chuckled and said, "I told you she was gorgeous."

"And after five seconds I wanted to believe she was completely innocent. She even made herself a suspect, and I still want to believe she's innocent."

"I know. I want to believe that Colin is completely innocent, too, and that he'll ask me to dinner."

Jackson took one look at the grin on her face and started laughing. A moment later, the door opened and one of the Javits Center security guards brought in a couple bottles of water for them. After nodding his thanks, Jackson took a long draught before picking up his phone and dialing Chang.

"Yeah, we need you to find Steve Jenkins, he's the creator—" Laughing, he added, "Okay, fine. Apparently, I'm the only one on the planet who didn't know. As soon as you find him, let him know we have a few questions for him."

"Peter gave you crap about not knowing who Jenkins is, didn't he?"

"Yep, and Looch was in the background piling it on."

"That's a crack team you've got there, boss."

"Don't make fun, Julia. You're part of that crack team."

Sitting down, Diaz took a sip of her water and asked, "So, who do you think did it?"

"Too early to tell, but we need to have someone look into who if anyone at the network might be involved. We can't just say the network is a suspect."

"I bet it's someone at the network."

"Didn't you know? It's always someone at the network." With a smirk, he raised his water bottle and took another gulp.

Chapter 15

Jackson paced the small security office. The florescent lights and white walls made the room seem more a part of an institution than a place where such amazing creativity and diversity was being encouraged this weekend. The old saying 'different strokes for different folks,' played through his mind as he thought about all of the people here celebrating something he didn't know anything about. Tens of thousands of people lined the Canyon of Heroes for a parade whenever the Yankees won the World Series, and even though he'd prefer a parade for the Mets once in a while, at least he understood the draw. This was all new and foreign to him.

His phone buzzed and he answered the call. "Did you find him yet, Pete?"

"Yeah, but he's being a bit difficult. He's refusing to leave his booth. Says we need to interview him here. There are a lot of people around his booth, and after the mayor's suggestion about keeping any disturbances to the con to a minimum, I wasn't sure I should, um, ensure his compliance."

Jackson could hear a lot of people in the background and thoughts of a tongue-lashing from Chief Alvarez should this become a circus made the decision for him. "We'll interview him by his booth then. We're on our way."

Casting a quizzical glance at Jackson, Diaz said, "On our way? What did Peter say?"

Returning his pen and notepad to the pocket of his jacket, he grabbed his water and stood. "Looks like Jenkins isn't willing to come to us, and Pete didn't want to cause a scene, so we're going to him."

Placing her notepad in her back pocket, Diaz pushed her chair in and started to follow. "Maybe I should take the lead on this interview."

As they exited the hallway leading from the security office back out into the bustling Javits Center, the enormity of the event hit Jackson once again. Costumes he had never seen were proudly worn as far as he could see as people ambled about.

He canted his head towards Diaz and replied, "Any particular reason why?"

"I caught him checking me out when I was on line for the coffee."

"Diaz, I'm sure guys check you out all the time. What makes this different?"

Pushing past a group of people cosplaying Thanos and the Avengers, she replied, "This was different because I caught him a couple times and he never looked away. They usually look away after eye contact unless they're really sure of themselves. He seems like an alpha-type, and if he's already disinclined to help us, questions from you might not be as well received as questions from me."

"Okay, you take the lead on this."

"Just like that?"

"You made a compelling case."

Smiling, he continued through a crowd of furry somethings. There were people everywhere, and the closer he looked, the more he realized that most of them weren't in costume. Almost all of them were wearing some kind of sci-fi or anime or superhero apparel, but they were just normal everyday people gathering to celebrate their love of pop culture. His daughter was right, it was all in good fun. Many people were carrying bags which indicated the dealers in the convention hall were doing pretty good business.

She glanced at him still smiling and said, "Oh, I get it. It's my second day in the unit and you want to see what I got."

Before he could reply, a voice he thought he recognized screamed, "Cosplay is not consent!"

Turning his head, he saw a guy trying to touch his daughter while Amanda, in her Supergirl costume, shielded her as if she were actually made of steel. Jackson couldn't tell if the man was pretending to be Inspector Gadget or if he was just a creepy guy in a trench coat, but he started towards the brewing showdown. He suddenly forgot all about the case, and went into protector mode. If some creep thought he was going to put his filthy hands on Raina or Amanda, he had another thing coming.

"Leave us alone," Raina yelled, drawing the attention of several attendees, although none stopped to intervene.

The creep shoved Amanda aside and took another step towards Raina, but Jackson stepped in between them. It took all of his willpower to not lay the guy out with one punch, but as long as he was on duty, angry dad impulses needed to be pushed aside. Captain Wilson would have a big problem with his lead homicide detective being filmed beating up a citizen at the convention his team was not supposed to make waves at.

He let out a breath he had been holding. "I believe these young ladies asked you to leave them alone." Flashing his badge, he added, "If I see you near them or following them again, I'll arrest you for assault. Do you understand?"

Usually that line combined with his badge would send the creepy crawlies slinking back to wherever they came from, so Jackson was surprised when the man bowed up to him and yelled, "Oh I'm real scared of your fake badge! Why don't you mind your own business? I just wanted to feel the fabric to see if the costume was authentic."

He tried to brush past Jackson, but Jackson stayed firmly planted in his way. A quick glance at his daughter told him she was happy he showed up when he did. Amanda had joined her by her side, and he could see the trepidation in their eyes. With him in between them and the stalker, they were getting their confidence back, but they were still a little afraid.

Diaz badged him as well and said, "These badges are real. Now move along before we move you."

With an incredulous look, the creep looked at Jackson and Diaz and said, "And who are the two of you supposed to be Scully and Mulder?"

"Nope, just New York's finest. Walk away now or you'll be taken out of here in cuffs," Jackson said.

"Get out of my way!" he yelled as he tried to push through Jackson and Diaz.

A moment later he was on the floor with Jackson cuffing his left wrist behind his body. After cuffing the right one, he got on the radio and said, "McGinnis, we've got an EDP in Aisle A eleven out in front of a booth called Enterprise Exhibits. Can you send an officer over to escort him out?"

"No problem, Detective. Should I send a Red Shirt?"

Jackson looked over at Diaz and shrugged. "I don't know what that means."

Throwing her hands up, frustration evident on her face, Diaz said, "Oh my God, you're hopeless. She was making a joke about Star Trek because we're in front of a Star trek booth."

"Officer's on his way."

"Thanks, McGinnis," he replied and noticed several people that had crowded around the spectacle shaking their heads in disappointment. A few ticks later, a young officer arrived and took the creepy Inspector Gadget away.

As the crowd began to disperse back into the flow of foot traffic, Raina hugged him and let out a sigh. "Thanks, Dad," she said as she held the hug for a few moments. He could tell she was frightened, but she was putting on a brave face.

"No problem, Peanut," he replied. Looking over to Amanda, he said, "That was very brave of you to stand up to that guy, Amanda. You were just like the real Supergirl."

"Yeah, except he pushed me aside like he was carrying kryptonite," she said with a note of dejection in her voice.

Raina hugged her and said, "At least you did something. I was all frozen and scared."

"Correct me if I'm wrong, but didn't I warn you about basement trolls this morning?" Jackson said with a hint of a smile tugging at the corners of his lips. His quip was rewarded with a snort of laughter from Amanda and a smile that Raina tried but failed to hide. "You want me to have Sergeant McGinnis keep an eye out for you guys?"

"No. That's all right, dad, but I do have a huge favor to ask."

With an exaggerated grimace, he reached for his wallet and said, "How much?"

Clasping her hands together as if praying, she replied, "Only forty. Please, Dad. I can give it back to you tomorrow. I have money set aside for each day."

With a raised eyebrow, Diaz nodded and said, "That's actually good planning, Raina. Kids your age usually don't think ahead like that."

"Well it didn't quite work out because I'm forty short for today's photo op." Turning back to her father, she said, "Pleeeeease!"

Looking over to his partner, he joked, "I guess you're buying lunch today, Julia." Handing Raina the money, he said, "Consider this part of your sweet sixteen present."

She looked down and upon seeing four twenties; she wrapped him up in another embrace. "Thanks, Dad. I love you."

"I know, Peanut." With a sigh, he added, "I hate to break up this Kodak moment but we're actually here on a case. I'll see you tonight. I want to hear all about the rest of your day."

"Okay, Dad. We'll have lots of pictures, too." Taking Amanda's hand, she turned to leave, and a moment later, they disappeared into the crowd.

"I hope that guy didn't ruin their day," he said as he began walking towards Jenkins' booth.

"Nah, those two seem pretty resilient. The money probably helped, too." Diaz said with a chuckle.

"That's why I gave her more than she asked for," he said, tapping his finger against his head. As they continued walking, he added, "You probably already know the answer to this, but Amanda yelled something at that guy. Something like cosplay is not —"

"Consent," she finished.

"What does that mean?"

"I'm sure you've noticed that some of the costumes are a tad revealing," she replied. He nodded his head affirmative and she continued, "Cosplay is not consent means that just because someone's wearing a costume, doesn't mean it's okay to touch them or harass them."

Jackson's furrowed brow and narrowed eyes conveyed his feelings on the matter as he said, "People actually need to be told that it's not okay to touch a sixteen-year-old girl?"

"Unfortunately, some do."

"I think I am going to have McGinnis look out for Raina and Amanda after all."

He frowned as he continued walking towards Jenkins' booth. What the hell was wrong with people? There were always a couple people in a crowd this size to watch out for, but to actually have a slogan because touching people without their consent was an issue seems like it ran deeper than a couple people.

Chapter 16

The autograph tables were quite a way from the photo-op area, and it was slow going. People were packed into the Javits Center like they were on a Japanese subway car, and it was difficult to fall into a good walking rhythm. Passing a guy who had to be on stilts, he was dressed in blues and purples, and he was wearing some light purple headgear that sported what looked like a purple boomerang protruding from each ear. He was holding a globe in his hands and licking his lips as several people stopped to take pictures delaying his trip even further.

"Who's this guy supposed to be?" Jackson said.

Diaz laughed. "Galactus. He's a cosmic powered bad guy from the Fantastic Four comics."

"Why's he looking at that globe like it's a steak dinner?"

"He eats planets. It's sort of his thing."

Shaking his head, he finally saw Lucco and Chang and picked up his pace.

"What took you guys so long? Did you stop for lunch?" Lucco said as he fell into stride with Jackson and Diaz.

"Raina and Amanda ran into a bit of trouble, and we happened to be close enough to lend a hand," Diaz replied.

"Are they all right?"

"Yeah. They're fine. Now, where is this Jenkins guy?" Jackson said.

Lucco and Diaz both started cracking up as Diaz pointed to a man that looked like some sort of Nordic warrior standing about four feet away with a crowd of people hanging on his every word. "Steve Jenkins is the guy on all of these posters and cut-outs," she said.

With a sad shake of the head, Lucco said, "Seriously, Jackson. Have you never even seen a commercial?"

"I don't really watch TV; just the occasional Mets game. You know that most of what little time I have is dedicated to reading Grisham." Stepping over to the warrior, he said, "Mr. Jenkins, I'm Detective Winters and this is my partner Detective Diaz. Mind if we ask you a few questions?"

A hint of annoyance flickered in his eyes as he leaned in closer to them and whispered, "Do you mind calling me Grimwolf in public? I've gotta maintain the image and all." His eyes settled on Diaz for a long moment before he took a step back.

Jackson nodded and Diaz took the lead. "Grimwolf, when was the last time you saw Garrison Williams?"

Giving her another once over, he said, "Yesterday morning I briefly saw him in the hotel lobby. I waved and he waved back, but he had his arm around Jasmine, whispering in her ear all cozy like, so I decided not to interrupt. Truth be told, I had a lot of work to do setting up for today anyway."

"We heard that you were mad at Garrison. Could you explain what that was about?"

"I hate to speak ill of the dead..."

A hint of a frown formed on Jackson's lips as he said, "I don't think he'll mind." Jenkins was oozing alpha, but it seemed like he was trying a little too hard to do it. Alpha didn't seem to be his natural state, and a little cop sarcasm might remind him of that.

Leaning in close to Diaz again, he whispered, "I was mad at him because he was being an idiot. I don't know exactly what happened, but I know he was being blackmailed by someone who has a video of him doing something he shouldn't with someone he shouldn't."

Pinching his fingers close together, he continued, "Hero TV was this close to canning him for violating the ethics clause in his contract and this could have cinched it. I even heard the execs were going to kill him off and bring his character back using a different actor, Dr. Who style. Jimmy Shultz in particular was gunning for him. The guy had it all, a successful show, adoring fans, and the hottest girlfriend on the planet, and he was bound and determined to throw it all away. That's why I was mad at him. I mean, come on. How do you cheat on Jasmine Connelly?"

Still writing, Diaz looked up and said, "That's interesting, but how do you know all this?"

"I saw him arguing with some chubby Deadpool. I don't know who the guy really was, I never saw his face. I heard Gar saying he didn't have that kind of money and the other dude said, 'If you know what's good for you,

you'll get it to me by the end of the weekend.' After he was gone, I asked Gar what the hell he had gotten himself into this time and he told me, minus the details, and that's when I got pissed at him."

Jenkins seemed to be leaning closer and closer to Diaz with each question. Jackson stepped in close enough to make Jenkins take a step back from her as she said, "Did he say how much he was being blackmailed for?"

"Hundred K. I was like, dude, you're so screwed." With a grin on his face, he tapped the back of his hand on Jackson's chest as if they were frat brothers having a brewski.

Annoyance flared, but Jackson was quick to push it down as he said, "Did it occur to you to lend him the money? With the number one video game in the world, I'm sure a hundred grand is chump change for you."

"I'm not as liquid as you might think, but under normal circumstances I definitely could have swung it. Problem is, I have half of my net worth tied up in real estate, and the other half I sunk into a movie project I'm putting together based on the game. I may have a nice-looking net worth, but I'm cash poor. I could have gotten him ten maybe twenty grand tops on such short notice."

Diaz looked up at the large celebrity and decided she didn't like the cocky look he was wearing. "Do you know who else he would have gone to for that kind of money?"

"Maybe Jasmine or Colin. I'm not really sure, but that would be messed up if he was trying to get it from Jasmine considering what it was for." The smile was back, and this time he was nudging Diaz with his elbow. Pointing to his line of fans waiting for an autograph, he said, "Listen. As you can see, I'm pretty busy. I need to get back in the booth. Maybe we can finish this later over drinks, or breakfast if drinks go well."

Jackson was still getting to know Julia Diaz, but he could sense she was about to erupt on Mount Jenkins, so he stepped in and said, "Thank you for your cooperation, you've been very helpful." He and Diaz turned to leave, and then almost as an afterthought, he said in a voice a little louder than he needed to, "One last question, Mr. Jenkins. Where were you between eight and ten this morning? We have to ask everyone."

A small grimace crossed Jenkins' face at the use of his real name in front of his fans, and Jackson felt a nudge of contentment at the unlikable star's frustration as Jenkins said, "Yeah. I left my room about six-thirty to go work out." Pointing to himself as if he were selling a car, he added, "This don't happen on accident, you know. I got back to my room, took a quick shower, threw on the costume, and came back here."

Diaz jumped back into the conversation. "Can anyone verify your whereabouts?"

"I'm sure my room key logs what time I come and go and the gym will log what time I arrived. I know a bunch of people saw me there, but I don't think they keep track of what time you leave."

"Thank you for your time," Jackson said as he turned with Diaz to leave.

"He's given us a lot of leads to run down," Diaz whispered.

"I know, but did he do it by design?"

"That's the question," she said with a shrug.

Chapter 17

Glancing around at the controlled chaos also known as the Manhattan Comic Expo, Lucco looked back and forth between Jackson and Chang. "So, we're looking for a chubby Deadpool? He shouldn't be hard to find at all."

"Yeah, there's only going to be a couple hundred Deadpools here," Diaz added as she pointed to a conga line with a few dozen people dressed as the beloved character causing a commotion.

"That looks like as good a place as any to start," Jackson said with a laugh. "Remember, we're looking for a heavier one, so that should narrow it down a bit."

They approached the conga line and began to spread out. Every once in a while, one of them would stop one of the Deadpools, discreetly flash their badge, and ask a few questions before letting the suspect rejoin the conga party. Some of the Deadpools, remaining in character, were complete wiseasses with their answers, but were also not the one they were looking for. After making their way through the whole line, they came back together.

"I guess we should have known it wouldn't be that easy," Jackson said as he continued scanning the convention center. "Let's split up. Any sign of a suspicious overweight Deadpool, radio it in."

Jackson roamed the convention center struck by how many people were jammed in to celebrate this culture he knew next to nothing about. It certainly was a colorful crowd, and everyone looked like they were having fun. Weirdoes like the one he and Diaz had confronted earlier were probably the exception to the rule, but he still had his eyes open for trouble. With over a hundred thousand people on the premises, it was a sure bet not all of them would be at the convention for some innocent fun.

A short time later, Jackson noticed a Deadpool wearing a sombrero and bandoliers approach a man in a uniform similar to those he spotted in the Star trek store. The man had a pretty blonde draped on his shoulder wearing an outfit he prayed his daughter would never even consider, and he seemed unhappy with whatever the masked man was telling him. Another woman in a red and black jumpsuit with a jester hat and a huge mallet stormed away from the conversation and out through a restricted access doorway. A look of angered shock crossed the Star trek guy's face as he violently shrugged the blonde off his shoulder. The suddenness and severity of the motion momentarily drew a few spectators who all watched the scantily clad blonde saunter off into the crowd.

He started towards the conversation but was spotted. Star Trek waded into the crowd, and Mexican Deadpool let his gaze linger on Jackson for a moment before he left through the same door the angry woman had used. Whatever it was he had just witnessed was the very definition of suspicious and fit with what Jenkins said. Apparently, Garrison wasn't the only one being blackmailed. Thumbing his radio, Jackson called his team as he picked up his pace towards the door.

"This is Detective Winters. I've got eyes on a suspicious Deadpool wearing bandoliers and a sombrero heading out of the building." After a quick glance around, he continued, "I'm one aisle over from the Tower of Tees under the D47 banner and heading out the restricted access doorway. Sergeant McGinnis, if you have anyone on the outside of that location, get them over there."

Clipping the radio back to his belt, he approached the doorway. The costumed suspect was exiting the building in a hurry, and Jackson rushed to follow. As the door closed behind him, he was met with a giant wooden mallet to the face. Stunned by the blow, he stumbled and fell into a pile of empty boxes as the woman in red and black ran out of the building. Trying to rise, the world started spinning around him and he slumped back into the boxes as his eyes slid shut.

"Winters! Jackson can you hear me?" Diaz tapped his cheek with her palm as his eyes fluttered open. Wondering where he was, he noticed the concerned look on Sergeant McGinnis' face as Diaz was asking, "What happened?"

His mind was sluggish as he replied, "Wha, um, just give me a second."

"We need to get the paramedics in here," McGinnis said as she pulled her radio off her belt.

The mention of paramedics seemed to snap him out of his funk. "No! No paramedics, I'm good."

"You're not good, Jackson," Diaz said. "You're bleeding from a cut above your eye, and you were unconscious a minute ago. You need to see the paramedics."

Standing slowly, Jackson relented. "Fine, but I'm walking over to them. I can't have Raina see me on a stretcher; it would ruin her weekend." Without waiting for a reply, he walked out the door on unsteady legs. McGinnis stepped up and steadied him as he walked.

Following behind him, Diaz said, "Tell me what happened."

"That was definitely our guy. We need to comb the area before he gets too far away. Also get Peter or Looch to get the convention center's surveillance on that door. It's restricted access, so it should be monitored. Our suspect was arguing with a guy in what looked like a Star Trek suit and two girls in outfits you'd probably be able to identify, but would be difficult for me to explain."

Diaz called the order in to Chang as they approached one of the onsite medical tents. "So how did you get hurt?"

"The one girl looked like some kind of black and red court jester was out in that hallway arguing with our suspect, and I lost sight of her as our guy was leaving the building. As I passed through the door, she hit me with something. The last thing I remember seeing was her running out the door as well."

"Sounds like she was dressed like Harley Quinn, and she probably hit you with a mallet or a bat," Diaz replied as a paramedic stepped up to Jackson and began looking at his eye.

"Come have a seat in the tent. Can you tell me what happened?" the medic said.

Before Jackson could answer, Diaz said, "He was hit with something and knocked unconscious for a couple minutes."

A frown formed on the medic's face as she said, "We need to check for signs of a concussion."

"Fine. As long as we do it here. I'm too busy to go to the hospital, and can we close this tent? I can't have my daughter see me in here."

"I'll get the precinct on the Deadpool hunt," McGinnis said as she exited the tent and pulled the flap closed.

Leading him over to a bench covered in white paper, the medic sat him down and began to shine a light in his eyes; first the left eye and then the right. They weren't overly sensitive, which was a good thing, but he could feel a headache coming on. The paramedic slipped on a pair of latex gloves and started to feel around the wound which caused a flinch followed by an unhappy growl. She flashed him an unnerving smile as she continued.

"You really should go get checked out, Jackson," Diaz said as she watched the medic clean the wound above his eye. The cut wasn't nearly as bad as it looked, but a nice bruise was developing around his eye.

"No can do, Julia."

A hint of frustration passed through her dark eyes as she put her hand on her hip. "Don't be so stubborn. There are plenty of people out looking for the suspect."

"I'm not being stubborn, and I know we have the best cops in the world out there searching, it's not that. Raina would be devastated if I wound up back in the hospital; even though it's minor."

Looking up at his new partner, his features softened and he continued, "She cried for days when I was shot, and Jacob cried when I went back to work yesterday. I can't put them through that again; not this soon."

Diaz held up a mirror and pointed to the bruise on his face. "How are you going to explain that?"

"I'll tell them I walked into a door or something. It doesn't really matter. As long as I walk through our front door on my own two feet, I'll be able to spin it in a way that won't upset them. There may need to be some ice cream involved, but it'll be fine."

"If you say so."

"I say so. Now can we drop it?"

Looking at the paramedic, Diaz queried an eyebrow.

"His pupils are responsive and the cut doesn't require any stitches. He should be fine, but if he exhibits any confusion, memory loss, or lack of coordination, bring him to the hospital immediately."

Jackson nodded his thanks to the paramedic and looked back to Diaz. "Satisfied?"

Her eyes held concern mixed with disappointment as she said, "No, but it'll have to do."

"Okay, as soon as Peter has the footage, we'll head back to the precinct. We still have to give the network a call, and we can set up the murder board and compare notes."

"Let's stop on the way back and grab something to eat. It's getting close to dinner time, and I feel like this is going to be a long night."

"Good call. Find out what the guys want and we'll pick it up."

"I'm driving," she said as she held out her hand for the keys. The look of concern on her face told him it wasn't up for discussion.

Understanding she was only being a pain out of concern, he knew she was going to be a great partner as he handed her the keys to his Challenger and said, "Thanks."

Chapter 18

Jackson and Diaz stepped into the squad room with arms full of take out. The individual odors of the dinners didn't mesh well, and they were happy to put the bags down on the conference table. Chang was already going through the video footage Jackson had asked for. As usual, he had gone the extra mile already having started on the traffic cam footage.

Before Jackson could unpack the food, he drifted over to the desks and said, "What do we have, Chang?"

"Looks like the suspects fled down West Thirty-Fifth Street, but they went into Sam Ash and we lost them. We're trying to get their footage right now, but it seems as though they may have been having technical difficulties with the bulk of their cameras."

"Sam Ash, we can work with that. Great work, Chang," Jackson said as he and Diaz unpacked their dinners.

"Meatball Sub," Diaz said as she held the sandwich out toward Chang and Looch.

"That's me. Thanks," Lucco replied while accepting his dinner. He took hold of the hero and caught a good whiff of the aroma of the homemade sauce before sitting down with a content sigh.

As he unwrapped his sub, he said, "I got a date next week with that Psylocke we saw. Her name is Tiffani, with an I."

"That's great, Looch, but have you gotten in touch with the Hero Network executive yet?" Jackson replied as he handed Chang a grilled chicken salad.

"I've left four messages. The last one hinted that if I had to leave another, they wouldn't like the consequences," he said as he took a huge bite of his meatball hero getting sauce all over his chin.

Diaz shook her head as she tossed him a napkin and said, "Seriously? What are you five?"

His mumbled reply was cut off by Captain Williams asking, "What the hell happened to your face, Winters?"

"Harley Quinn kicked his ass," Lucco replied with a laugh. Jackson frowned at him which brought on more laughter.

"We have the footage here to prove it," Chang added with a smile.

He turned his laptop toward the group and pressed a button. They watched the girl exit first followed by the chubby Deadpool. He moved past her and said something as she lifted her weapon into a waiting position. A moment later, Jackson hurried through the door only to be met with a mallet to the face. Diaz grimaced, but the rest of the team laughed at Jackson.

"What is she like ninety pounds?" Captain Wilson said with a wicked grin as he patted him on the back.

"Alright. Laugh it up, guys," Jackson replied as he took a bite of his burger, knowing they'd do their best to remind him of this for a long time. He knew if it had happened to one of them, he'd be piling it on right now, too.

"In all seriousness, where are we on the case?" Captain Wilson asked as he picked at Jackson's fries.

"Does Belinda know you're back to eating fries?" Jackson said with a wry grin.

"No, and she's not gonna know."

"Oh, she'll know," Diaz said. "You guys think you're all so slick, but women know. We always know," she added with a wink as she offered the captain a slice of her pizza. His frown let her know the temptation was not appreciated as he shook his head and she took a bite of the greasy cheesy goodness.

"As far as the case goes," Jackson said, trying to restore a modicum of order to the meeting, "Our Prime suspect is this guy pretending to be Mexican Deadpool."

"Cosplaying Mexican Deadpool," Diaz corrected.

"Cosplaying. Whatever. We have several other suspects, but this guy and his minion jumped to the front of the list when they assaulted me and ran."

"Technically, only the little girl assaulted you," Captain Wilson said to more laughter from Lucco and Chang.

"Speaking of that. No one is to mention what happened to Raina or Amanda, got it?" Captain Wilson queried an eyebrow and Jackson continued. "I don't want to ruin their weekend because I got hurt on the job. It's too soon after all they've been through. I'm just gonna tell them that someone slammed a door in my face or something."

The team nodded their understanding and Jackson stood to roll the whiteboard up to the conference table. Taping a picture of Garrison Williams to the center of the board he looked at his team and said, "Let's go through our suspect list."

Diaz taped a picture of Colin Stone to the top left corner of the board, and her gaze hung there for a moment longer than necessary as she said, "He was overheard arguing on a phone call with the victim the night before he was killed."

"We also have Jasmine Connelly," Jackson said as he taped her picture to the board.

"She implicated herself by telling us Garrison may have been cheating on her. She also mentioned there might have been some tension between Garrison and Steve Jenkins." He taped a picture of Grimwolf to the board remembering how much he disliked the man.

"And Steve led us to this man over at the network," Diaz said as she taped a picture to the board. "Jimmy Shultz was allegedly gunning for Williams."

"And we have yet to hear back from the network, so first thing in the morning, we'll be making their day difficult if they still haven't replied," Lucco added.

He wrinkled up his sub wrapper and tossed it into the trash can across the room. His arms shot up indicating the three was good and Chang gave him two thumbs up for the effort. Diaz frowned as she looked back and forth between Lucco and the garbage can. It was a long way, but Jackson was used to seeing him make that shot.

Ignoring Lucco's display, Captain Wilson glanced from picture to picture and said, "Why is Jenkins a suspect?"

"According to Connelly, he was mad at Williams, but she didn't know why," Diaz replied. Moving back towards her desk, she picked her water up off the table and took a sip before screwing the cap back on.

"Jenkins told us it was because Williams was cheating on Connelly, but I'm not sure I buy it," Jackson said. "I'm not sure if he's lying, hiding something, or if I just don't like him, but he's definitely a suspect."

"Agreed," Diaz said with a shake of her head.

"So, five suspects with Deadpool in the lead," Captain Wilson said. "Looks like you've got your work cut out for you." Walking back towards his office, he turned and added, "Keep me posted."

"Will do, Cap," Jackson replied. Turning to his team, he asked, "Did any of your canvassing turn up anything?"

"Possibly," Chang replied. "We found several people who remember a Deadpool leaving the Javits center in a hurry around nine this morning. None of them mentioned bandoliers and a sombrero, though."

"Adding those props would take the killer all of five seconds," Diaz said.

"It's a brilliant disguise. A totally different look in just a few seconds," Lucco replied

"Yeah, it's starting to look more and more like we need to find this guy," Jackson said as he finished his water and sat on the edge of the table. Closing his eyes, he rubbed his temples for a moment before going to his desk and pulling out some Tylenol. Catching his team's worried glances, he said, "Do we know which way Deadpool was heading when he left the Javits Center?" He swallowed three pills and dropped the bottle into his desk draw.

Looking back through his notes, Lucco tapped one of the pages with his pen and said, "Three of the witnesses put him exiting on Thirty-Eighth onto Eleventh Avenue and heading uptown."

"Okay, you guys head back over and canvas the area while Diaz and I go see the Medical Examiner."

"You sure you don't want us to go see the M.E.?" Chang said as he shifted uncomfortably in his seat.

"Yeah. She kinda bailed on you while you were in the hospital. We can take this if you want," Lucco said.

"No. Dr. Jensen and I are both adults doing a job, it'll be fine."

He tried to sound cavalier, but he wasn't sure who he was trying to convince. For their part, Chang and Lucco didn't say anything about it, but he couldn't avoid her forever even if he had a reason to. Still, if he was wrong, his headache would be getting a whole lot worse.

Chapter 19

By the time they left the precinct, the sky had turned a dark blue as day gave way to night. Street lights were on, and there were a few less cars on the road. The smell of exhaust still filled the air along with the ripe aroma of the piles of garbage waiting to be picked up by sanitation that night.

"So, what was that about?" Diaz said as she walked to the Challenger with Jackson.

Still rubbing at his temples, he replied, "What was what?"

"All of that stuff about Dr. Jensen and bailing on you."

Diaz still had Jackson's keys so she pressed the unlock button and moved towards the driver's side. When Jackson didn't say anything, she slid into the driver's seat.

Jackson opened his door and stepped into the car with a sigh. "Dr. Jensen and I used to date. It's always been an on and off thing because we always realize after a few weeks that it's not working. She was seeing someone else when I was shot, but she still came to visit me a couple times. I told her not to mess up a good relationship by staying by my side so she didn't. Now the guys think she ditched me and that I'm pissed about it. I've given up trying to set them straight, but things are actually okay between us... I hope."

"I guess we'll find out," she replied with a slight frown as she started the car.

"It'll be fine."

When they arrived in the M.E.'s office, the smell of chemicals hit them like a mallet. Jackson opened the door and was greeted with an awkward hug. "Jackson, it's so good to see you back on your feet."

"Thanks, Kari. It's good to be back."

A look of concern colored her face as she looked at his eye and touched his face, "What happened here?"

"Nothing major. Just walked into a door. You know me."

"I do know you, and that's how I know you're lying. You're not going to try and peddle that load of crap to your kids, are you?"

"Thank you," Diaz said as she entered the conversation. "I thought I was the only one who thought that was a terrible idea."

Jerking his thumb towards his colleague, Jackson said, "Dr. Kari Jensen, I'd like to introduce you to my new partner Detective Julia Diaz."

After shaking her hand, she Looked Diaz up and down, turned back to Jackson, and said, "Wow. Captain Wilson really hooked you up. She's gorgeous and smart."

"Thank you, Dr. Jensen."

"Please, call me Kari."

Tapping his foot impatiently, Jackson said, "I appreciate your concern, but I just can't let this weekend be ruined for Raina. After the last three months, she really needs this."

"She needs her father to tell her the truth, but that's none of my business," Dr. Jensen replied with a little bit of frost in her tone as she turned away.

Diaz' eyebrow rose and Jackson shrugged at her. "Kari, are we okay? Did I do something?"

"No. Of course not. I'm sorry. It's just been a hectic week. I assume you're here for my report?"

"Yes. ma'am. Just the highlights," Jackson said with an easygoing smile hoping to ease some of the sudden tension.

"Cause of Death is blood loss from the laceration on his throat. I found a small piece of plastic in the wound and sent it to Rivera. Based on liver temp and lividity, I place time of death between eight-thirty and nine-thirty a.m. Also, the bruise on his face was pre-mortem and had not yet fully developed. My guess would be that someone hit him in the face moments before they killed him."

"That all fits what we were thinking, and we also found a piece of plastic at the scene. Looks like someone used a toy sword as a real sword. Thanks, Kari."

Stepping over to her desk, she picked up a report and handed it to him. "No problem. Now, if you'll excuse me, I have a traffic fatality to attend to."

Surprised at the abrupt dismissal, he looked at Diaz and then back at Dr. Jensen. "Um, sure. I'll let you know if we need anything else."

Before he could exit the office, Dr. Jensen called out, "Jackson, if you get a few moments free in the next couple days, I'd really like to sit down with you."

Not sure what brought about the sudden thawing, he replied, "I'd love to. I'll give you a call."

She smiled and nodded, and he continued out to the car.

As they were driving back to the precinct, he looked at Julia and said, "Was that weird? That was weird, right?"

Keeping her eyes on the road, she replied, "No comment."

"I wasn't imagining that was I? That was kind of Jekyll and Hyde, right?" When no reply came, he added, "Maybe I did get hit in the head harder than I thought."

Stopping at a red light, she turned to him and said, "This! This is what I was talking about outside your house last night."

"Would knowing that I used to date the Medical Examiner have affected your decision to join the unit?"

"No. I guess not, but that was super awkward, and I hate awkward."

"I'm sorry about that, but I think something is going on with her that has nothing to do with me, but that she didn't want to talk about in front of you."

"Is that what your keen detective mind is telling you?" she replied as a smile tugged at the corner of her lips.

"Indeed it is," he replied with a smile of his own. "Seriously, though I can go back to her alone next time if you don't want to chance going through that again."

As the light turned green, the car started moving and her eyes were back on the road as she replied, "No. I'm an adult with a job to do as well. I can handle it if you can."

"I appreciate that, and for the record, Dr. Jensen is the only person we have any affiliation with that I used to date. My ex-wife, however is married to a real jackass in IA."

"Ooh, that sucks to be you," she said with a laugh. "And for the record, I had a short relationship with a guy in the Seventeenth precinct. It didn't end well, but I also haven't heard from him in a couple of years. He's the only guy I've been with since my husband died."

"Okay. Now that all of that is out of the way, let's head up to Thirty-Eighth and see if Looch and Pete have found anything."

"Are you sure you don't want to go home? You've been rubbing those temples a lot, and you did take a pretty good hit today."

Rubbing his temple again, he decided that in the spirit of team building, it might be a good idea to follow his new partner's advice. "You know what? You're right. If they find anything important, they'll call. Let's just stop back at the precinct so I can pick up a few things and then call it a day."

"Sounds good," she said.

"And, Julia... thanks. I know this hadn't been an easy day for you either, seeing one of your favorite celebrities cut down and wondering if one of your other favorites was responsible. If you need to talk about it—"

"No. I'm fine for now. I guess I'm still processing it. I'll let you know."

Chapter 20

Jackson walked into the house to the smell of pepperoni pizza wafting out of the living room. Raina and Amanda had changed out of their costumes and into some comfy-looking sweats and their outfits for the next day were laid out on the dining room table. They were sitting on the floor showing Jacob the day's pictures and eating their not-so-healthy dinner.

"I hope you saved a slice for me," Jackson said as he hung his coat on one of the hooks near the door.

"Dad!" Jacob yelled as he ran towards Jackson. Stopping short, his smile changed to a frown as he looked up at his father and said, "What happened to your eye?"

Raina suddenly seemed more interested in her dad than she was in her pictures. "Did that happen on your case today? Are you okay, dad? Let me get you some ice. Amanda, could you bring my dad a slice of pizza?"

She was already in the kitchen before he could respond to any of her queries, and he knew he had to handle the situation carefully. Raina had fallen into the pattern of dropping everything to tend to him after he was released from the hospital. It got to the point where he had to order her to go out and have some fun with Amanda. His injuries were difficult for her to handle, and it killed him that she was so upset. Today's injury was minor, but he hated the thought of it bringing back any of those feelings.

Amanda handed him a slice of pizza as she said, "Are you okay, Uncle Jax?"

Jacob looked up at him, worry evident in his cherub face, and Raina handed him an ice pack and folded her arms waiting for the explanation. Throwing his hands up in surrender, he said, "I'm fine." Noticing the apprehension in his daughter's eyes he added, "Really. Let's go sit down in the living room and I'll tell you what happened. It's pretty funny actually. The guys haven't stopped teasing me about it all day." Taking a bite of his pizza, he trotted into the living room and sat down on the couch. The kids sat down on the floor in front of him and waited for him to spin his tale.

With what Kari said about the truth still ringing in his ears, he decided to give it a try; omitting some of the details of course.

Before he could begin, Jacob piped up, "So what happened, dad?"

"I was at Comic Expo and as I was leaving the building, there was this little lady, not much bigger than Raina, dressed as Harley Quinn in a red and black onesie swinging a big mallet. I didn't see her and I walked right into it. It knocked me over and left me with this small cut and a big black eye. She must have felt really bad about it because she ran away before I could even get up. I walked over to the medical tent with Sergeant McGinnis and Detective Diaz, and the medic gave me a band-aid and told me I was fine. So that's it. Everything is fine, except for my reputation. Looch and Peter have been telling everyone I got my ass kicked by a ninety-pound girl. Even Captain Wilson teased me."

Amanda laughed and said, "Sucks to be you, Uncle Jax."

"Thanks, Amanda. Supportive as always," he replied and laughed as she stuck her tongue out at him.

"Can I buy a big mallet, dad?" Jacob asked as he crawled into his sister's lap.

Jackson's laugh turned into a guffaw as he looked at the mischievous look playing across his son's face. "That would be a big no."

"Aww."

Raina still looked pensive, so he said, "You don't have to worry, Peanut. Detective Diaz made me let her drive the rest of the day. I've got a good partner looking out for me again, okay?"

Her trepidation seemed to melt away as she hugged her brother tight and said, "Okay. Just please be careful, dad. Me and Jacob don't have anyone else."

Hearing that hit him harder than the mallet had. The fact that their mother had abandoned them still stung. That fact that she still lived in Brooklyn and rarely even tried to see her children hurt even more. Hearing his daughter say they had no one else meant she had given up on ever having a relationship with her mother and Jackson wanted to scream. It was never supposed to be this way, but Raina had been the one to catch Emma cheating and Emma all but disowned her after she let her father know. The whole situation was a mess, and he wished his daughter had never been tangled up in it. If he had been the one to catch her, she might still have a relationship with Raina.

Mustering as much cool as he could, he took his daughter by the hand and replied, "I'll be as careful as I can, Peanut. Now, let's see those nerd con pictures."

"Dad," Raina said with as much chastisement as a sixteen-year-old could muster while Amanda laughed.

"Sorry sweetie," he said, and winked with his good eye at Jacob.

A few minutes later, Jackson had to admit he was impressed with the lengths some of the people in Raina's pictures had gone to for their cosplay. He also found it somewhat amusing that he even knew what cosplay was. Picture after picture displayed immense talent and creativity along with a joy for what they were doing. It was hard not to be impressed.

"These costumes are fantastic, Raina. I take back everything bad I ever said about Comic Con."

"Yeah right," she said with a dubious expression on her face.

"No. Seriously. Some of these people are really talented, and I'm not gonna lie, some of these women are pretty attractive."

Before Raina could voice her displeasure with that comment, Jackson's phone rang. It was his neighbor Olga, and the only reason she would be calling this late was if she couldn't watch Jacob tomorrow. It was late, and he wasn't sure he'd be able to get another sitter on such short notice, but he would have to try.

Picking up the phone, he said, "Hey, Olga. What's up? Oh, your daughter's in town without the kids, and she's taking you to Atlantic City tomorrow? That sounds great... No, please don't worry about it. I'll make other arrangements for Jacob. It'll be fine... Okay, have fun... Yep, same time Monday... Goodbye."

Standing, he started towards the kitchen and said, "Keep your place on those pictures, Peanut. I want to see the rest of them after I get Jacob squared away."

With a heavy sigh, he made the call he always dreaded making. Part of him hoped his ex-wife would miss the call, but there was no one else he could call on such short notice. His other two options were going to be at the comic expo all day.

"What do you want, Jackson?" the grating whine on the other end of the call said.

"And hello to you, too, Emma."

"Whatever."

"Listen. I'm working a case, and Jacob's sitter cancelled for tomorrow. Is there any way you can pick him up and spend the day with him?"

"Sorry, I've got my weekly spa appointment booked and I'll lose the deposit if I cancel."

Annoyance flaring up instantly, he replied, "Seriously? I'll reimburse you for the deposit, how's that?"

"No, and I don't appreciate you calling last minute like this."

"You don't appreciate— maybe it's last minute because his sitter called me about thirty seconds ago, did you think about that?" Trying to keep control over his voice, he added, "When was the last time you even saw Jacob anyway?"

The angry reply shouted through the phone, "Oh don't you dare start that crap with me. You call me last minute. You ask me to cancel my plans, and now you're trying to guilt trip me into doing what you want. I don't think so."

"Guilt trip? You think it's a guilt trip for me to ask for a little help once in a while? He's your son, too, and you haven't seen him in over seven months. The whole time I was in the hospital, you couldn't even be bothered to poke your head in and say hello to your kids. They really needed you by the way."

"Stop it, Jackson."

"Seven months! And you live in the same damn borough. Great job, Emma. Sorry I burdened you with the hardship of seeing your own eight-year-old son."

"Screw you, Jackson."

"Right back at ya."

At times like this, he really missed being able to slam the phone down for emphasis. Pressing a button to end the call just seemed inadequate even if she was still talking when he did it. Leaning on the counter rubbing his temples and taking a few steadying breaths, he hoped his kids had missed that exchange. His hopes were dashed when Raina appeared in the doorway, cheeks flushed and eyes red.

Looking down at the white tile floor she said, "Amanda and I will take him with us to comic con tomorrow, dad."

Swallowing something that tasted rancid, maybe it was the last of his pride, he replied, "You heard that, Raina?"

"We all did. It took Jacob a minute, but he worked it out that mom doesn't want to see him, and he's not too happy about it."

"Damn it," he replied under his breath. Gently placing his hands on her shoulders, he looked her in the eyes and said, "I'm so sorry you guys had to hear all of that. I should have been mature enough to talk to your mom in a more civilized tone. I'll work something out for Jacob, don't worry, and please don't let this ruin your weekend."

"It's okay, Dad. I don't blame you. We already told Jacob that if mom couldn't pick him up that we would take him with us."

"Sweetie, this is not your responsibility—"

"Yes. It is," she replied in as stern a voice as he had ever heard from her. "He's my brother and I love him, and I don't mind if he comes along." With her shoulders beginning to shake, she added in a voice that cracked, "And I don't want to be like her."

Jackson wrapped her up in a bear hug. "Oh, Peanut. I'm sorry. I'm so sorry."

Drying her eyes, she said, "It's not your fault, dad. You stayed." With a kiss on the cheek, she added, "I love you, daddy." Turning, she padded back into the living room, but there was solitude in her steps and it broke his heart.

Chapter 21

Jackson's phone buzzed, waking him from a troubled sleep. It took him a few moments to get his bearings and figure out he was in his bedroom. Raina's words were still weighing heavily on his mind. Wiping the sleep from his eyes, he looked at the screen and saw it was Chang calling. He relished the idea of new information about the case taking his mind off of the night's events.

"What's up, Pete?" he said a little groggier than he intended.

"Sorry, Jackson. Did I wake you?"

"Maybe, but it wasn't good sleep anyway. What's up?"

"I just came across an interesting tidbit?"

"Chang?"

At one-seventeen in the morning, Jackson was in no mood to try and guess the information, or wait for it to be disseminated in a round-about way.

"Jimmy Shultz over at Hero TV took out a twenty-million-dollar life insurance policy on Garrison Williams less than two months ago."

"Is that normal?"

"It is normal for networks to take out insurance policies on some of their stars to protect their investment in the show. It's a variation of the key person insurance policy."

"Key person?"

"Basically, if a company has an employee whose death would lose them a lot of money, they can take an insurance policy out on that person to recoup some of their potential loses."

"Okay, it sounds straightforward enough. Why is this newsworthy?" Jackson could almost hear Chang's brain churning as his colleague prepared to answer.

"A couple of reasons really. From everything we've heard, it seems like Williams was going to be canned for repeated infractions of the ethics clause in his contract."

"So, he couldn't possibly fit the key person role the insurance policy would require," Jackson said. Standing, he walked out of his room to get a glass of water and saw Raina's light still on and made a mental note to check in on her after he finished with Chang.

"Also, the timing of the policy makes it suspicious."

"Agreed. Has anyone from the network ever replied to Lucco's calls?" Starting down the stairs, he glanced over to Jacob's door. How could Emma be so cold towards such an amazing kid?

"Not yet."

"Does Shultz live in the city?"

"Let me check," Chang replied. The sound of computer keys being tapped filled Jackson's ear. Not quite as soothing as most hold music, but infinitely better than waiting on hold. A moment later, he was in the kitchen and Chang was back on the line.

"Yes. He's on Park Avenue. Ooh, fancy."

"Sure is. And if he's not at the precinct by nine a.m., have a uni drag his fancy ass out of his apartment by nine-oh-one."

"Sure thing, boss."

"How did the canvas on Thirty-Eighth go?" he said as he filled his glass from the refrigerator water dispenser.

"Nothing yet, but one person did mention a homeless man who's fairly regular on that street in the mornings. We'll send someone over tomorrow to see if he noticed anything."

"Sounds like a long shot."

"Pretty much, but it's worth a try."

"Copy that. See you in the morning, Chang." Ending the call, he started towards his daughter's room, water in hand.

A gentle rap on the door was followed by the whispered words, "Come in."

He opened the door and Raina and Amanda were sitting on the floor with several boxes in front of them. Most of which were in various stages of being painted. A quick glance at the rug revealed a clear plastic tarp keeping the carpet safe from stray paint drops.

"What's going on, girls?"

"We're making Jacob's costume for tomorrow," Raina said.

"It looks interesting. Am I allowed to know what it's going to be?"

Raina pulled last Halloween's Optimus Prime mask off her bed followed by the spandex Captain America outfit he had bought Jacob for this Halloween. With as big a smile as her tired face could muster, she said, "We're making him a mash-up costume."

"Mash-up?"

"It's when you combine two separate characters into one cosplay, Uncle Jax."

"We're calling it Captain Prime. He'll wear the Captain America suit and carry the shield in one hand, but on his feet and the other hand he'll have transformer parts to match his Optimus Prime mask. What do you think?"

"I think it's going to be fantastic girls, and thank you so much for helping me out and doing this for Jacob. I'll let you get back to it." With a smile he added, "Goodnight. Don't stay up too late."

"We won't, Dad."

Closing the door behind him, he took a sip of water and trudged back to his room. Seeing the girl's smiles might help his sleep come a little bit easier this time.

Chapter 22

Jackson stepped into his kitchen to see three costumed heroes, and one of those heroes had put coffee on for him making them a real-life hero. The aroma hit his nostrils and it reminded him of how tired he was. He needed to get that caffeine in him quick. Raina approached him with a tired smile holding a cup and handed it to him.

"Here you go, Dad. It looks like you really need it."

"Yeah, Uncle Jax. You look like crap," Amanda said with a laugh.

With the bruise circling one eye, and the bag under the other, he knew she was right, but he tapped into his most positive voice and said, "Thanks, Amanda, and thanks, Peanut." Taking a sip of his coffee, he looked over the trio before him. "So, who are we today? Spiderman's sisters?"

"No. I'm Spider Woman, the Jessica Drew version. Amanda is cosplaying Spider Gwen," she said as she and Amanda positioned themselves in front of Jacob.

Jackson's eyes lit up and he said, "Is Spider Gwen related to Tony Gwynn?"

"Who's Tony Gwynn?" Raina replied.

"Never mind," he said, shoulders slumping in the knowledge that he had failed to pass on his love of baseball to his daughter.

"I like the platinum wig, Amanda."

"Thanks, Uncle Jax."

A smile spread across her face, and it must have been contagious because Raina had one, too. They parted like the Red Sea to reveal Jacob in all of his costumed glory.

With a theatrical bow, Raina said, "Allow us to present for the first time anywhere, Captain Prime!"

Jackson stood there impressed. The robot boots and gloves the girls had made looked professional. He had no idea they were so talented. They had even made a robot looking belt to go along with the costume.

Optimus Prime's red and blue colors meshed perfectly with the Captain America costume, and Jacob lifted the mask to reveal a proud grin.

"You look incredible, Jacob. Great job, girls." Stepping forward, he held out his hand and Jacob gave him an enthusiastic high five.

"He looks really good, right, Dad?" Raina said.

Jackson could barely contain his smile. "He sure does. You two should design costumes for a living."

"It's really more of a hobby, but we love doing it," Amanda said.

"Okay, pictures." Taking out his phone, he found his smile growing as his kids struck their best superhero poses and he snapped off several pictures.

After returning his phone to his pocket, he pulled out some money and said, "Okay, Sergeant McGinnis will have a ticket waiting for Jacob, so be sure to give her this." Handing Raina a fifty-dollar bill he added, "And don't let her refuse, okay?"

"Okay, Dad."

Handing Raina some more money he said, "I threw in twenty bucks for each of you to get lunch, and an extra fifty for Jacob to get some souvenirs. Is that going to be enough?"

"Yeah. It should be fine, thanks," she replied.

"You don't have to pay for my lunch, Uncle Jax," Amanda said.

"What happened to not turning down free money?"

"That was before you gave Raina all that extra yesterday, and now you've gotta pay for Jacob, too."

"Don't worry about it, Amanda. I know your dad would do the same for Raina and Jacob. Now, if I'm driving you in today, we have to leave in two minutes."

Finishing the last of his coffee, he checked to make sure he had his case file with him. By the time he had his notes organized and the newspaper in his hand, his three heroes were lined up right behind him ready to go. He grabbed his keys and took his coat off its hook as he held open the door and watched his kids pass through and walk to the car. To his surprise, their excitement was contagious, and he caught himself wishing he could go with them just to see the smiles on their faces.

After dropping the kids off, and asking Sergeant McGinnis to keep an eye out for them if possible, he drove back to the precinct. It was another perfect fall day, and the sun glinted off the skyscrapers as he drove with the windows down. Cool air rushed into the car helping wake him up a bit more. To his disbelief, the cherry on top of a great Saturday commute, he found a parking spot less than a block away from the precinct. Walking into the squad room at eight-thirty-nine, Chang was the only member of his unit present, and he wondered if the man even went home last night.

"What are you sleeping here now, Pete?"

A humble smile pulled at the corners of his lips as he looked up and said, "No. I left right after we spoke last night, and this morning I caught a lull in traffic on the BQE. Sailed right in."

Raising an eyebrow, Jackson replied, "That was lucky. I can't remember the last time there was a lull in traffic on the BQE."

"Well there was no lull for me," Lucco complained as he stormed into the room. "Seriously every asshat in New York was on the BQE today."

"You know that includes you, right, Looch?" Chang said.

"Yeah, funny!" he replied as he popped open a can of cola and chugged.

"Traffic was so light today," Diaz crooned as she breezed across the room, coffee in hand. "I thought I was toast because I couldn't get Hector going. I got to my parents fifteen minutes later than usual, but then it was easy like Sunday morning."

"So, everyone had an easy commute except me? That sounds about right," Lucco said.

"How's your eye? It doesn't look like you slept much." Diaz said to Jackson as she sat down at her desk.

"Still hurts but it's fine. I didn't sleep much, but that has more to do with my ex than my eye."

"You spoke to your ex?" Lucco asked with a healthy amount of skepticism in his voice.

"More like yelled, but that's expected. What sucked was Raina and Jacob heard and they were pretty upset. I try to never say anything bad about Emma in front of them, but I was in another room and didn't realize my voice had risen. They had already pretty much guessed that their mother wants nothing to do with them, but hearing me confirm it in angry tones really brought it home for them. I've never in my life felt like more of a jackass than I did last night."

"Yeah, but they'll love you more for it in the long run because they know how much you love them," Chang said. Straightening up, he nodded towards the Captain's office and said, "We should probably pick this up later."

"No. I'm pretty much done talking about it," Jackson said.

Following Chang's line of sight, he saw Chief of Detectives Alvarez marching into Captain Wilson's office with a look on his face that suggested he was angry. Chief Alvarez was always angry, so this was nothing new, but Jackson knew that anger had to do with him being the head of the unit, and it wasn't likely to end any time soon. With a controlled exhale, Jackson stood up and waited for the inevitable summoning.

Chapter 23

"Winters," Captain Wilson called across the active squad room. Jackson looked up and Wilson waved him over.

"Here goes nothing," he mumbled to his team.

Lumbering across the room to meet with the Chief of Detectives, he nodded to two uniformed officers as he walked. He stopped at the door and waited for Captain Wilson to bid him enter before shuffling into the office. Chief Alvarez closed the door behind him and they all took a seat. Jackson was surprised that Chief Alvarez had let Captain Wilson remain behind his desk. The man's ego knew no bounds.

Without preamble, Chief Alvarez turned to him and said, "Where are we on the Garrison Williams investigation?"

"We have five clear suspects, but our primary suspect's identity is unknown?"

"Unknown? Why?"

"He's always in costume. So far, it's only been a character called Deadpool. And he's been seen with two college age women also in costume as Harley Quinn."

"Who are the other suspects?"

"Colin Stone, Jasmine Connelly, Steve Jenkins and a Hero TV exec named Jimmy Shultz who should be on his way in now."

Chief Alvarez let out a low whistle and said, "Tread carefully, Detective."

Jackson wanted to roll his eyes. As if they were going to be anything but careful. Did he really think they were just going to march several celebrities out of the con in cuffs and start a riot? Maybe he did think that. He was known to be the kind of boss who thought no one else really had any idea of how to do the job which led to many redundant comments like that.

Nodding, he said, "Yes, sir. We've conducted all interviews on site as per your orders, and we've barely caused a ripple to the flow of the convention."

"You understand how much money this convention brings to the city, right? We can't have any of your cowboy crap jeopardizing that," he said with a hard edge to his voice.

"Excuse me?" Jackson replied before he could stop himself.

"You need me to spell it out for you, Winters?" Chief Alvarez said in a menacing tone.

"No. I think he's got it," Captain Wilson said glaring a warning at Jackson.

Ignoring the Captain's attempt to diffuse the situation, he pressed forward. "I'm not sure I do, Captain. I'd like an example of this cowboy crap so I know how to avoid it." Jackson knew he was treading close to the edge of some dangerous waters, but Chief Alvarez' rebuke was completely uncalled for and he was already in a bad mood.

"Winters!" Captain Wilson bit out, but Chief Alvarez was out of his chair.

Poking his finger into Jackson's chest, he growled, "You need an example? How about getting your partner killed? Is that a good enough example? You went off book and your partner died. How's that? No one else wants to say it, so I will."

Now it was Jackson that was out of his chair, and Captain Wilson was already moving out from behind the desk to step in between them. "What did you just say to me?" Jackson said voice rising.

"You may have gotten the headlines, and the commendations, Winters, but the reality is if you were half as good a detective as Boyd was, he'd still be alive right now." Chief Alvarez was now squared up to him and in his face.

Not backing down, he squared up to the Chief and replied, "I didn't ask for any commendations. I even asked Captain Wilson to give them all to Buddy. Don't try and come in here and act like this was something I wanted."

Captain Wilson stepped in between them and yelled, "That's enough, both of you." Lowering his voice, he added, "Boyd was the senior detective on the case, and he ordered Winters to split up. We even have Winters' protest on record. What happened to detective Boyd was tragic, but it was Boyd's decision to split up and go in without backup, not

Winters, and he left plenty of blood in that alley as a result of Boyd's decision, too."

Hearing his captain stick up for him melted some of the anger, and Jackson took a step back. "We'll go about this investigation as quietly and efficiently as possible, sir," he said in a conciliatory tone.

"See that you do," Chief Alvarez said. Turning to Captain Wilson, he said, "And Captain, you'd do well to keep better control of your people." Without another word, he spun on his heel and stormed out of the office.

Jackson moved to follow, but Captain Wilson grabbed his arm and spun him around. "What the hell is the matter with you? You don't get into the face of the Chief of Detectives ever! Do you understand? He says something to you like that again, you take it without a word, document it, and I bring it to the commissioner. That's how a chain of command works. As it is, I may have a hard time keeping you from getting your ass busted down to traffic duty. Now, get out of here and go solve that case."

"Yes, sir."

Jackson marched out of the office with several sets of eyes pretending not to look in his direction. When he reached his desk, Lucco looked up with a smirk plastered to his face and said, "So, good meeting?"

Lucco was probably the only one in the unit who would say something like that, but it brought a hint of a smile to his face. "You guys heard that?"

"You don't really have an indoor voice when you're angry, do you?" Diaz added to a round of subdued chuckles.

"Apparently not. Now, what's next?"

"Shultz is on his way in," Chang replied.

Chapter 24

With a clear sky and the sun out, this was shaping up to be a nice fall morning in New York City. It almost made him like the place a little. He would still be on the first plane out as soon as his obligations for the weekend were met. For now, however, he was interested in something that could prove useful to him. A Deadpool met with two Harleys on the corner of Thirty-Fourth Street and Tenth Avenue, and he was very interested in what they were talking about.

Discretely handing Red Harley a picture, Deadpool said, "Our target for today is Gene Ludwick. He'll be finishing a panel in room 1A18 at ten-thirty."

"Ludwick? As in the tech billionaire?" Red Harley blurted, failing to hide her shock.

Glancing around in a surreptitious manner, he put his hand on her arm and said, "Easy. Not so loud. We don't want anyone else knowing our business."

"There's no way he'll be there without some of his bodyguards," White Harley said.

"That's why there're two of you. Give it your best shot. I'm sure it'll be more than enough. Have sex with his bodyguards if you need to; just get Ludwick to the Collingsworth."

Folding the corner of his newspaper down to have a peek at the interesting conversation playing out in front of him, he just had to hear the rest of it. Pretending to turn to the sports section as he leaned on the hood of his red Prius, he kept a keen ear tuned to the costumed figures in front of him. People had been passing by in colorful attire all morning, but this was the group he had been waiting for. This was the group that might wind up giving him the opportunity he needed to get away with murder.

"The cops are onto us, Edgar. We should quit while we're ahead," White Harley said as she held her arms close to her body against the chill in the morning air.

Edgar has a room at the Collingsworth. Now he had a name and a place. Folding the newspaper in half, he walked around to the edge of his rental car and shuffled into the driver's seat to wait and see which direction Edgar went in. He rolled the window down and opened the newspaper once again to see if anything else of note would be said, but he knew he already had all the information he needed.

"The cops couldn't find a pimple on their ass with a magnifying glass," Edgar replied.

Stepping closer to the girls, he gently took each of them by the hand. "Don't worry. No one knows who we are or where we are, and I'm paying you more than enough to take a little risk. Now go, and if you can't find Ludwick, try to find Ray Sanderson. He's a closet Anime fan, and a retro Sailor Moon panel is letting out of room 1A24 at eleven."

Letting go of their hands, Deadpool turned and began walking away from the Javits Center while his two companions reluctantly headed towards the convention.

He figured Garrison's blackmailer wouldn't be working out of the Marriot which was the official convention hotel, but he figured the guy was in the area. The idea of the blackmailer had been planted in the cop's minds when they questioned him. Since that time, he had been hoping to find the blackmailer, so he could feed him to the police and better his chances of getting away. Having found the perpetrators, it looked as though his plan would work. Now all he had to do was get a burner phone and leave a trail of breadcrumbs for the police to follow before getting back to the convention.

Prepaid phones were a criminal's best friend. Not that he was planning on becoming a criminal. Garrison had been a one-time venture into a life of crime, and while it was a doozy, he wasn't planning an encore. With everything this Deadpool wannabe was into, hopefully the cops would be convinced they had the right guy long enough for the con to end and for him to get back to the normal ebb and flow of his life.

Wearing a ball cap with his hood pulled up over it and a pair of Oakleys, he hoped no one would pick up on who he was as he entered the convenience store to buy his first and hopefully his last burner. Entering the store, he noticed merchandize stacked everywhere. One side of the store was dedicated to snacks and drinks, while the other side seemed dedicated to chaos with a dizzying array of anything you could think of. Pencils next to purses, glasses next to screwdrivers, there seemed to be no rhyme or reason to the set up. Finding what he was looking for by the counter, he pointed to the haphazard stack of phones behind the older Asian woman working the register and said, "I'd like to buy a phone."

"What brand?" she replied without looking at the phones.

"Doesn't matter."

"What color?"

"Doesn't matter."

"What size screen?"

Starting to get frustrated, he said, "Doesn't matter. Actually, look behind you." Waiting until the woman complied, he added, "I will take the phone sitting on the top of the stack."

"That phone is $49.95."

"That's great. I'll have that one."

"Would you like to add data?"

"No. Thank you."

"Would you like to purchase insurance?"

That question almost struck him as funny. There was no way a forty-nine-dollar burner phone in a convenient store came with an insurance plan, or at least no way any of their customers had ever purchased it.

"No. Thank you, ma'am. Just the phone please, and I'm in a bit of a hurry."

Scanning the phone and looking back at him, she said, "$54.94. Cash or credit?"

Handing her three twenties, he looked down at his watch.

"Would you like paper or plastic?"

"I don't need a bag. I'll just take the phone." Starting to get frustrated, he thought that if she asked him one more question, he might be committing his second murder.

Handing him his change and the phone, she said, "Thank you. Please come again."

I sure won't, he thought as he hurried out of the store. Tearing open the box, he jumped into his rental car and took off to find a more secluded place to make his call. After driving a few blocks, he made the call.

"Nine-one-one, what's your emergency?" the tinny voice answered as he glanced around making sure he was not being captured on surveillance.

"I think I just saw that Deadpool guy the cops are looking for going into the Collingsworth hotel. He was with two young women dressed like Harley Quinn, but they went towards the Javits Center."

"Can you tell me what he was wearing?"

"He was wearing a regular Deadpool costume, and he was a little over weight, so the spandex was a little tight."

"Can you explain what a regular Deadpool costume looks like?"

Frustration began seeping in again. Was everyone in New York this thick? "It's a red costume. Just Google Deadpool and look at the first image."

"Would you mind holding, sir?"

With a smile, he ended the call. This was even better than he had hoped. That inept operator would probably take several hours to get this information to the police, and that would give him all the time he needed to get his ducks in a row to get away with murder. He was so happy about the stupidity of the nine-one-one woman; he almost didn't see the car stop at the light in front of him. Hitting the brakes a little harder than necessary, a short screech grabbed several people's attention.

"Watch where you're going, jackass," a middle-aged man in a cheap suit yelled as he crossed the street flashing him a New York salute.

"Nice driving, moron," a woman trying to look classy, but was obviously anything but, yelled as she jogged across the street in high heels.

Having no choice but to sit there and take it, he just smiled hoping for the light to change soon. The longer he stayed in this city, the less he liked it. He was already about to be late to his next convention obligation, but he knew his fans would wait.

Chapter 25

Edgar arrived back to his hotel room. The maids had just left, and there was a hint of a bleach smell near the bathroom. He lit a candle, and the cinnamon aroma would all but eradicate any residual cleaning odors. Making sure the blinds were still closed, he was checking on his cameras when Red Harley walked in, and he could tell she was unhappy.

With as soothing a voice as he could muster, he said, "Karen, what are you doing here? Where's Leena?"

Stepping closer, she replied, "Leena's at the con waiting on Ludwick. I needed to talk to you."

"About?" He continued checking his cameras to make sure they were all operating correctly. It would be a shame to lose out on a payment because of equipment failure.

"About our financial arrangement," she said placing her hands on her hips for emphasis.

Stopping in his tracks, he turned slowly to face her and bit out the words, "What about our financial arrangement?"

"It sucks and I want more money, that's what."

"We already have an arrangement in place," he said carefully.

Fixing him with a hard glare, she said, "An arrangement that greatly benefits you, not me."

"Twenty thousand dollars is not enough?"

"Not compared to what you're making it isn't. I know you're blackmailing the guys we're sleeping with, and I didn't sign on for that. It's bad for business. I only signed on because you said we were just here to sweeten a corporate deal. After this, I won't be able to work in this city again. Besides, Leena and I are doing all the hard work we should be entitled to some of the profits."

Sitting on the edge of the bed, he tapped the comforter next to him. "Sit down for a minute, Karen," he said, but his voice had taken a menacing turn.

With some apprehension, she sat on the bed next to him and he continued, "Let me explain something to you. I've been working on this plan for months. It was a painstaking process figuring out ahead of time who was going to be here worth bribing. I had to bribe people that work for the con to leak some names to me. I had to get the van and learn how to use all of this equipment that I had to purchase, and I face the bulk of the risk. Blackmail carries a far higher sentence than prostitution. Compared to what I've had to do, what you're doing is easy."

"You think what we do is easy? Have you seen some of the men we've had to sleep with?"

"I didn't hear you complaining when you were having sex with Garrison Williams," he quipped. Seeing her face harden, he continued, "You are a whore. Sleeping with people is what you get paid to do. I hired you because your ad said no questions and no hassles. Not only did I agree to your rate, I practically doubled it. I am paying you five thousand a day to sleep with two or three guys. You won't have to work again for weeks if you don't want to, and you'll have more than enough money to resettle if you need to. Now please, enough of this nonsense. Go meet Leena at the convention."

With a sigh, Karen stood and started towards the door. Edgar had already returned to his equipment check. Turning back to face him, she said, "It's not right. You're using us just like everyone else. All I'm asking is double. That can get me out of the life and away from here. You'll never see or hear from me again."

"What about Leena?"

"She's naïve. She actually thinks twenty grand is a lot of money."

"From where I'm standing, Leena seems like the smart one."

With a theatrical sigh, he took a step towards Karen and said, "Since you're here instead of working, I'll give you a choice. You can stay here and help me relieve some of my stress, or you can go find Leena and do your job. Hell, I'm feeling generous. I'll even throw in an extra five K since you made such a compelling argument. Now what's it gonna be?"

"There's a third option where I go to the police and let them know what you're up to," she replied, defiance coloring every word.

Rounding on her, he had her pressed up against the wall before she could move. "You just passed the point of no return, Chica," he growled as he put his hands around her throat and began to choke her.

Clutching at his hands, fear filled her eyes as she squeaked, "Edgar. Edgar, I can't breathe."

"That's the point," he snarled. "Greedy whore like you needs to be taught a lesson."

"Edgar! Stop," she wheezed, fighting for even a tiny breath of air. Her struggling hands found a vase of flowers. Frantically grabbing for it, her fingers finally closed around it and she swung with all her might; hitting him in the head. Shattered glass, water, and flowers cascaded down Edgar's body as he released his grip and clutched at his head.

Gasping for air, she tried to reach the door, but Edgar was on her too fast. "You're gonna pay for that!" he said as he threw her across the room.

Her foot caught the edge of the bed and she fell forward; hitting her head on the corner of the dresser and landing in a heap next to the bed. Blood spread quickly on the brown carpet as Edgar stared down at Karen with a mixture of horror and grim satisfaction. A moment later, he realized that his rash action had effectively ended his get-rich-quick scheme.

"No, no, no. This can't be happening," he mumbled as he tried to think of a way to keep his scam rolling.

Leaning over, he checked Karen's pulse confirming she was dead and began to sop up the blood with the hotel towels. The trunk he had used to bring all of the equipment into the room was still in the closet and should fit Karen's body. After folding the body into the trunk and cleaning up the broken glass and flowers of the vase, he still had to figure out what to do with the bloody section of carpet. He couldn't have Leena bringing high profile marks in and seeing that. As he was closing the door to the closet, he looked at the carpet and a thought hit him, but he would need some tools.

Edgar wheeled his trunk through the lobby of the Collingsworth and out to his van. After loading the trunk into the van, he drove several blocks away and backed into a construction site with four dumpsters lined up near an open gate. After a long glance in each direction, he decided the coast was clear. Hoisting the trunk out of the back of the van, he hefted it into a half-full dumpster. Peering around the area one last time, he closed up his van and drove back to the hotel. Retrieving a level, tape measure, and a box cutter from the van, he started back up to the room. On his way to the room, he saw an unattended maid's cart and grabbed a few towels.

He entered the room and tossed the extra towels on the bed. Placing the level on the floor, he cut a straight line into the bloody carpet with his box cutter. After cutting a rectangle out of the carpet, he lifted the corner of the dresser to remove it. Going over to the closet, he cut a piece the same size. Placing the bloody carpet in the waste basket with the bloody towels, he took another towel and wiped up the blood that had seeped through the carpet. With a frown, he tossed that towel in the basket and wrapped up the bag. Lifting the edge of the dresser again, he slid the new piece into place and surveyed his handiwork.

"No good. The edges look cut," he said under his breath.

Taking a gander around the room, he saw Karen's bag. He placed the bag over the carpet and looked again. "It'll have to do. It's not like they'll be checking out the floor," he mumbled as he placed the plastic bag full of evidence into a backpack and left the room looking like just another fan on his way to a day of Comic Con fun.

Leena's next mark would have to be the last one because he suddenly felt a strong desire to leave town as quickly as possible.

Chapter 26

Jackson sat at his desk waiting for Hero TV executive Jimmy Shultz to arrive. Chang spoke on the phone with an officer who was looking for the homeless man on Thirty-Eighth, and Lucco was going through more convention footage trying to see if he could spot their prime suspect. Diaz was leaning over Lucco's chair sipping coffee and peering over his shoulder while Jackson went through his case notes. Soft sunlight drifted through the window lighting up the desk as he read.

Something about this case was not sitting well with him, and he couldn't put his finger on it. At first, he thought that it was because it was his first case back, and then he thought maybe it was because his kids were at the Javits Center when it happened. Now he knew that there was more going on with this case than he could see at the moment, and it bothered him.

Chang's voice broke his concentration. "IA in the house," he whispered as he glanced towards the door to the squad room.

Jackson looked up in time to see Joey Sambino storming towards him. "This day just keeps getting better and better," he mumbled as he shot his team an exaggerated eye roll.

"Who's that?" Diaz whispered.

"The guy Jackson's ex cheated on him with, and to make it more fun, they're married now," Lucco replied.

"Even more fun, he's IA," Chang added.

"Jackson, we need to talk, now!" Sambino said, drawing most of the squad room's attention.

"I'm kinda busy. Come back later," Jackson replied as he looked back down at his case notes.

"No. Now," he said again, snatching the folder from Jackson's hands and tossing it on the desk.

"You might want to take a step back, Joey."

"Why? What are you gonna do?" he replied, and now the entire room was focused on the brewing showdown.

"I might just have to give IA a call to find out why they're hassling me in the middle of an important investigation."

Puffing out his chest in defiance he said, "Oh, so you're a snitch now, Jackson?"

Standing up, he replied, "No, Joey. That would be you. What do you want?"

"You can't be calling my wife and starting trouble."

"This isn't the time or place for this conversation, Joey."

"I disagree. Call her and bother her again, and we're gonna have problems."

"You want to talk about this here? Fine! We'll talk about this here. Sorry if asking her to take a little responsibility for her children is such a bother to her. Sorry that you married a crazy cheater who would abandon her own children. Is that the apology you're looking for?"

"What the hell did you just say to me?"

"What are you deaf and stupid? I called her a cheater. You know she is. What do you think it was you two were doing while she was still married to me?" The rest of the squad room suddenly seemed busy.

"You better watch yourself, Winters."

"Or what? You'll have Emma ignore my kids some more? I don't know what you thought you were going to accomplish coming here like this; calling me out like some tough guy in front of my team, but I'm not playing your stupid games or hers. You don't want me to call and ask her to watch her own son anymore? Fine, I won't."

Taking his phone out, he made a show of deleting her number. "There, I deleted her number. I'll never call her about anything having to do with MY kids again, but don't be bringing her by the house on the rare occasion she wants to pretend she's a real person and actually see her children."

Sambino looked like he wanted to throw down right there, but he held his composure and growled, "I hope you're ready for the hell I'll make your life if you call her again."

Jackson rolled his eyes and replied, "Yeah, and I hope you signed a pre-nup because once a cheater always a cheater."

Joey took two quick steps towards him, but was stopped short by the booming voice of Captain Wilson. "Is there something I can help you with, Officer Sambino?"

"No, sir," he replied while continuing to glower at Jackson.

"Good. I'm sure you can find your way out then."

Begrudgingly, he said, "Yes, sir." Turning back to Jackson, he added, "This isn't over, Jackson."

"As far as I'm concerned it is," Jackson replied and grabbed the folder off his desk as Sambino stalked out of the room.

"Winters, a moment please," Captain Wilson said.

Jackson hurried over and said, "Sorry about that, Cap. I had an uncomfortable conversation with Emma last night, and I guess Sambino thought here and now was a good place to talk about it."

"And that's why you were borderline insubordinate with Chief Alvarez this morning, isn't it?"

"Yeah, I'm really sorry about that, Cap. I hate to make things more difficult for you. I'll write a formal apology to Alvarez if you need me to."

"No. He was out of line, too. Just tread lightly. Remember, Alvarez is already gunning for you because he wanted his guy in your seat, but the commissioner wants you, so you're okay for now, but you don't have a lot of rope if you know what I mean."

"Understood."

"Jimmy Shultz is waiting for you in interview room three," he said as he withdrew to his office and closed the door. Jackson waved Diaz over as he started out of the squad room.

"Did you wake up this morning and decide you were going to piss everyone off, or is it more of a whack-a-mole approach?" Diaz asked as she walked beside him to their next interview.

"Funny."

"I'm just saying."

Chapter 27

Jackson opened the door to interview room three and walked into a wall of cologne. The smell almost caused him to take a step back. Maybe the stench was intended to be pleasant had it not been so liberally applied. Diaz stifled a sneeze as she entered the room. Sitting on the other side of that aroma was a short, smug man wearing navy blue Canali slacks and a white dress shirt with thin red pin stripes by Hugo Boss. The top two buttons had been left open with a pair of Ray Ban sunglasses hanging off the shirt, and the man was fidgeting with a pair of gold cuff links. Jackson didn't get a look at his shoes but had no doubt they would probably cost him a full pay check or more. Jimmy Shultz clearly wanted people to know he was wealthy.

Sitting down across from Jimmy, Jackson opened his folder to reveal the crime scene photos of Garrison Williams. Diaz watched Jimmy's reaction closely as her partner slid the photos across the metal table. So far there was no reaction except maybe a little disdain.

Through pursed lips he let out an exaggerated sigh and said, "If we could skip the theatrics. This is a rather busy weekend for me."

"Sorry if the murder of one of your stars has put a crimp in your plans, Jimmy," Diaz said while Jackson laid out a couple more photos.

"Why am I here?" he asked, his face still betraying no emotion at the gruesome photos.

"We were hoping you could help us figure out who did this?" Jackson replied.

"Oh, and here I thought it was because of the insurance policy Hero TV took out on Garrison a couple months ago."

"You've gotta admit the timing does look a bit suspicious," Diaz replied as she continued to study his face.

"Twenty million dollars for a person you were about to fire anyway seems like a very fortuitous coincidence," Jackson added.

"We hadn't decided to fire Garrison."

"Maybe not, but you were close," Jackson said.

Leaning forward, Diaz added, "Especially given the rumors floating around the con this weekend."

Jimmy queried an innocent eyebrow and said, "What rumors?"

"C'mon, Jimmy, you don't really expect us to believe you haven't heard Mr. Williams was being blackmailed for partying with two college-aged cuties dressed as Harley Quinn?"

"I have, but much like your justice system, we prefer our employees be considered innocent until proven guilty."

The pair on this guy, Jackson thought as he leaned back in his chair and said, "Can anyone verify your whereabouts yesterday morning between eight and ten?"

"I was with several of our other executives in a meeting. We were making a last-minute adjustment of the information we are going to release on Hero TV's third original program today."

"And what information would that be?" Diaz said.

"The show is going to be about Raging Bull and will be the first ever superhero television show to cast a Native American in the lead role."

Jackson knew Diaz had only asked to satisfy her own curiosity, but he wanted to see how easily the information rolled off Jimmy's tongue. Sliding a pen and paper towards their aroma-challenged person of interest, he said, "I need a list of people who can verify you were there."

"No problem," he replied as he took the pen and wrote down five names. Sliding the pad back towards Jackson he added, "There might have been an intern there bringing our coffee, but I'm not sure what her name is."

"So, what prompted the insurance policy in the first place if you guys were so unhappy with Mr. Williams' behavior?"

"Can I be honest?"

"We'd prefer it," Diaz deadpanned.

"I think the ethics clauses in these contracts aren't worth the paper they're written on. They're there because these actors are supposed to be role models, but we're not really holding them accountable to any sort of standard. Bottom line is Garrison's negative press was costing the network money. I could care less if he wants to have an orgy with a whole

113

sorority. It's none of my business, but it becomes my concern when it starts affecting the network's bottom line."

"Fine, but why take the policy out on him? You get nothing if you fire him," Jackson said.

"Because I'm a cynic, and I figured at the rate Garrison was self-destructing, the network could make a little money if he went too far. And it looks like I was right."

"Are you serious?" Diaz said, popping out of her seat as if a timer had just gone off. "You're betting against his life? How about getting him some help? Did you ever think about that?"

Raising his hands in mock surrender, he said, "Take it easy there, little lady. We tried several times, but he wasn't having it. I mean he was a nice enough kid, but he had no idea how to handle his fame and wasn't about to let anyone help him. I saw that and made a gamble, but that doesn't mean I didn't care. I'm the one who hired him. We were friends, but this is business."

Diaz looked like she wanted to rip Jimmy's arms off, but before she could, Jackson stood and said, "Thank you for your time, Mr. Shultz. You're free to go."

Chapter 28

"What a jackass," Diaz yelled after Jimmy exited the interview room.

"Agreed. He's slimy, but I don't think he did it."

"And who is he calling little lady? Guys like five-six, tops. Sexist pig!"

"Relax, don't worry about him." Jimmy had fired his partner up, and he wanted to chuckle, but he didn't know her well enough to yet.

"We're still gonna run down his alibi, though, right?"

"Of course, I just don't think it's going to end with Jimmy behind bars for murder. Sorry, Julia."

Sneezing again, she said, "And that much cologne on anyone should be illegal. What did he fall in a vat of it?"

"Maybe he was trying to get superpowers?" Jackson replied with a smirk.

Stopping with a theatrical sigh, she hit his arm and said, "You just made a comic joke, Jackson. I'm so proud of you. The guys are going to be so happy about this."

As they were walking back to the squad room, Diaz' phone buzzed. "What's up, Looch?"

"Are you with Jackson?"

"Yeah, I got you on speaker."

"We just found a dead body stuffed in a trunk in a dumpster. She's dressed as Harley Quinn."

Exchanging a look with his partner in the hallway, Jackson said, "You think it might be the one who hit me?"

"Maybe, you two should get down here."

Before Jackson could answer, his phone buzzed. "Hang on, Looch. I have another call coming in." Accepting the call, he said, "Detective Winters."

"Hi, detective, this is Officer Watkins over at the Tenth. We received an anonymous nine-one-one call at eight-forty-five this morning that we believe is connected to your case. It took a while for the call to get routed here because the operator didn't believe it was legitimate."

"What was the call about?"

"A man said he saw the Deadpool the cops were looking for with two Harley Quinns."

At that, Jackson's eyebrows rose, and he reached into his jacket for his pen while holding the phone to his ear with his shoulder. "Anything else, Watkins?"

"He said the girls went off to Comic Con and he saw the Deadpool go into the Collingsworth Hotel on Thirty-Fifth Street."

"We'll check that out, Watkins. Thanks."

"What was that?" Diaz said as they stepped into the squad room.

"Anonymous nine-one-one call this morning gives us a possible location for our killer. The Collingsworth hotel."

Through the speaker on Diaz' phone, Lucco said, "That could be something."

"Agreed, but we'll check it out after we meet you and Pete. Where are you?"

"West Thirty-Sixth between Tenth and Eleveth."

"We'll be there in ten," Jackson said as he unlocked his desk draw and removed his firearm.

"Sounds good," Lucco replied.

Diaz ended the call and retrieved her own weapon. "Things are starting to move fast. We better catch a break quick or Alvarez is gonna chew your ass out again."

"Thanks for the reminder."

The temperature had dropped a little from the morning which meant that a cold front was on its way, but the sun was still out among some fluffy white clouds. Jackson silently wondered how long the good weather would hold out. As they drove over to their new crime scene, they passed several buildings that had serious renovations going. Most of the construction sites had fences around them, and most of those fences had privacy fabric. The splotches of color broke up the monotony of the buildings. There wasn't a lot of traffic because it was the weekend, so they made good time.

Jackson glanced at Diaz and said, "If our tipster is right, then our Harley's death is sometime between eight-forty-five and now."

"Do you think our suspect is killing off his accomplices so no one can ID him?"

"It's too soon to say. Let's wait and see if this is one of our girls before we go in that direction."

The crime scene turned out to be another fenced in lot holding building supplies for one of the several projects underway near the Javits Center. With blue tarp zip tied to the eight-foot chain link all the way around the lot, the chances anyone noticed anything hovered near zero. Four green dumpsters emblazoned with an Atlas logo stood side by side near the gate. From the size, Jackson estimated them to be thirty yards each. As he and Diaz approached the entrance to the lot, Chang waved them over, hefting the yellow tape for them to step under.

"Right over here," Chang said pointing to a sheeted body in front of the third dumpster.

"Did anyone see anything?" Diaz said as she took in the scene.

"Couple construction workers think a white work van may have dumped the body around nine-forty-five, but they were too far away to say for sure or get a plate."

Lifting the edge of the sheet, the face of a beautiful young woman peered up at Jackson through dead eyes. He immediately recognized her and lowered the sheet. "Yeah. She's the one that hit me yesterday."

"So, we can say conclusively that Deadpool is involved in all of this," Chang said as he stepped around the body.

"Did our suspect leave anything for us?" Jackson asked Rivera as the man snapped photos of the scene.

The young crime scene tech looked up at him and replied, "Nothing yet." Before Jackson could object, Rivera added, "I'll get my report over to you as soon as possible, Detective. I know this is a high priority case."

"Thanks, Rivera, and make sure the medical examiner knows this is related to the Williams case." Jackson said as he and Diaz began walking back towards the car. "Pete, stay here and continue canvassing. We're going to the Collingsworth."

"Will do."

Tossing the keys to Diaz, Jackson took out his phone and said, "Captain's gonna want an update." Nodding her understanding, she slid into the driver's seat while he closed the passenger's side door and made the call. "Cap, looks like the vic on Thirty-Sixth is one of our suspect's accomplices. She's definitely the one who hit me yesterday."

"What do you think this means?" Captain Wilson replied.

Looking to his partner as she turned onto Thirty-Fifth Street, he said, "Diaz thinks he might be getting rid of his accomplices so less people can ID him, and I'm inclined to agree with her."

"It's a sound theory. What's the next step?"

"We're heading over to the Collingsworth to check out an anonymous tip that puts our suspect there, and after that, we're going to try and find his other accomplice before she winds up dead."

"Keep me posted."

"Will do, sir."

"So, you're on board with my theory now?" Diaz said as she stopped for the light.

"Now that I know for sure who the victim is, it makes sense. It might also be that they had a disagreement that the other young lady wasn't a part of."

"If that's the case, it's likely she doesn't even know her coworker is dead."

Dozens of people crossed in front of their car in each direction. If this had been a weekday, that number would have been hundreds. Even the foot traffic in the area felt a little light. People who weren't a part of the convention were probably avoiding this area altogether. That would be the smart thing to do, and he hoped that would be the trend for the weekend because they were making decent time without having to use the lights.

As they pulled up to the Collingsworth, Jackson surveyed six white work vans in various parking spots near the hotel. Three of the vans contained business logos while the other three bared no distinct markings. Stepping out of the car, he motioned to the vans and said, "Let's get a patrol car down here to run the plates on these vans. "

"Good idea. We may get lucky and find one that doesn't belong."

Chapter 29

"Cap. Hotel employees confirm our vic has been hanging around the hotel with another girl dressed like Harley Quinn. One of them even remembers the two of them leaving with a Deadpool a couple nights ago. Chang and Looch are going to sit on the hotel while Diaz and I go back to the convention and try to find our remaining Harley."

"Good work, Winters," Captain Wilson replied.

"Good work, Winters," Diaz mouthed as she queried an eyebrow. "We didn't really do anything yet."

"Alvarez is probably with him. He's still doing damage control for my little outburst this morning," Jackson whispered.

"Let me know as soon as you have anything else."

"Yes, sir," he replied. "We should be meeting up with Sergeant McGinnis at the convention in about ten minutes." The call ended and Jackson turned to Diaz with a bewildered look on his face. "Alvarez must really be up his ass. Let's pray we break this case soon."

When they arrived at the convention center, they noticed an impromptu memorial shrine to Garrison Williams had been started in front of the building. Photos of the actor with fans were stapled or taped to plywood, candles were crowded around a headshot, and stuffed animals in sci-fi gear were placed around the display. People waited in line to leave more items around Garrison's picture. Fans embraced each other, and some cried as they mourned the loss of one of their heroes. It was a somber scene marring what should have been a fun-filled weekend.

As they moved through the crowds, Jackson and Diaz were mobbed by reporters lobbing question after question at them.

"Detective Winters, do you have any leads as to who killed Garrison Williams?" Mike Urbanich from the New York Times asked with his pen and pad ready for a reply.

"Detective, who is the prime suspect?" Sandy Cavanaugh from ABC News called out as her cameraman filmed.

Bethany Hernandez from the New York Daily News sidled up to him as he eased his way through the group and said, "Detective Winters, do you think the murdered cosplayer is connected in any way to the Williams case?"

He wondered how she knew about that already. Several other reporters called out to them until Jackson stopped and said, "The NYPD has no comment at this time." Several other questions were tossed at him as he and Diaz turned and walked past security.

"I guess the cat's out of the bag," Jackson quipped.

"This morning's Daily News headline was **DEATH CON ONE**."

"Brass can't be happy about that. I wonder what tomorrow's headline is going to be?"

As they worked their way through the over-crowded convention center, Diaz' head was on a swivel as she looked at every interesting costume. "Where are we meeting Sergeant McGinnis again?"

"She said to meet her over by the autograph area."

"Great, more crowds."

"I thought you'd be okay with the crowds being a regular at these events," he said as he pushed past some medieval warriors.

"It's actually the one part of the con I hate. My legs get so tired after four days of shuffling around in these never-ending lines," she said.

As they worked their way over to the autograph area, Jackson's eyes widened as he noticed a name he recognized. "Lisa Saranna!" he exclaimed. "I'm not gonna lie, Julia, I kinda have a crush on her."

"She's the sorceress from The Ultimate Quest, right?" With a suspicious squint she added, "I thought you didn't like sci-fi."

"I don't know anything about a quest, but she played the Medical Examiner in a cop show called Big Time. It's the one show I've actually watched in the last ten years, and it's mostly because of her."

"Is she why you dated Dr. Jensen?"

Thinking about Diaz's question for a long moment, he turned to her and said, "You know, I've never thought about that. If I was subconsciously wishing Kari was more like Lisa's character that could explain why our relationship has failed repeatedly."

Diaz chuckled and said, "You're a mess, Jackson."

"Guilty as charged," he replied.

Looking around, she said, "The autograph area is huge. I'm going to tell McGinnis to meet us by Lisa Saranna's table." A mischievous smile played across her lips as she called the sergeant.

"Seriously?"

Before she could answer, Raina, Amanda, and Jacob approached them. "Dad," Raina beamed. "I got Lisa Saranna's autograph for you, and she said she wanted to meet you."

"Meet me? Why?" he replied, looking at Diaz to see if he was being set up.

"I told her you were a big fan, and when I told her your name, she remembered that you were the Detective who killed Tanner Hodges. I think she's going to do another cop show and wants to pick your brain."

"Here she comes, Dad," Jacob said from behind his Optimus Prime mask and Captain America shield.

"Guys, I'm working a case right now."

"Maybe you can pump her for information, Uncle Jax," Amanda said, raising her eyebrows and failing to hold back a grin. Diaz snorted a laugh prompting an even bigger smile from Amanda.

"Yes, Detective. Please pump me for information," Lisa Saranna said in a playful voice as she threw her arms around Jackson in a friendly embrace. "It is very nice to meet you, Detective Winters. You have some very cool kids."

"Yes, and I'll be sending them away to boarding school on Monday," he said as he scowled in their direction.

Ignoring the jab, Raina took out her phone and started snapping pictures. "Say cheese, Dad."

Untangling himself from the lovely television star, he smiled and said, "It's great to meet you, Lisa." Looking at her again, he added, "And I really wish I could stay and talk, but we are here on a case."

"I understand," she said as she slid a business card into his jacket pocket. "I live local, so maybe you can give me a call when the case is over. I'd love to get drinks and talk."

"That sounds amazing."

"I'll make sure it happens," Diaz added with a smile that suggested she was very much enjoying the situation.

A moment later, she pointed and said, "Here comes Sergeant McGinnis, and we need to go over some details of the case with her."

As they walked away, Jackson pointed to a group of reporters and said, "I'm so screwed."

"It'll be fine," Diaz said as they approached Sergeant McGinnis.

"Follow me," Molly said. She led them to a well-lit room in a restricted area so they could speak without worrying about the press or convention goers overhearing them. Three officers were already in the bright room waiting.

Jackson looked at the assembled officers and said, "Okay, guys. We're looking for a college-aged woman dressed as Harley Quinn."

"The movie version," Diaz said.

Nodding thanks to his partner, Jackson continued. "Right. The movie version. Apparently, there's a difference." Two of the officers chuckled as he continued. "Any points of clarification you need, ask Detective Diaz. I'm not exactly an expert when it comes to superheroes or sci-fi."

Sergeant McGinnis glanced at the officers then back at Jackson. "Is this young lady a suspect in either murder?"

"No. We believe she is our suspect's accomplice in the blackmailing but not in the murders. In fact, we think her life may be in danger," Diaz replied.

"So, you believe him to be good for both murders," a young officer said more than asked.

"It's just speculation at this point, but there's a good chance," Jackson replied.

"I know there's probably a lot of them out there, but we need to keep an eye out for this Harley," Diaz said.

"Stop any combination of Harley and Deadpool that you see together and question them. If they're still at the convention I want them found," Jackson said.

"We'll do our best," Sergeant McGinnis replied.

Chapter 30

Raina held Jacob's hand as they made their way through the dense crowd. His eyes were big as they took in all of the costumes, artwork, and merchandise. She loved seeing him this excited. They followed close behind Amanda as she weaved her way towards the exhibition floor's exit. There was a cosplay creation panel they really wanted to get to, and even though she knew Jacob would be bored, it couldn't be helped. As much fun as they were having with Jacob today, this panel was the thing they were most looking forward to, so he would have to deal. He had been on his feet all day and needed to rest for a little while anyway.

"Hey, little dude. That's a great costume. Would it be all right if I take a picture of you with my daughter?" a man in a Green Arrow costume said. His daughter looked to be about seven and was wearing a pink transformers costume.

Jacob smiled and looked at Raina and said, "Can we take a picture, Raina?"

"Of course, but let's be quick. The line for the panel is going to be long." Digging her phone out of her clutch, she stood next to the little girl's father as his daughter and her brother posed for a picture. After snapping a couple, she looked to the man and said, "Did you get it?"

"Yes. I did. Thanks. That's a great costume he's wearing. Do you mind if I ask where he got it?"

"My sister and cousin made it for me last night," Jacob said as he took Raina's hand.

Looking at Raina and Amanda, the man was clearly impressed. "That's a great job."

With a shy smile, she brushed a stray lock of hair behind her ear and said, "Thanks, but we only made the boots, gloves, and belt. We already had the rest of the stuff."

"We had to throw it together last minute because we didn't know he would be coming with us until last night, but it turned out pretty good," Amanda said as she rustled Jacob's hair.

"Well it looks great," the man said as he took his daughter's hand. She hefted a pink robotic arm and waved as they merged back into the crowd.

"We did a good job," Amanda agreed. "All day, people have been taking pictures with Jacob. He's gotten more love than we have."

"I know right. It's crazy, and it's really made it fun for him," Raina said. Jacob beamed as they talked about him.

"For me, too. We did this and people love it. I didn't think that would make me so happy, but it does," Amanda said with a smile.

"Well let's get to that panel and see how we can make more fun stuff like this. Maybe we can make Jacob the coolest eight-year-old in the neighborhood for Halloween."

Taking her brother's hand once again, they began to make their way through the crowd when suddenly; she felt a hand on her shoulder. Turning her head, her eyes went wide and her throat went dry as she recognized the creepy guy in the trench coat.

"You got me in trouble yesterday, young lady," he hissed as he tried to spin her around. Having a spandex costume came in handy as she was able to slip his grip and pick up her pace.

Pushing Jacob forward, Raina called out, "Amanda, get Jacob out of here, quick. I'll meet you at the panel."

"What? Raina what are you...?"

Her question was answered when she saw the man from yesterday. Nodding her head in agreement, she reached for Jacob and started walking in the opposite direction.

Raina paused until she saw Amanda take Jacob's hand before merging into the crowd going the other way. Her hope was that her stalker would follow her and not Jacob and Amanda. Glancing back, she was almost relieved to see him following her. His jaw was set in concentration and his eyes held malice. She thought she was going to start tearing up, but she knew she needed to keep her emotions on lockdown if she wanted to get away. Picking up her pace, she weaved through the crowd trying to lose him, but he kept coming.

Mind racing, she wondered what she could do. *Maybe I should call dad? No, even if he's still in the building, he's probably far away. Should I call Sergeant McGinnis? She probably has an officer near here.* With her head on a swivel, she finally saw what she was looking for; the beautiful blue uniform of one of NYPD's finest. The creeper was still behind her as she made a beeline for the officer. Her stalker had yet to notice the policeman, and she hoped he would remain oblivious until it was too late.

Picking up speed, she purposely bounced off the officer and fell to the floor. Annoyance flared in the man's blue eyes until he saw who had walked into him. Reaching out a hand, he helped her up and said, "Are you okay?"

Pretending to be flustered, which wasn't difficult under the circumstances, she brushed herself off and said, "Yeah. I'm fine."

"Maybe slow down a little."

Tears started to form in her eyes as she pointed at the creepy guy and said, "I'm sorry, Officer. That guy keeps trying to touch me and I was trying to get away from him."

The man stopped short, and several people in the crowd were now glaring at him so Raina added, "Sergeant McGinnis had him tossed from the con yesterday for pushing my cousin and trying to touch me, and now he's bothering me again today." She hadn't realized she was shaking until she looked at her hands. All of the emotions she had tried to keep in check were starting to flow.

The man began backing up, but the officer took two quick steps towards him and said, "Is this true? Are you harassing this young lady?"

"I've never seen her before in my life," he growled.

"He's lying," Raina yelled, and now the tears were flowing. "Just call Sergeant McGinnis. She'll remember him from yesterday."

Pointing at the man, the officer said, "Don't you move." A crowd was starting to form around the showdown as the officer turned to Raina and said in a much gentler voice, "It's okay. No one's going to hurt you. What's your name?"

Taking a deep breath to calm herself, she replied, "Raina Winters."

"Winters?"

"Yeah. He's my dad," she said as she wiped at her eyes.

Moving back to the creepy guy, the officer called into his radio, "Sergeant McGinnis. This is Officer D'Agostino. We've got a man in a trench coat bothering Raina Winters. She says you tossed the guy from the con yesterday."

"Is Raina there with you?"

"Yeah, and she's a little shaken up."

"Cuff that creepy bastard and get him out of here. He's gonna spend a night in the tank. And let me speak to Raina"

"Yes, ma'am." Handing the radio to her, he stepped forward and said to the man, "I'm sure you know the drill." The man turned around, the whole time glaring at Raina and let Officer D'Agostino cuff him without further incident.

"Raina, where are Jacob and Amanda?"

"I sent them up to the panel when I noticed the man following me," she replied, her breath catching several times. "I figured he would only follow me."

"That was good thinking. You're a very smart young lady."

"Thanks, but I was just doing what my dad taught me to do."

"I'll be there very soon, and we'll get you up to that panel."

"Thanks, Miss McGinnis."

"No problem, sweetheart."

Raina handed the radio back to the officer and watched as he escorted her would be attacker from the premises. A few moments later, Sergeant McGinnis appeared wearing a look of deep concern. She approached, and pulled Raina into a comforting embrace.

Chapter 31

For the second time in two days, Jasmine Connelly walked through the door of the Javits Center security office to answer questions. Weariness covered her like a cloak, but she seemed to be doing better than yesterday. Her movements were halted and unsure, not what you would expect from a television star but understandable considering the circumstances. Her outfit was similar to yesterday except she wore a white tee instead of black, but she looked no less stunning. The faint white orchid scent that accompanied her was such a contrast to the overwhelming aroma of Jimmy's cologne. It was nice to know some people still knew how to apply their perfume for the best result.

Jackson hadn't planned to speak to her again today, but she called him and asked to meet. As the celebrity sat down, Diaz slipped into her seat directly across from her with the box of tissues within easy reach, although it didn't look like she would need them today. Jackson closed the door and sat next to Diaz placing his forearms on the edge of the table and leaning forward just enough to encourage conversation without seeming intimidating.

"What can we do for you, Miss Connelly?" he asked as he held out a bottle of water towards her.

Taking the water, she nodded her thanks and began to unscrew the cap as she said, "I talked to a few people yesterday and found out some information I think might be pertinent to your investigation."

"What information," Diaz replied with her pen and pad at the ready.

Jasmine took a long sip of her water and carefully placed the bottle on the table. Looking at Jackson, she answered Diaz's question. "For starters, I know what Garrison and Colin were really arguing about the other night."

"And you're not worried that telling us this might get Mr. Stone in trouble?" Jackson said.

"I don't think it will," she replied. "Colin was mad because he had to loan Garrison a hundred grand."

"And did he tell you what the hundred K was for?" Diaz said.

Taking another sip, she looked over to Jackson and leaned in. He could tell the move annoyed Diaz, but she was doing a good job of not showing it. "He said Garrison had lost big in Atlantic City. He also said this was the last time he would be bailing Garrison out."

"Atlantic City? Do you think that's what the money was really for?" Jackson said as he leaned in a little further.

"I don't see why Colin would lie about that," she replied.

Maybe to spare your feelings, he thought. "Why do you think Colin was done bailing him out?"

"I guess even a nice guy like Colin has his limits, and Gar was screwing up more and more," she said.

Digging into her purse, she produced a sheet of paper. "But that's not the big news. This is." She handed the paper across the table to Jackson with a satisfied smile.

"What is that? "Diaz said as she looked over Jackson's shoulder at the paper.

Pointing to the paper, Jasmine looked at Jackson and said, "That is a memo sent out to the writers by Jimmy Shultz asking them to begin thinking of ways to recast the character without messing with the continuity of the show. He wanted it to be creative and soon."

Nodding his head as what she said began to sink in; he looked to Diaz and said, "So they were going to fire him."

"Look at the date on the memo," she replied.

"Three days before the insurance policy was taken out." A smile crossed his face as he said, "Jimmy's gonna need a better explanation than he gave us yesterday."

"I just hope he's not wearing that cologne again when we interview him," Diaz said as her nose scrunched up in displeasure at the memory.

Jasmine smiled and waved her hand in front of her nose. "I know right? It's like the guy's sense of smell doesn't even work."

They both chuckled and Jackson smiled as he said, "Can we get back to this?"

She smiled a shy smile and said, "Right. Apparently, the network was going to fire him over his shenanigans, and they didn't even know about the hundred grand yet. It wasn't just the behavior either. Apparently, Gar was becoming very difficult to work with."

"Where did you get this memo, Miss Connelly?" Jackson said.

"I'm friends with the writers. I remembered the commotion this caused when it first circulated and asked one of them to forward it to me."

"That was a great idea," Diaz said.

Her eyes brightened and she sat a little straighter at the encouragement. "Is any of this helpful, Detective Winters?"

"Very. Thank you so much for bringing this to us," Jackson replied. He couldn't help but notice that she seemed to be addressing only him; even when Diaz was asking the questions.

"Anything to help catch Gar's killer. Am I free to go? I have to be at my table to sign autographs in ten minutes."

"Certainly, and thanks again." He stood and held the door to the office open for the beautiful celebrity.

She stopped and gave him a hug. A moment later, she breezed past him and was back with her waiting entourage. Turning back, she said, "It's the least I can do for the famous Detective Jackson Winters."

And there it is, he thought. Even celebrities are fascinated by serial killers and the people who catch them. "Thanks again, ma'am," he replied with a smile as he closed the office door.

"So that's why she prefers you to me," Diaz said with a chuckle. Imitating Jasmine, she clasped her hands together and looked up at him doe-eyed and crooned, "Is any of this helpful, Detective Winters?"

"Stop. It was helpful," he said with a laugh.

"And you got a hug from another celebrity."

"Yeah, I didn't mind that so much," he deadpanned.

"I bet you didn't," she replied with a raised eyebrow that said Jasmine's hug was probably the highlight of his year.

"At least she wasn't obnoxious about it like that Jenkins clown was yesterday." Imitating the man's voice, he said, "How about we talk about it more over drinks, or breakfast if drinks go well?"

"Not funny," she replied with a frown.

Chapter 32

Holding his phone tight to his ear against the noise in the convention center, Jackson said, "Hey, Cap. Diaz and I just spoke to Jasmine Connelly again. She told us that Colin Stone was lending Williams the blackmail money, but she thought it was because he lost big in Atlantic City."

"Makes sense that Stone wouldn't want to hurt her with the truth."

"It's also possible that that's what Williams told him. Connelly let us know that Stone was done with all of Williams hijinks, so I'm inclined to think he wouldn't be lending him blackmail money for getting recorded having sex with two prostitutes. We're on our way over to talk to him."

"Good. Anything else?"

"She also showed us a memo Shultz sent to the writers telling them to write Williams off the show. It was dated three days before he took out the insurance policy. I'm gonna have Chang and Lucco talk to him while we talk to Stone."

"Good. We need something to drop soon."

"Is Alvarez still pissed?"

"Just solve the case and let me worry about Alvarez."

"Will do." After ending the call, he took out the memo Jasmine Connelly had given him and snapped a picture of it before dialing Chang. "Pete, I need you and Looch to pick up Jimmy Shultz and ask him a few more questions."

"No problem. Do we have new info, or is this a follow-up?"

"I'm sending you a copy of a memo that Jimmy wrote asking the writers to write Williams off the show. It's dated three days before he took out the insurance policy."

"Yeah, that's a red flag. Are we doing the interview on the premises or at the station?"

"Do it here."

"Okay."

Dropping his phone into his pocket, he turned to Diaz and said, "Let's go talk to Colin Stone."

The autograph line for Colin Stone was long, and several of the people crowded in between metal stanchions glared as he and Diaz walked up to the front of it. Colin had yet to emerge from behind the heavy blue curtain, so he flashed his badge to the young volunteer and strode past the booth. Holding the curtain back for Diaz to pass through, he could see curiosity coloring the faces of many of the people queued up waiting for the star before he ducked behind the curtain.

A few moments later, Colin Stone, flanked by a well-dressed man and a beautiful woman, approached. When he saw Jackson, his shoulders slumped a bit and a sigh escaped his lips. "Can we make this quick? There are a lot of people waiting for me."

Diaz stepped up to him and said, "Okay. We'll get right to it. What was the hundred grand you were lending Garrison for?"

Jackson was surprised the actor's composure held. Stone certainly was good. If he hadn't been looking right at the celebrity's eyes when his partner asked the question, he would have missed them widen just a fraction at the mention of the money. "Who told you that?"

"Do you really want to play that game?" Jackson said. "I thought you wanted to make this quick?"

"Fine," he snapped. "Garrison told me he lost big in Atlantic City and owed a guy who was going to go to the press unless he paid him this weekend. He couldn't afford the scandal, so I was helping him out, but I told him this was the last time."

Diaz' eyes narrowed as she studied the actor's face. "And you're sure that's what it was for?"

Throwing his shoulders up in a shrug, he said, "No, but that's what he told me."

"So, you have no knowledge of the video of him with the two escorts or the blackmail?" Jackson said, studying his reaction for any hint of deception.

Colin's eyes softened and his shoulders relaxed as he said, "No, but it doesn't surprise me. I never would have loaned him the money for that, and he knew that. Please tell me Jasmine doesn't know. This will crush her."

"We haven't told her," Diaz said. "Why did you leave the hundred grand out of the first interview?"

"I didn't think it was relevant," he said with a shrug.

"Everything is relevant in a murder investigation. Especially large sums of money. Try again," Jackson said with an edge to his voice.

"I didn't want it getting out, at least not from me. My friend is dead and I wasn't in a hurry to let people know his last act in this world was to lose a hundred K gambling so I left it out because I figured why would a blackmailer kill someone he was about to get a big payday from? I would think they would at least wait 'til after."

"If you think of anything else at all, please call us," Diaz said as she handed him her card. "I know this has been a tough weekend for you. I'm a big fan and I'd hate for you to have to see us again." With a hint of a smile, she added, "At least in an official capacity."

Colin smiled back and looked over to Jackson, "So, am I free to go?"

"Yeah. If we have any further questions, Diaz will call you. Thank you for your time."

Colin slipped through the curtain and a loud cheer erupted from the fans in line. As Jackson turned to go, he felt Diaz' elbow hit his gut. "Diaz will call you. Really?"

A smirk formed on his lips as he looked at his partner, "You know, in case he wanted to talk in a less official capacity." Those last two words were accompanied by air quotes and his smirk turned to a smile as her face flushed. "For the record, I believe him that he didn't know about the video and the escorts."

"I do, too. He also makes a good point that blackmail schemes traditionally don't end well if you kill the victim before you get the money."

"I agree." As they walked his phone buzzed. Reaching into his pocket, he dug it out and said, "Detective Winters."

"Jackson, I have something for you."

"On my way, Kari."

Chapter 33

"I hope this isn't awkward again," Diaz said as she stepped out of the Challenger.

"You and me both. You don't have to go in if you don't want to," Jackson replied as he walked towards the door.

The Building which housed the Medical Examiner's office loomed like a grey cloud bringing ill tidings. The open loading bay sat perched like a mouth that could never consume enough. Most medical examiners offices had a similar vibe. Dr. Jensen's office was in the basement and assessable through the rear of the building.

"No. It's fine, and I can always duck out to take a call if I need to."

"Sounds like a plan." Pushing through the door, he was greeted by the smell of death mixed with antiseptics and bright fluorescent lights. He always hated coming to the morgue for that reason, but the reason he didn't used to mind coming to the morgue was entering from the other side of the room.

"Jackson, hi," she said as she approached holding a file. Stepping around the table containing the victim's body, she handed him the folder before adding, "And Detective Diaz, it's good to see you again."

"You as well, Doc," she replied as she looked down at the young victim's body.

Jackson glanced down at the body. With all of the makeup removed, it struck him just how young this girl looked. She should have been in college hanging out with friends eating pizza and talking about boys, not in a morgue.

"Can you give me the highlights," he said with a sad shake of the head. He had seen too many kids on these tables over the years.

"Well for one, it's not the same M.O. as the Williams murder. The cause of death was blunt force trauma to the head. The angle of the wound suggests she fell and hit her head on the corner of something."

"Could it have been an accident? If she was part of the blackmail scheme, there's no way the perp could have reported this, so he would have had no choice but to dump the body," Jackson said.

"I don't think so," she replied as she pointed to the victim's neck. "Do you see the bruising on her neck? She was being strangled by someone, probably someone strong. It's more likely she blacked out and fell, or she was pushed and stumbled. Either way, she had help falling into whatever killed her. I put the time of death between eight-thirty and nine-thirty a.m."

"Thanks, Kari."

Jackson turned to leave, but she caught his hand. Looking at Diaz, she said, "Detective Diaz, would you mind giving us a minute?"

"No problem. I'll call this into Wilson," she said as she took out her phone and left the room.

As soon as the door closed, Dr. Jensen said, "Jackson, I'm sorry about yesterday."

"There's no need to apologize."

"I have no right telling you how to talk to your kids. I was out of line."

"Really, it's no problem. In fact, I took your advice for the most part." A quizzical look crossed her face so he elaborated, "I told them everything exactly as it happened, coming through the door, getting hit with a mallet, the girl running away, all of it. The only thing I didn't mention was that it was case related."

"And they were okay with it?"

"Raina suspected there might be more, and Jacob asked me to buy him a mallet."

A hearty laugh escaped her lips as she smacked his arm and said, "And what did you say?"

"I said no chance," he replied with a laugh.

"Jackson, I think I was so short with you yesterday because of Paul."

"Paul? What's going on?"

"I'm pretty sure he's cheating on me."

"Kari, I'm so sorry."

"Me, too. I think I was projecting my general disdain for men at you. I'm sorry."

"It's fine. No worries."

"No. It' not fine. Even though we've never been able to figure it out, you've always been considerate and fair. My ire should not have been directed at you."

"We all have bad days, Kari. And we know each other well enough where one bad day is not going to ruin the friendship. Now, how bad do you want me to harass Paul?"

A smile played across her lips and she hugged him. "Very bad, but for now I think I can deal with this on my own."

With a chuckle, he shook his head and turned to leave.

"I mean it, Jackson. Let me handle it."

Hoisting a wave, he pushed through the door. Waiting by the car, his partner waved him over. "What have we got, Diaz?"

"Wilson wants us back at the station to give an update."

"Was the phone call not enough?"

"Apparently not."

"I bet Alvarez is riding his ass."

"That's what I was thinking."

Chapter 34

Staring at the murder board, Jackson knew they were missing something. His fingers were drumming on the conference table as his eyes moved from suspect to suspect.

"If you stare any harder, you're gonna burn a hole in it," Diaz said as she put a cup of coffee down in front on him.

Rubbing his eyes, he looked up and said, "I know, but Colin was right. It just doesn't make any sense for Deadpool to kill Garrison before he got the money which puts us back at square one."

"So, you're thinking Shultz or Jenkins," Chang said as he dropped into the seat across from Jackson.

"I bet it was that gorgeous blonde Jasmine," Lucco said as he leaned on a column across from the table. "Hot chicks can be deadly, and Garrison was double dipping."

"Could you be any cruder?" Diaz said with a frown.

"Less speculation and more police work," Jackson said. "All of our other suspects have alibis. Let's see if we can start poking holes in them. Julia, check the hallway footage for Stone and Connelly. Find out if there's any possible way those time stamps could be altered. Looch, talk to every person on Shultz' alibi list, and see if you can find the intern he didn't seem to remember. He didn't necessarily need to be at the Javits to be involved. Pete, run down Jenkins morning. Hit the gym he said he went to and find out if anyone there remembers seeing him, and how long he stayed. If there's no way to log him out, that leaves him with a lot of time between when he said he went to the gym, and when he went back to his room."

As his team hurried to their tasks, he walked over to Captain Wilson's office and rapped on the door. A moment later, a weary Captain Wilson opened the door and waved him in. The lights were a little dimmer than usual, and the look on his face implied it had been a rough day.

Taking a seat at the desk, he said, "Cap, I'm starting to think that this Deadpool impersonator didn't kill Garrison Williams."

The sad shake of his head indicated that comment had made his day worse. "What makes you say that?"

"He was blackmailing him. Why kill him before he got the money?"

"Maybe Williams threatened to go to the police."

Shaking his head, he stood and started pacing the office. "I don't think so. Colin Stone was lending him the money. All indications are that he was going to pay. There was also his ethics clause. No way he risks losing his job."

With a deep sigh, Captain Williams pushed away from his desk and leaned back in his chair. "You may be right. Who's your next best guess at this point?"

"Either Shultz or Jenkins. I've got the team going through everything on them, and they're also rechecking Stone and Connelly's alibis."

"Do me a favor. Work all of your leads, but publicly act as if this Death Pool player guy is still your number one suspect."

He thought about correcting the captain's error, but thought better of it. "Alvarez isn't letting up, is he? I'm sorry, Cap."

"At this point, if you don't catch Williams' killer, the very least you're looking at is a reprimand for insubordination in your permanent file, but it'll probably be worse than that."

"Understood."

Pointing to the door, he said, "All right, get out of here and catch this guy. The rest will take care of itself."

With a nod, Jackson turned to leave. As he opened the door, he turned back and nodded again to his captain. Chang almost ran into him as he made his way back to his desk.

"Big break, Jax. That homeless guy we were waiting on from Thirty-Eighth told us he saw a guy dressed in red spandex and a mask dump a toy sword in a dumpster." Tilting his head, he laughed and said, "If this case wasn't at comic con, that would have been the weirdest sentence I've said in a long time."

"Still might be," Jackson said with a chuckle.

"Anyway, it's chipped in the right places. Rivera is going over it now, but it looks like we have our murder weapon."

With a hearty pat on the back, he said, "That's great work, Pete. Take Looch and go see Rivera. Let's see if we can get any leads on this toy sword."

"Sounds like a plan. Also, Looch has found a few witnesses that saw Jenkins at the gym bright and early yesterday morning. They said he was gregarious and talked to a lot of people, but none of them remember seeing him leave or even how long he stayed. His room key puts him back in at nine-thirty-five, and back out again at nine-fifty-five, so he did go back like he said he did."

"Sounds like he wanted to be seen; he could have easily had the time to kill Williams and get back to his room. After you get the ball rolling on the sword, I want you guys to watch him."

His money would have been on Shultz, but it was starting to look like Jenkins might be their guy, although he wasn't quite ready to put all his money on that number.

"Good call, boss," Chang said as he began to walk towards his desk.

Calling after him, he added, "But don't look like you're watching him. Don't let him see you."

Chang's thumbs up let him know he had been heard as he sat down at his desk and looked over his notes. Things were starting to move, and each new development was cementing the fact that they had two separate cases.

Diaz padded into the room, phone in hand talking as she walked. Sitting down at her desk, she looked at him and said, "Stone and Connelly check out. There was no tampering with the time codes of the footage in their hallways or the key logs on their doors."

"That's good news. We're down to two suspects, Shultz and Jenkins with Jenkins in the lead."

"So, we're treating this as two unrelated murders with chubby Deadpool being our only suspect for Harley's murder."

"Fingerprints got a match in the system. Her name is Karen Matthews, and she was only twenty-one years old."

"That's a shame. Do we have any idea who the other girl he's using is?"

"Not yet."

Chapter 35

Jackson glanced up from his desk and saw a young woman standing at the door of the squad room. Glancing in several directions, she looked scared and was looking for someone. Pretty with long blonde hair, she seemed familiar. It hit him who she was, and he all but jumped up and hurried to the door. She noticed and a hint of recognition played across her face as she started into the room to meet him.

"Detective Winters?"

"That's me," he said in a casual tone. She looked a little jumpy and he didn't want to spook her.

Still looking in each direction, she found a spot on the floor to stare at as she said, "Is there somewhere we can talk?"

Pointing to the middle of the room, he said, "Is the conference table okay, or would you prefer something a little more private?"

"Conference table is fine," she replied as she trudged over and plopped down in one of the seats. He could tell she was barely keeping it together

Waving Diaz over, he said, "Is it okay if Detective Diaz sits with us?"

Peeking up at Diaz, she nodded and said, "Yeah. It's fine."

Jackson sat down across from her and Diaz sat down next to her. "Can you tell us your name," she said.

"My name is Leena and I think something terrible has happened to my roommate." Holding back tears, she wiped at her nose and said, "I think Edgar killed her."

"Edgar who?" Jackson said as he slid a box of tissues towards her.

"I don't know. He never told us."

"I know this is difficult, but if you could start at the beginning, that would be really helpful," Diaz said.

Looking around the room, she leaned in and in little more than a whisper said, "A few days ago Edgar called Karen and me from the number on our website and asked to hire us for four days. We're escorts and we charge three thousand a day. He was offering us five thousand a day and he paid half up front. I thought this might be enough to get me out of the life so I jumped on it, but Karen didn't seem to trust him. I think she only went along with it to protect me."

Wiping at some tears, she sniffled and continued, "It was all going well. We even got to sleep with Garrison Williams, but then Karen found out that Edgar was blackmailing the people we slept with. Edgar told us they were potential investors in his company and that he hired us to sweeten the deal. I asked why it had to be at comic con, and he said his company was a tech company and those types of investors would be there. He had us dress up and everything."

"Did that seem a little off to you?" Jackson said.

"Not really. To be honest, companies do that sort of thing all the time, and he was paying us a lot of money."

Jackson opened a bottle of water and offered it to Leena. She waved it off and he took a draught. Putting the bottle on the table, he said, "Was Edgar dressed up as well?"

"Yeah, he was this guy Deadpool. He kept saying it just made sense, but I didn't know what he meant by it. Anyway, after the fifth or sixth guy, we found out that Edgar had actually been filming us and was blackmailing the guys. Karen went to confront him while I was seducing the next guy. I told her we should just leave because blackmail is bad for business and I didn't want to be wrecking people's lives, but she said Edgar knew where we lived so we had to keep going until she figured something out."

"Do you always follow Karen's lead?" Diaz said.

"Pretty much. She's like a big sister to me. She got me off the street and into a nice apartment, and she always takes care of me. I trusted that she would have some kind of plan before we bailed. She was supposed to meet me back at the room when I brought the next guy, but she didn't. After the John left, I noticed that her bag had been moved over to the dresser. I thought that was weird, so I checked it out and under the bag, the carpet had been cut."

Tears started to flow down her pink cheeks as she choked out the words, "I lifted up the carpet and there was blood underneath, and now I can't get in touch with Karen at all." Her tears were flowing freely now as she rubbed at her eyes with her fists.

Diaz rubbed her back for a few moments before she said, "I'm so sorry, but is Karen's last name, Matthews?"

The look on Leena's face suggested she knew what was coming next. "Y...yes" Her voice was barely audible and the tears continued to stream down her face.

Jackson gave her his most compassionate look as he said, "We are so sorry for your loss, Leena. I know this is difficult, but could you tell us where the room is that you and Karen were using? We would love to catch the guy that killed your friend."

"Room 1704 at the Collingsworth."

"And what does Edgar look like?" Diaz said.

"He's a Hispanic guy; average height, dark hair, a beard, and a bit of a belly."

"Thank you, Leena. Diaz, get a uni over to that room. Have Rivera start processing the scene and have a couple plain clothes officers out on the street waiting for this clown."

As Diaz moved to her desk to make the call, Leena cast a sheepish look up at Jackson and said, "Do you think I can stay here for a while. Edgar really scares me, and I don't want to go back outside until he's in jail." The tearful pleading eyes broke his heart.

The look of fear in Raina's eyes when that creepy guy was trying to touch her yesterday flashed through his mind as he looked at the fear in Leena's eyes. She was only a few years older than his daughter, but she didn't have anyone like him looking out for her. In that moment, all he wanted to do was make sure this kid was protected. "Of course. We'll need you to give us a positive ID on Edgar when we catch him anyway." Seeing the worry in her eyes, he added, "Don't worry, he won't be able to see you at all. I'll make sure of it."

"Thank you, Detective."

"No problem. Detective Diaz is going to sit with you while I go speak to my captain, and he's going to make sure you're safe until Edgar is caught, okay?"

She nodded her assent and he talked to Captain Wilson. It didn't take much convincing. Captain Wilson thought it was a good idea to keep her around until she needed to identify the suspect, and if they let her wander off, she might not come back, so he would have a female officer sit with her until they caught Edgar. After Jackson was sure Leena was comfortable with the arrangement, he and Diaz left the station. The temperature had continued to drop from the morning and was now bordering on cold as they walked to the car.

While they were walking, his phone buzzed. "What's up Rivera?"

"Room 1704 is definitely the crime scene and the blackmail location. We've found prints belonging to both Karen Matthews and Leena Van Deen along with prints from half a dozen men. We've also found several hidden cameras, and the prints on the cameras belong exclusively to an Edgar Ramirez."

Jackson pumped his fist and said, "That's good work, Luis. We're on our way over." Turning to Diaz, he added, "Put out a BOLO for Edgar Ramirez wanted for questioning in both murders." Flipping on the lights and sirens, he took off for the Collingsworth.

With a confused tilt of the head, Diaz said, "Both murders. I thought we didn't like him for both?"

"We don't, but Alvarez is riding Wilson hard, and he'd prefer the chief of dicks not know we're further on the Matthews murder than we are with Garrison Williams. Plus, I want the murderer to see Ramirez' face plastered all over TV and the internet and think he can relax."

"If he thinks we're not looking, he might make a mistake. Good call."

Pulling up to the Collingsworth Hotel, they parked in the fire lane and entered the building. Jackson walked up to the counter and flashed his badge to the young woman. "Hi, I'm sure you've seen all of the police in and out of here in the last hour. We're investigating one of your guests. Could you tell me who paid for room 1704?"

Tapping a few keys, she traced her finger down the screen and said, "I have a credit card for and driver's license for an Edgar Tejada."

"Tejada? Did you get a picture of the license?"

"I think so. Let me check." Thumbing through a file, she stopped and extracted a piece of paper. "Here it is, Detective."

"It's a match for Ramirez," Diaz said. Pulling out her phone, she added, "I'm going to add Tejada to the BOLO."

Looking back to the young woman behind the counter, Jackson smiled and said, "Thank you very much."

He led Diaz to the elevator and pressed the button for the seventeenth floor. By the time they arrived, Diaz was finished updating the BOLO. They walked into room 1704 and took in the blur of activity before walking over to Rivera. There was a whole team of techs processing the room, and Jackson knew it was because Chief Alvarez was on everyone about the Williams murder. Too bad this was actually another case altogether. Rivera was practically lying on his stomach on the floor to photograph something under the bed. They waited until he was finished, and when he saw them, he stood up.

"Detectives, we've been unable to find any hard drives these cameras were recording to, but they are wireless, and the model he used boasts an impressive range."

"Break it down for us," Diaz said as she studied the room.

"It could be broadcasting to another room in this hotel, or anywhere else within a three-block radius."

A low whistle escaped Jackson's lips. "Is there any way you can trace the signal or pick up anything receiving these transmissions?" Something caught the corner of his eye and before he could stop himself, he said, "Hmm, Ramirez really did cut the carpet."

Diaz looked over as Rivera smiled and said, "Yeah, he cut out the bloody carpet and tried to replace it with a piece he cut out of the closet. I don't know how he was expecting this to fool anyone. Anyway, we have traced the signal to a vehicle parked on Thirty-sixth between Tenth and Hudson."

"Nice, I bet it's a white van. Diaz, get the Captain to send an unmarked to watch the cars on that street, especially if it's a white van. As soon as the BOLO hits, he's going to be looking for a quick exit."

"Got it."

"One more thing," Rivera said as he held up his finger. "We've found two phones in the room. One belongs to Karen Matthews. Assuming

Ramirez and Leena have theirs, this last one may belong to one of the men they were blackmailing."

He wasn't ready to declare it was Williams' phone yet, but he was a little excited and had reason to hope. "Let us know as soon as you crack it." With that, he turned to leave.

Chapter 36

Edgar counted off the ticks of the clock above the fifties style counter of the diner he had chosen for the payment drop. He sat on a chrome stool with a fire engine red leather cushion. The booths had the same white top and chrome trim of the counter while the seats were cushioned with the same red leather upholstery. This place was known for its coffee and pie, and having just finished two slices of drool-worthy apple pie, he could attest to the truthfulness of the claims. Halfway through his third cup of black coffee, he glanced up at the chrome-trimmed clock one more time. His army helmet sat on the stool beside him, today he was Army Deadpool.

Congressman Vasserman was due in a little over two minutes and knew not to be late. The door chimed, and his eyes traced the checkerboard tiles up to the front of the restaurant, but it wasn't his man. Lifting his mask up over his lips, he sipped at his coffee again. The waitress arrived to top off his cup, and he glanced at the time again. The congressman wasn't the only one he was waiting on. Leena had yet to contact him on the completion of her last assignment and he was starting to get a bad feeling. She should have called him half an hour ago, although Sanderson wasn't a bad looking guy. Maybe she was enjoying his company a little longer than she had to.

He was considering getting this payment, finding Judge Hastings for his payment, and skipping town with a little over half of what he had initially hoped to get. It would still be more than enough to live in Mexico for a long time. Karen's death had not been planned and could be traced to him, and sooner or later, the cops would figure it out. Sadly, Leena would probably need to follow in her footsteps to give him the time he needed to get away. Maybe he would just tie her up in the room to get a head start. She was a good kid after all, and she hadn't tried to shake him down for more money. He would make the decision if their paths crossed before he left.

Another long sip of his coffee calmed him, if only a little. When had he become the type of guy who even contemplated killing another human being? Karen's death had been heat-of-the-moment, accidental even, but anything he did to Leena would be pre-meditated. People were glancing in his direction. Even for New York, his camouflage jacket over red spandex get up was a little out there, and he wasn't exactly close to the con. The door chimed again, and the congressman strode towards him. It was go time. Wearing the standard ball cap, sunglasses, please-don't-recognize-me combination, he slipped a thick manila envelope out of his Yankee jacket.

"It better all be here, amigo," Edgar whispered as he slipped the payment into his backpack in one deft motion.

"It is. And if I ever see your face again, my reputation be dammed, I will see you in jail. Do you understand?" he snarled as he stood to leave.

Edgar knew this was just bravado but decided to mess with him just a little. "No promises!" A chuckle escaped his lips as the other man stiffened a smidge. Turning an intense glare at Edgar, he waited a moment before leaving. The chime on the door signified his exit.

Edgar took another long draught of his coffee and was about to stand when he saw his face on television. He was wanted for not one but two murders. Stunned, he almost stumbled as he stood. The mask covered his shock, and he was thankful for it because his reaction would have been suspicious. The police were wrong, he only killed one, but how had they figured it out? What was he going to do? Taking a deep breath, he let it out slowly and prepared to leave. Walking with a steady confidence he didn't feel, he pushed through the doors of the diner, hearing the chime one last time, and stepped out onto the crowded street. The temperature had dropped a bit over the last day, and he was reminded of why he wanted to leave the city so bad.

After walking for several minutes, he had his phone in his hand and dialed the judge. The phone was answered on the fourth ring with one word from a self-important voice. "Hastings."

"Hello, Judge. It's Deadpool. I need you to meet me with your payment at the corner of Thirty-Eighth and Eleventh in twenty minutes. If you're not there, the video gets released in twenty minutes and one second."

"You're wanted for murder and you're still trying to shake me down? Are you crazy?"

"Yes. I am. And since I'm wanted for murder, you know I have nothing to lose by releasing the footage, so no cops. I have it set up so with the push of a button, your pervy secret gets sent out to all the networks. If I even get a whiff of law enforcement, your career and your marriage are over. As you can imagine, I'm in a bit of a hurry as well, so you better not be late."

After a long pause, Hastings bit out the words, "Fine. I'll be there, just don't do anything stupid."

"Twenty minutes starting now."

Hanging up his phone, he set the timer and leaned against a tree across the street from Clyde Frasier's restaurant on Thirty Eighth Street. He would wait eighteen minutes and walk to the corner. With hundreds of people in Deadpool costumes, he knew it wouldn't raise any red flags for him to mix in with the convention crowd, but he didn't want to loiter across the street from the convention center with all of those cops outside either.

Nineteen minutes later, he was standing on the corner, and the judge was plodding towards him with a grimace fixed firmly in place. Edgar checked the area and was certain he had not brought any of the police with him. Without even trying to be subtle about it, the judge handed him a small green duffel bag and muttered, "I hope you choke on it."

"Nice doing business with you, Judge Pervs-a-lot," he said as he turned and strode away. He was now carrying two hundred thousand dollars in cash and had another three hundred thousand waiting in his apartment. Heading towards his van, he knew it was time to get out of the city. The address listed on his license was different from where he actually resided, so it would take the police a while to figure out where he lived. He pondered his getaway as he walked towards West Thirty-Sixth Street.

As he turned the corner onto Thirty-Sixth Street, he looked up to see his stolen van right where he'd left it. A smile spread across his face under his mask accompanied by a bounce in his step as he realized he was about to get away with five hundred thousand dollars. His happiness was short lived when he saw two men walking towards him. One looked Italian and the other was Asian. One of them spoke into his phone, and Edgar knew they were cops.

With as much nonchalance as he could muster, he crossed the street and tried to turn back towards the Javits Center. A glance behind him told him they were onto him. "Damn cops!" he mumbled as he broke into a run.

"Edgar Ramirez! NYPD. Stop right there," one of the cops yelled as they chased him.

He was only a block from the convention center, and he had a good lead on the dynamic duo chasing him, so he was confident he could get lost in the crowd.

Chapter 37

Standing out on the convention floor, he was too wrapped up in his thoughts to enjoy the weekend. Fortunately, he only had another day or so to fake it, and then he was sure he would get away with murder. He only needed to buy a little more time, and he was unsure his ploy to frame chubby Deadpool had worked, but he would keep checking his phone every couple hours to see if there was anything about him on the news. Word around the con was a second body had been found, so hopefully that would lead the cops further away from him. He didn't care who they went after as long as they had stopped sniffing around him.

A Deadpool flew past the photo op area towards the autograph booths. As he ran, he took off a green army helmet and a camouflage jacket and tossed them aside. He took an envelope out of a backpack and placed it in the duffel bag he carried and tossed the backpack aside as well. Another person in a Deadpool costume picked up the helmet and jacket and put them on and mimicked a crazy run like the one who had just passed. He hoped this meant the cops were after the blackmailer instead of him.

His hopes appeared to be answered as two men arrived sweating and a little out of breath. He recognized them as two of the cops who had interviewed him. One took off after the first Deadpool while the other took off after the one who picked up the helmet and jacket. Both characters sped off in opposite directions while the frustrated cops followed, talking on walkies the whole time. Several additional police joined in the chase and it was starting to cause a little bit of a commotion. The bigger the ruckus the better as far as he was concerned.

True to character, several additional Deadpool cosplayers started running around and giving the police reason to chase them, and suddenly, it was as if he was watching a live version of the Keystone Cops. The bigger the spectacle, the longer it would be before they came back around to him, and these cosplayers were causing quite the spectacle. These morons were unwittingly helping him get away with murder, not to mention helping the shady blackmailer avoid the cops. Being 2019, people had their phones out filming the action instead of trying to help the police as the chase had just become the convention's biggest attraction. Suddenly, he couldn't wait for the six o'clock news.

A grin spread from ear to ear as he watched the mayhem. A pretty Irish officer stopped near him and he heard her say into her phone, "Jackson, you need to get down here. Lucco and Chang chased your suspect into the convention center, and now dozens of Deadpools are making a pain in the ass of themselves. It's starting to get a little out of hand, and the captain is not going to be happy. The original suspect was wearing an army helmet and a camouflage jacket, but he ditched it. He didn't ditch his green duffel, so I'm telling my guys to focus on the duffel."

He wished he could hear Jackson's reply. That smug arrogant bastard thinks he's all that because he shot a serial killer. That guy was as clueless as the rest of them, and he couldn't wait to see him knocked down a few pegs. The pretty cop moved on, barking at her guys to stop chasing any skinny Deadpools or any that were not carrying a duffel bag. His smile continued to grow as he stepped behind the curtain to move on to his next convention obligation.

Nodding to people who belonged behind the curtain as he walked where the crowds were not allowed to go, he couldn't contain his smile. *I'm really gonna get away with this. These stupid cops have no idea. The attractive one could have actually reached out and touched me, but she looked past me as if I wasn't even there.* "This is too good," he mumbled.

"What's too good?" a cute volunteer said as she sidled up to him. Perky with long brown hair and all the right curves in all the right places, she looked to be about twenty. *I've had younger*, he thought. *Heck, the blackmailer could have just as easily trapped me as he did Williams. I wouldn't have said no to those two Harley cuties, and I won't say no to this cute thing talking to me now.* He never knew if they were after him or his money, but he never cared either.

Giving her a long once over, which she seemed to enjoy, he said, "Those idiot cops chasing all the Deadpool cosplayers around. That was the funniest thing I've ever seen."

A frown formed on her face as she looked at him. "Damn, I always miss all the good stuff. What happened?"

"I'm still not sure. Two detectives chased one Deadpool past the autograph area, then suddenly, dozens of Deadpools started running all over the place and the cops didn't know who to chase." A deep laugh escaped his lips.

"Why were they chasing the first one?" she asked as she walked a little closer.

This was really turning out to be a good day. She might just have to come to the break room with him. "I don't know why they were after the first guy. All I know is I would hate to be them when the video of them being super incompetent breaks the internet."

Another deep laugh erupted and this time she laughed with him. "I can't wait to see that online."

"Come to the break room with me. I bet they already uploaded some of the videos. We can watch them and laugh together."

A mischievous gleam formed in her eyes and she said, "I can think of some other things we might be able to do in the break room, too."

Yes. It was turning out to be a good day indeed.

Chapter 38

Jackson watched the madness unfolding at the Javits Center with a look of shock and the sad resignation that he was about to get his ass chewed out by Chief Alvarez again. The only way to avoid it at this point would be to actually bring in the subject. Molly's info came through the radio loud and clear, yet there were still dozens of cops chasing the wrong suspects. People laughed, people ran, people ignored and went about their day, but worst of all, people filmed the action on their phones. When this hit the internet, the joke would be on the NYPD, and he'd be up the creek without a paddle.

"What the hell are they thinking?" he said to Diaz who wore a similar expression of shock on her face.

"I don't know, but they better have a good story. The brass can't blame you for this can they? You weren't even here when this started."

"But I'm in charge of the guys who did chase Ramirez here, so it's my responsibility."

An officer caught hold of a skinny Deadpool right in front of him, and he waved the officer off the kid. Bringing his radio up to his mouth he growled, "This is Detective Winters. Next cop I see chasing a skinny kid through here is gonna have my foot stuck so far up their ass, they'll need surgery to remove it. If the perp isn't chubby and isn't carrying a bag of some sort, stop chasing them immediately, you're making us look like a bunch of idiots. Do you understand?"

Several yes, sirs filtered back through the radio and most of the action died down. Shaking his head, he scanned the crowd. Most of the cameras were back on normal convention activities, and there were only a few chases still happening.

"Chang, what's your twenty?" he said.

"I'm by the side exit onto Thirty-Fourth Street chasing the original suspect," he replied, struggling to catch his breath.

Jackson started to run around the outside of the building from the exit closest to Thirty-Fifth Street with Diaz hot on his heels. They burst through the doors into the sunlight drawing the attention of dozens of costumed fans. Thumbing the button on the radio, he said, "Diaz and I will meet you on the outside. Let me know when you're about to exit."

"Will do."

"Looch, what's your twenty?"

"The original guy was wearing a helmet and a camo jacket. He must have dumped it when we lost sight of him and another dude picked em up. I didn't want to take a chance of losing him, so Chang and I split up. I caught the kid, but it's not Ramirez. I'm bringing the props back as evidence, but I'm all the way up by Thirty-Eighth."

"Alright, head back this way, check in with McGinnis, and be ready if Chang's guy changes direction."

They rounded the corner as the doors on the Thirty-Fourth Street exit were flung open. Chang's voice came through the radio, but they could already see the suspect. He was looking backwards to see if Chang was still on his tail and appeared to be unaware of Jackson bearing down on him until it was too late. Jackson speared him in the midsection like a linebacker flooring the quarterback. The bag went flying from the suspect's shoulder as he folded in half and hit the cement hard. The cameras were back out as Jackson flipped him over and cuffed him fast.

Standing, he hauled Edgar up and said loud enough for the lookie loo's, "Edgar Ramirez, you are under arrest for the Murders of Karen Matthews and Garrison Williams. You have the right to remain silent. Anything you say can and will be used against you in a court of law..."

"I didn't do it," he yelled, trying to get the crowd on his side. "Police brutality! You all saw him tackle me without cause."

"Nice try, Edgar," Diaz said with a smile as she held up his bag. "We also got you on blackmail." Thumbing her radio, she said, "This is detective Diaz. Can we get a squad car over to Thirty-Fourth please?"

McGinnis replied a heartbeat later, "It's on the way."

Edgar wasn't done with his show. The crowd was growing by the moment and he wanted to play to them. "You planted that!" he yelled. "These crooked cops are setting me up."

Fortunately, the crowd wasn't buying his nonsense. "Shut up, dude. You ruined the con for everyone. I hope your fat ass rots in jail," a college guy in an NYU sweatshirt yelled.

Several other people heckled Ramirez, and he finally shut up. Bethany Hernandez and a cameraman from the Daily News arrived on the scene while Edgar was still screaming.

"Detective Winters, is this the man who killed Garrison Williams?"

"No comment."

"Why is this man under arrest, Detective? The people have the right to know."

She walked right alongside him, and the cameraman stayed a few paces ahead to continue focusing on the perp-walk. The crowd followed as well, and he wondered how long it was going to take to get a squad car a couple blocks. He didn't want this to turn into even more of a debacle than it already was.

"Why won't you answer the question, Detective Winters?"

Edgar started up again. "They think I killed Garrison Williams, but I didn't. You have to help me."

Bethany Hernandez got excited as she stuck the microphone in Jackson's face. "Is this true, Detective Winters? Did you arrest this man for the murder of Garrison Williams?"

"You know we can't comment on an ongoing investigation, Miss Hernandez."

She smiled at him, and he wanted to smile back. She was a looker, and they ran into each other a lot. The only problem was that he'd never be able to trust that she wasn't just with him to get a story. The wrong pillow talk could end his career, so he resisted the temptation, but he still liked the game.

A cruiser pulled around the corner, and Jackson pushed Ramirez into the rear seat. There was still a crowd of people with their cameras out filming everything he did to be posted on the internet should one mistake be made. After the cruiser took off, Jackson, Diaz, and Chang returned to their cars. Lucco was waiting for them as they arrived. He was still sweating a little from the chase, but he wasn't out of breath like Chang was.

"Okay, you guys go pick up dinner while Diaz and I question Ramirez. Alvarez is probably already on site, and I don't want him to see your faces after what happened here with all the Deadpools, so stay scarce for a good hour or two. Maybe visit forensics or go back to the Collingsworth. I'll take whatever crap he flings, but hopefully since we have our prime suspect in custody, he'll be a little more civilized."

With a grateful nod, Chang jumped into his car and started the engine. Lucco mouthed the words; thank you, or it might have been, I love you. He was never quite sure with Looch. A few ticks later, they were driving off.

"What are you going to tell Alvarez?" Diaz said as she slipped into the passenger seat of the Challenger.

"The truth. That the clowns who dress up like the clown from the movie also act like the clown from the movie and saw an opportunity to make a pain in the ass of themselves. There's no way he can expect to have a clean take down when there are literally hundreds of people dressed exactly like the perp."

"Have you seen the videos online? They already have the bumbling music playing while our guys chase all the Deadpools all over the place. If I didn't think I was about to get my ass handed to me, I'd be cracking up right now."

Frowning, he said, "There's nothing we can do about that, and we got the right guy. That's gotta count for something."

Shaking her head, she held up her phone and said, "This one says, No Deadpools were injured during the making of this film. #NYPDfail. Where do people come up with this stuff?"

He felt his headache coming back. "This is going to be one of those nights."

Chapter 39

Jackson and Diaz strode into the squad room. It was time to face the music. Sooner or later, Chief Alvarez was going to have something to say, and the man had no patience, so it was likely to be sooner. Captain Wilson was the first to approach, and he was wearing a smile that said he hoped this collar would be good enough to negate some of the chief's fury.

With a pat on Jackson's back, he said, "Jones dropped Ramirez off in interrogation room three. Good job, Winters."

"Thank you, Captain. We're going to let him sit for a few minutes before we go down. I want to make sure we have our evidence compiled from the Collingsworth. His prints and DNA are all over that scene, so I want to lead off with the slam dunk and see what he has to say."

"I'm going to check in with Rivera now," Diaz added as she picked up the phone on her desk.

A slow clap started from behind Captain Williams, and a moment later, Chief Alvarez came into view. Jackson wanted to punch the smug right off his face, but did his best not to show it. He knew this was coming, and after his outburst this morning, he had no choice but to take it.

"Well, well, well. Another smooth takedown for NYPD's finest, Jackson Winters. That was about as low profile as we ever could have hoped for with you leading the charge, right Winters? Memes, video's, and a police department that will have to work hard to have the word laughingstock removed after the display at the Javits center today thanks to you."

Sarcasm was better than yelling, so Jackson continued to hold his tongue, although by the look on Captain Wilson's face, he wasn't the only one who wanted to throw down with Chief Alvarez. A smartass comeback was tugging at his soul, but he resisted. His captain had already put enough on the line for him this week, and he wasn't going to repay that kindness by getting in the chief's face again, no matter how much he wanted to.

"What? Nothing to say? No pithy comebacks? The great Jackson Winters has finally learned to hold his tongue? What the hell is wrong with you?" He yelled loud enough for the whole squad room to hear.

Getting into Jackson's personal space, he continued using his outdoor voice as he added, "What part of low profile do you not understand, Winters?"

Before he could say anything, Sergeant McGinnis— who he didn't even know was in the room— stepped in front of him and said, "With respect, sir, Detective Winters wasn't even on scene when the incident occurred. He and Detective Diaz were still wrapping up at the Collingsworth. Detectives Chang and Lucco were there and they were chasing the correct suspect. It was the uniform guys who got it wrong and made the mess. I failed to get them under control, and it was actually Detective Winters who brought the whole fiasco to an end as well as captured the suspect. I accept full responsibility, sir."

Chief Alvarez stared speechless at the feisty sergeant. Jackson could see he wanted to jump down her throat for butting in where she was unwelcome, but what she said was accurate so there wasn't much he could say. Another dressing down wasn't very far off, but Jackson was okay for now.

With a hard glare at the unblinking Sergeant, Chief Alvarez said, "That'll be all, Sergeant. Dismissed!"

Sergeant McGinnis spun on her heel and exited the squad room. Jackson could actually see her shaking a little, and he wished she had not just fallen on her sword for him. Now, she was on the chief's radar which was not a good place to be. He was ready to take whatever the ass cannon dished out, but he wasn't ready to see her have to deal with it. He was going to have to call her later to thank her and also to make sure she never did that again.

Diaz broke into his thoughts. "We've got everything we need."

"Let's do this."

"Captain Wilson and I will be right on the other side of the window. Don't screw this up!" Chief Alvarez said with a frown.

Jackson was flipping him off in his mind as they entered interrogation room three. Sitting on a metal chair and chained to the metal table, Ramirez was still in his spandex minus the mask. Jackson pulled out a chair for Diaz on the other side of the table and then took the remaining seat. His eyes never left the suspect. Diaz arranged a bunch of papers in a file, while Ramirez looked despondent. Nailing this clown was going to be rewarding no matter how much Chief Alvarez tried to beat him down. He had killed a twenty-one-year-old kid and needed to pay for that.

After several tense moments, Jackson looked at the dingy white wall, then back to Edgar and said, "So, Edgar, you've been busy. Stolen van, six counts of blackmail, two murders, what else are we going to find if we keep digging into your life?"

Diaz was arranging some photos in front of him. The photos showed Karen Matthews in the trunk, the bruising around the neck, the wound on the head, and the dresser she hit her head on. He looked away and wouldn't meet their eyes. It was if he was afraid that eye contact would be an admission, or he was too big a coward to face what he had done. Jackson waited for a few moments after Diaz was finished before smacking the table really hard. The sound reverberated through the interrogation room and Edgar visibly jumped.

"Look at the photos, Mr. Ramirez. Why did you take Karen Matthews' life?"

Ramirez still refused to look, and he shouted again, "I said look at the photos. What? You're a big enough man to kill a little twenty-one-year-old girl, but you can't even look at your handiwork? Why is that?"

Edgar tried to shove the photos off the table, but his hands were chained to the table, so the gesture was in vain. Sweat formed at his brow and on his neck as his situation was becoming more and more real in his mind. They had him and he knew it. There was nowhere for him to go, nothing left for him to do. He had killed this girl and now he was scared to face the consequences, but Jackson was going to make him face those consequences.

Looking Jackson in the eye, he yelled, "Because it was an accident."

Jackson stood and yelled, "Accident? Your hands accidentally found their way around that kid's neck? Try again, Edgar!" Gripping each side of the table, he leaned in staring daggers into the prisoner.

Ramirez crumbled under the intense gaze. "We were arguing about money and I wanted to scare her. She said she was going to go to the police, but I needed her to finish what we had set out to do. I choked her to let her know I was serious, but she hit me in the head with a vase and I shoved her. She lost her balance and hit her head, but I didn't mean to kill her. I just wanted to make some money off wealthy people with no self-control, but she got greedy. I was already paying her almost double her rate but she said blackmail was bad for business so she needed more. I didn't mean to kill her."

"No. You only meant to force her to have sex with people so you could get rich," Diaz said with a scowl as she picked up the photos.

"She was a whore. That's what whore's do."

"But she didn't know you were blackmailing people, did she? She found out and got mad," Jackson said.

For the next fifteen minutes, Edgar detailed his blackmailing scheme. The victims he collected money from, the ones he had targeted, but did not get before he was caught, where the copies were, everything. Captain Williams knocked on the window and Jackson left the room for a moment. Stepping into the viewing room, he saw Leena standing in between Captain Wilson and Chief Alvarez. She was in tears as she gave a positive identification of Edgar as the man who had hired them and given them their assignments. An officer escorted Leena out, and Captain Wilson shot Jackson an encouraging nod.

"Good work, Winters."

"Thanks, Captain. He's in a chatty mood. I think I'm going to blindside him with Garrison's picture now, but I'm starting to think he didn't do it."

Chief Alvarez glared at him and said, "You better hope he did it."

Was this jack wagon kidding? Was he really so worried that we solved the wrong case first that he couldn't be happy a murderer was off the street? This guy is a joke, and he doesn't belong anywhere near law enforcement. How is it that the mayor and commissioner were unaware that this clown is a total moron? No one wants to work with him or for him. That should be an indication he's not fit to lead, but in the NYPD culture of failing up and political postings, the likes of Chief Alvarez were allowed to thrive.

Shaking off the negative thoughts, he replied, "Don't worry, sir. We've got a much better suspect in mind for Williams' murder." Without awaiting a reply, he left the room and returned to interrogation.

"You're going away for a long time, Edgar. I only have one more question for you, and if you give me an answer I like, we might be able to knock a few years off that life sentence."

A long pause had Edgar looking up in anticipation, hoping against hope he would escape a life sentence. His eyes blinked rapidly several times, but Jackson saw his heart sink when he smiled.

"Why did you kill Garrison Williams?"

He knew that Edgar didn't do it, but he had to ask. He had to put on a show for the chief, dot all the eyes cross all the tees. Edgar's face went blank. Looking back and forth between him and Diaz, confusion played across his face.

"Well? Why?" Jackson yelled.

"I didn't. He said he was going to give me the money tomorrow. Why would I kill him before he gave me the money?"

"Maybe he was going to go to the police? We've seen how you react to that." Diaz said.

"No. He told me if this got out, he would be ruined. He would have never gone to the police. He was going to give me the money."

Edgar switched from afraid to indignant in an instant. "I already told you everything, but I'm not going to let you pin another body on me. I'm not going to be your fall guy so you could look good for the press. I didn't do it."

Jackson and Diaz stood and left the room, Edgar continued yelling behind them, "I didn't kill Garrison Williams. Do you hear me? I didn't kill him. I want a lawyer."

Chapter 40

When Lucco walked into the stationhouse, Chief Alvarez was fuming that they still had no one in custody for the murder of Garrison Williams. The target of his ire was of course Jackson. He took it like a champ without saying a word. Even Diaz seemed impressed with Jackson's newfound self-control. The temperature in the room was dropping fast, so he and Chang were probably better off not sticking around. After dropping off dinner, they took off in a hurry. They had found out that Jenkins was supposed to be at an after party in the ballroom of the Marriot and had finagled some tickets to better keep an eye on him. Jackson gave them his blessing, and they were on their way to the store to get some comic appropriate party outfits.

"Alvarez is really coming down on Jackson. It's like his second day back. Why can't he lay off already?" Lucco said as he drove to the nearest store.

"Jackson did get in his face this morning. It's not like he's forgotten that. Remember, Chief Alvarez is all about the politics, and Garrison Williams' killer still being on the loose is bad for Alvarez politically."

"Yeah well if he doesn't let up, I'm making a complaint. This is not how you should be running a police department. It's bad for morale."

Chang looked at him and stifled a laugh. "Who are you? And what have you done with my partner?"

Smacking the steering wheel, he said, "I'm being serious, damn it. Alvarez' attitude is bad for the department."

Nodding an apology, he said, "Sorry, Richie. I'm just not used to seeing you this serious. I didn't know this was weighing on you so heavily. "

"It's just not cool. Not after everything Jackson has been through." After a long pause, he said, "You know I was on vacation when they killed Hodges. I'm in the Bahamas screwing around, and my team is getting shot up. I've never forgiven myself for that."

The car slowed to a stop at a red light, and Chang put a hand on his partner's shoulder. "You can't blame yourself for that, Looch. I had my appendix out. I was on my couch eating Jell-O with Junie. They moved on the information when they got it. We couldn't have predicted when that would be."

The light turned green and the car started moving again. "I know, but it sucks, and I'm like five minutes away from smacking the stupid off Alvarez' face. That guy better move his ass along. I'm sick of him sniffing around our station. Go back to One PP already."

"Amen to that."

They pulled up to the Marriot at nine-thirty. Chang walked in wearing a flash cap, a flash zip up hoodie, black jeans, and a pair of red Chuck Taylors. Even in his mid-thirties, he still passed for his mid-twenties. Lucco went all out dressed as Batman with a full body suit.

"Not a word to Diaz about this," he said to Chang as Chang's phone snapped a picture of him.

"Yeah, I'm not sure that's gonna be possible," he replied as he hit send and laughed. "Seriously, bro. You could have just picked up a batman hoodie and wore some jeans. There's no way I'm letting this opportunity slip by after the Chick Flick Chang nickname." His phone pinged and he smiled at the text. "Diaz wants to see the bat ass. Turn around."

"Ha-ha," he said, but his tone indicated he didn't find it funny. "Let's just find Jenkins."

As he turned to go into the party, Chang snapped off another picture and sent it to Diaz.

"Would you cut it out," Lucco said.

They weren't quite ready for what was going on when they entered the room. Lasers bounced off the walls while robots on stilts danced on the stage. The DJ played sci-fi theme songs mixed in with techno, and costumed convention goers partied like it was 2099. Bars were set up all around the outskirts of the ballroom, and people drank, danced, and talked pop culture, but mostly the first two. Storm Troopers danced with X-men and Robots danced with Anime characters. Avengers danced with Teen Titans, Aliens danced with Steam Punk pirates, and there was a T-Rex running around the room grinding up on random partiers. Chang must have snapped a hundred pictures already, and Looch knew that Diaz would be jealous she missed the fun.

Two scantily clad young ladies approached him to take selfies with him in his Batman costume, and Chang was relegated to taking the pictures while scanning the area for Jenkins. The girls pulled Looch onto the dance floor, and he smiled at his partner as if all his dreams were coming true at once. He noticed Jenkins dancing with a cute woman in a volunteer shirt. Her long brown hair was pulled into a pony tail that whipped around as they moved. Motioning Chang to get eyes on Jenkins, he went back to dancing. Chang continued snapping pictures, but several discreet shots were of Jenkins. He wasn't acting like someone afraid of being arrested for murder.

About ten-forty-five, Jimmy Shultz arrived with an entourage from the network and lots of nubile groupies on their arms. Jimmy's suit was easily ten grand, and he had two young women draped on him as beautiful arm candy. "And these guys have the nerve to put a morality clause into the actor's contracts?" Chang shouted over the music as he snapped pictures of the entire entourage.

Looch nodded his head in agreement as another costumed young lady handed him a phone number. "I'd never sign a morality clause," he said as he put his phone away. "I can literally date a different woman each week for the next year with all the numbers I've scored this weekend."

"Yeah, but how many of them actually live in NY?"

"You're right. I should try and get with some of the out-of-towners before they leave," he yelled.

"You'll never find happiness that way."

He was about to argue the point when he saw Shultz and Jenkins talking. Chang caught it, too and immediately started taking pictures. A few minutes into the conversation, an argument started, and a few moments after that, the shoving began. Chang continued taking pictures as Jenkins took a swing and connected with Jimmy's eye. Within seconds, several large bouncers were escorting both men from the property. Lucco and Chang moved to follow, but both of the men were whisked away in limos before the detectives could get to their car.

"Tell me you got that," Lucco said.

"Of course."

"My man!"

Lucco went back into the hotel and changed out of the Batman costume. He threw on a pair of jeans, a white tee, and a Yankee sweatshirt and put the costume in the trunk of the car. They left the party just before midnight and texted Jackson some pictures from the argument between their suspects on the way home. The party idea had been a good one. Now they just needed to figure out what it all meant.

Jackson texted back a minute later and Chang started laughing as Lucco pulled up to a red light.

"What's so funny?" he said.

"Jackson said good job and if he sees you in that Batman costume again, you're fired."

Lucco frowned as he turned his head to face Chang. "Seriously?"

Chang laughed as he said, "He said the NYPD can't have masked vigilantes running loose in the city."

Lucco chuckled. "Looks like he's finally warming up to this case. Forward that to Diaz, she'll get a kick out of it."

Chapter 41

Jackson was finally able to leave the station. Chief Alvarez had hung around the station forever, and there was no way he was leaving before the chief. His stubbornness wouldn't allow it. When he thought it was going to be one of those days this morning, he had no idea how right he would be. As he was approaching the Brooklyn Bridge, his phone buzzed. The caller idea showed it was Martin and he answered it by tapping a button on his steering wheel. He always told Raina that hands free was the way to be. Hopefully she would remember that when she started driving.

"What's up, buddy?"

A long pause like dead air on a college radio station followed. He almost thought his friend had butt dialed him. When it was just past awkward, Martin answered in a small voice, too small for the Martin he knew.

"Jax, I may be in some trouble."

Warning bells went off in his head. In the thirty-one years they had been friends, he had never heard Martin utter those words. His mind flashed back to the conversation he had walked in on during poker night and his gut told him it had something to do with that.

Without pausing to think about it, he said, "What kind of trouble?"

"I'm not sure. I think the deal Vince and I are working on for the firm is with some shady people."

The cop in him took over immediately. "What's the name of the company you and Vince are working with?"

The lights of the bridge flashed by as he enjoyed the low traffic flow and actually reached the speed limit. A sure indication he had worked later than usual. It was almost worth it for this commute, but he'd take massive traffic jams over even a minute with Alvarez any day of the week. The phone was silent again and he knew that wasn't a good sign.

"It's not a firm, it's a private investor."

"Did you suspect he was shady when you and Vince started working with him?"

"I didn't, but I'm beginning to think that Vince did. Jax, I think something's gonna go down and I'm meant to be the patsy."

"Who is the investor?"

"Jax, you know I can't reveal that information."

"Martin, you know it stays between us. It's not like I'm gonna go running to the SEC. Who is it?"

Another long pause told him his best friend might not have been as naïve as he thought.

"Dmitry Koslov."

He knew that name, and if he knew that name it meant this was no one his friend should be doing business with. "Russian mob? Are you serious? Of course, they're shady."

"I didn't know he was Russian mob until you just said it this second. I just thought he was a scam artist looking to make a quick buck at my expense."

"You need to extricate yourself from this deal as soon as possible. Take the financial loss. Go on report. Do whatever you have to do to get out of this. Do you understand?"

"I don't think I can. The deal is too far along. If I purposely tank it, I could get fired."

His drive home was no longer enjoyable, all he could think about was how much trouble his best friend was in. "Martin, fired is better than dead, and you're all Amanda has left."

"I need some time to figure it out."

"What do you need from me?"

"I just need to know that if anything does happen to me, you'll take care of Amanda."

"You know I will, but let's work on making sure nothing happens to you."

"I'm working on it, Jax."

The call ended about the time he was pulling up to the house. Catching Garrison Williams' killer was no longer the most important thing on his mind. How was he going to get Koslov's tentacles unraveled from his best friend's life? He was unsure Martin really knew how much trouble he could be in, and it was far worse than losing his job. You don't cross

Russians, and once you do a deal for them, they own you for life. It was close to five minutes before he pried himself out of his car grabbed his folders and trudged towards his house.

The door flung open and Raina and Amanda greeted him with big smiles which brightened his mood instantly. The smell of pepperoni pizza wafted out of the kitchen and tickled his nostrils. His stomach rumbled, and he remembered barely having time to touch the sandwich Chang and Lucco had left for him. Eating would have made Chief Alvarez think he wasn't working hard enough, so most of his food wound up in the squad room fridge for tomorrow.

"Dad, we heated up some pizza for you."

Pulling his daughter into a one arm hug, he kissed the top of her head and said, "Thanks, Peanut."

The weariness in his eyes must have been evident because Amanda said, "Is everything okay, Uncle Jax?"

He pulled her into a hug and kissed the top of her head as well. "It's just been a really long day, Kiddo, and tomorrow's probably not going to be much better." Releasing the embrace, he set his folders on the table and rubbed his hands together in anticipation. "Now, where's that pizza?"

While he was eating, Raina and Amanda bombarded him with details of their day, including another visit from the creepy Inspector Gadget at which point he flashed the time out signal.

"That guy came after you again?"

Raina shrank away a little and there was still a touch of fear in her eyes as she said, "Yeah, but Officer D'Agostino and Sergeant McGinnis took care of it. I really like Sergeant McGinnis, Dad."

"Yeah, she's great. So, do I need to send some sort of thank you out to D'Agostino and McGinnis?"

"I would, and if you do, I'd like to write them a note as well."

A smile crept up on his tired face. His daughter would always be a better person than he was. Taking another bite of his pizza, he was thankful they had ordered from Joey's. They had the best sauce, and he loved the fresh mozzarella they used. He tried not to eat pizza or fast food too often, not counting this weekend, but when he did have Joey's, it was a little slice of heaven.

"Okay, so do you guys have pictures?"

"We had so much fun, dad. Everyone loved Jacob's costume, and we already finished his costume for tomorrow."

"I really appreciate you taking care of your brother today, but you don't have to bring him with you again tomorrow. This was your big Sweet Sixteen gift. I can hire a service."

Both Raina and Amanda almost looked crestfallen at the suggestion before they regained their excited composure.

"No way, dad. We were like convention all-stars because of Jacob. All day people wanted to stop and take pictures of him in his costume. They even pointed it out as a great example of a mash up at the cosplay creation panel. We actually had much more fun because he was with us."

"You don't know how happy it makes me to hear that, girls. Now, let's get back to those pictures."

After close to a hundred photos, he came to the conclusion that in spite of the creep that tried to grab her, the kids had a great time. The girls kissed his cheek and ran upstairs to get some sleep before the last day of the convention, but he still had a little work to do. Pulling the laptop in front of him, he pulled up the pictures of Jenkins and Shultz fighting that Chang had texted him and planned to do a little internet surfing to see if there was anything tying these two together.

When he opened the laptop, he checked the internet history which was probably the lone way he spied on his daughter. At least that's what he told himself. It was the easiest way to see what she was into, as teenagers often left out a lot of information. The first site that popped up was an Amazon page for a costume design starter kit. The package included all kinds of materials, props, and directions for how to make costumes. He was sure that this item would make it onto his daughter's Christmas list in a couple months, but he was so thankful for how she stepped up with her brother that he was going to order it for her now while she was still so excited about the con.

As he was about to press the purchase button, he glanced at the price and froze. Two hundred fifty dollars plus shipping? "Why can't they ever have cheap hobbies like rock collecting?" he mumbled as he pressed the button.

The reality was that even with the extra money he had given her and Amanda this weekend, and buying the last minute ticket and souvenir money for Jacob, this convention was still thousands of dollars less than the party he would have thrown her, so he selected next day shipping realizing it was already Sunday and bought his daughter a well-deserved thank you present. He could already see her and Amanda up in her room coming up with some crazy and amazing get up for their next costumed affair, and the thought put a smile on his face as he switched his focus back to the case.

Chapter 42

Jackson picked the morning paper up off the stoop and groaned. In big bold letters taking up the top quarter of the page was the headline: **ACTION JACKSON**. A picture of Lisa Saranna embracing him took up half of the cover page, and the subtitle below was the one that was sure to get him an early morning reaming from Chief Alvarez. It read: *Detective Jackson Winters canoodles with local celebrity while Garrison Williams' killer remains free.* Unflattering would be a generous description of the article for both him and the NYPD, and it was written by his good friend Bethany Hernandez.

Trudging back into his house, he knew it was going to be another one of those days. As he reached for an oversized travel mug to pour lots of steaming black coffee in, three superheroes marched into the kitchen. His daughter's purple outfit and dark wig reminded him of one he'd seen the other day.

Studying Raina, it came to him and he said, "Psylocke, right?"

Beaming, she replied, "Dad, how did you know that?"

"Your old man's got a few tricks up his sleeve."

"No. Seriously, how did you know?"

With a laugh he put his hands up in surrender. "Okay, you got me. Looch pointed another Psylocke out to me on Friday. Her name is Tiffani with an I. He's got a date with her, too."

Raina and Amanda both laughed and Amanda mumbled, "I bet he did."

"So, who else do we have here?"

Pointing to Amanda, she said, "This is Dark Phoenix, and we made another mash up costume for Jacob."

"He looks like a green version of Wolverine. What's that symbol on his chest?"

"He is the Green Wolverine. We bought a Green Lantern spandex outfit on our way home last night, and we painted the plastic wolverine mask and claws he already had green. He really likes Green Lantern, so he can still use the costume for Halloween because we kept the green mask."

"Great job, girls."

After another round of pictures, he gave his enthusiastic son a high five and added, "You all look amazing. Are you ready to go?"

They followed him out of the house and all jumped into the Challenger to go back to the Javits Center one more time. As they crossed the Brooklyn Bridge, he looked in the rearview mirror and said, "Girls, if that guy comes anywhere near you again, call me immediately. And if I'm not nearby, call Sergeant McGinnis. Do you understand?"

"We will, Dad, but Sergeant McGinnis said his paperwork was going to get lost for a day and he wouldn't be able to make it back to the con even if he wanted to."

Breathing a sigh of relief, he realized he owed that woman a few rounds of drinks. "That's great news but stay alert anyway, okay?"

"We will, dad."

After dropping the kids off for the last day of the con, he sailed into work. Sunday morning was usually an easy commute on the rare occasion he worked them, but now the easy part of his day was over. Before his foot had even crossed the threshold into the squad room, Chief Alvarez had already bellowed for him to get in the captain's office.

Holding up the Daily News, he stepped into Jackson's personal space and yelled, "What the hell is this?"

"I believe it's a newspaper, sir," he replied, but a look from Captain Wilson told him to zip it.

"Oh, this is a joking matter. It's bad enough we had that debacle catching the wrong guy yesterday, but now the whole city gets to wake up and see you cozying up to an actress. You need to be solving the case, not rubbing elbows with celebrities!"

After a long silence he glared at Jackson and said, "Well? What have you got to say for yourself?"

Captain Wilson nodded, and he tried to hold his most respectful tone as he said, "Well first, I'd like to point out that we did not in fact arrest the wrong guy. We caught Karen Matthews' murderer at the convention. Second, Lisa Saranna came up to me and threw her arms around me. I immediately disengaged and gently let her know I was on duty. She asked me if she could shadow someone in the NYPD for an upcoming role, and I told her I'd get back to her when this case was completed. That's all that happened, and there's nothing I could have done differently. You know the news is just trying to stir the pot, sir."

"That's pretty much what Detective Diaz said, Chief. Looks like the reporters were just in the right place at the right time and caught an innocent exchange. They tried to turn it into something it's not to sell more papers. Won't be the last time, either," Captain Wilson said with an encouraging nod in Jackson's direction.

After what could only be described as a cross between a grumble and a growl, Chief Alvarez said, "Where are we on the case?"

Jackson smiled and said, "If you'll follow me, sir."

Being respectful and pretending he didn't hate the man was difficult, but he still felt bad about losing it yesterday and putting Captain Wilson in a difficult position. The captain deserved better than that from his lead homicide detective. They stopped at his desk, and he called up the pictures of Shultz and Jenkins arguing in the Marriot ballroom last night as well as some possible points of connection.

"These photos were taken last night by Detective Chang at a convention after party. Our two main suspects got into it pretty good as you can see. After Chang emailed me the photos, I did some digging and found out a few interesting tidbits."

"Such as?" Captain Wilson said, not wanting any dramatic lulls to be filled with the chief's nonsense.

"Such as, Jimmy Shultz pulled HERO's backing for a movie based on Jenkins video game character, Grimwolf."

"Why is that important?" Chief Alvarez said, and for once, he seemed more interested than aggravated.

"It's important because Garrison Williams had been tied to the project which is the only reason it got off the ground in the first place, and he recently pulled out giving both Steve Jenkins and Jimmy Shultz motive to kill him."

Captain Wilson's face morphed into another one of his famous toothy grins as he clapped Jackson on the back and said, "That's good work, Winters!"

"So, what's the course of action?" Chief Alvarez asked in an actual human voice. Was that hope in his eyes?

"We're going to bring Jimmy Shultz in first because we can already nail him on the insurance fraud. Maybe we can leverage that for something bigger. In the meantime, Detectives Chang and Lucco will be keeping an eye on Jenkins. His alibi is flimsy and they'll be digging, but right now, all we have is circumstantial. I think he's our guy, so the quicker we can eliminate Shultz, the more time we'll have to go full bore on Jenkins."

"I'll let you get to it then," Chief Alvarez said as he spun on his heel and marched out of the squad room.

Jackson's eyebrow rose as he watched him go. "Did that just happen, Cap?"

"What, the part where Alvarez was actually a human being for a few minutes?"

"Yeah, that."

Clapping his back again with big meaty hands, he said, "Don't get used to it, but if you can solve this case and grab him a good headline, we might not see the mean side again for a couple weeks."

With a grin stretching his lips, he said, "You sure know how to motivate a guy, Cap."

"That's what I'm known for," he replied with a chuckle as he turned to go back into his office. Calling over his shoulder, he added, "Update me after you speak to Shultz."

"Will do, sir."

Chapter 43

By the time Chief Alvarez left, his team was all accounted for and busy. Lucco was convincing Jimmy Shultz to come back in for a few more questions, Diaz was trying to put names to faces of Jimmy's entourage from the night before, and Chang was looking over some of the crime scene photos. Specifically, the toy sword that murdered Garrison Williams. Chang's interest drew his attention and he moved behind him to look over his shoulder at the picture. He had enlarged the magnification and was moving the mouse across the picture in a deliberate fashion.

"What are you thinking, Pete?"

"I'm thinking this sword came from somewhere."

"Probably the local toy store."

Chang stopped and looked up at him. "See, this is why you need people like me and Julia on a case like this. This is not a toy sword— at least not to the owner. It's a collectible replica. It's far more detailed, far more expensive, and probably a lot sturdier than a plastic sword a kid might buy for ten bucks."

"Okay, so?"

"So, if this is as expensive as I think it is, it had to come from somewhere, and they might keep records of who purchased it. A lot of replicas are limited editions so they can charge more for it. In this case, I'd guess the sword goes for just about four hundred dollars."

Jackson's jaw dropped and Chang caught it. "Supply and demand. If Grimwolf has ten million fans and they only create one hundred official replicas, they can charge a lot of money for them and they probably keep track."

"Good idea. And you're right, in my mind that was a ten-dollar plastic toy. I'm glad you're on the case, brother." Clapping him on the back, he continued watching for something that might give them a clue as to the owner.

After a few beats, he said, "Why do you think someone would pay so much for a plastic replica? I'm sure they'd rather have a regular metal sword for a replica."

From across the desk Diaz said, "Because Comic Cons don't allow real weapons to be brought on the premises. It's a big safety hazard, and there would be far too much liability involved. But the cosplayers still want to look as authentic as possible, so they'll buy the plastic just to complete the look."

Nodding at the rationale behind her answer, something in the picture caught his eye. "Hey, Chang, does the end of the blade seem off to you? Can you zoom in on it?"

Narrowing his eyes, he caught it too. "Looks like wear and tear on the edge of the blade, but it's too uniform to be, not to mention this isn't the type of toy you play with."

"If I didn't know any better, I'd say this blade was filed to be sharper than a plastic blade should be."

Surprise colored Chang's usually calm features and his eyes widened as he said, "You're right, Jackson. It has been filed. Good eye."

Lucco and Diaz came around to have a look. "That means whoever owns this sword intended to kill Garrison Williams with it," Lucco said.

"It also means that if they filed it down in their hotel room, there might be forensic evidence," Diaz said with a smile.

"Winters," Captain Wilson called from his office. "Jimmy Shultz and his lawyer are in interrogation room two."

"Yes, sir. Come on Julia." As they turned to leave, he stopped and said, "Chang, top priority is finding out where that sword came from and who owns it."

As they entered interrogation room two, a wall of cologne hit them even harder than the last time they met with Jimmy Shultz. This time he was a little disheveled as if anyone wearing a Kiton blue and navy plaid suit could be disheveled. His blue pinstriped Brioni dress shirt was untucked, and the suit jacket was unbuttoned. His hair was beyond tussled, and the face of his eighty thousand-dollar iced out watch was sporting a fresh crack. A dark blue coating ringed his left eye, and he slumped in his chair as if he meant to sleep.

His lawyer was dressed every bit as impressively as he was. Except for the disheveled part, he looked like he had gotten a good night sleep and had time for a shower. His Mark Cross black leather briefcase sat on the table. Calvin Dodd attorney at law was not one to put seven thousand-dollar briefcases on the dirty floors of a police interrogation room.

Glancing at Jimmy with a smile, Jackson said, "Tough night, Jimmy?"

"It is what it is," he replied with a casual wave of the hand.

"Don't answer any of their questions," The lawyer said. Trying out his most impressive glare on the detectives, his voice turned to ice as he said, "What is my client being charged with?"

"Insurance fraud," Jackson said unmoved by the lawyer's attempt at intimidation. After all, he had quite an impressive array of glares himself, and he was using one of them now.

A moment of confusion played across the attorney's face, but he was practiced enough to not let it linger as he figured out the game. This time, instead of a glare, he had more of a lets-make-a-deal voice. "And why are two homicide detectives interested in a lowly case of insurance fraud?"

"We're not, but it came up in the course of our investigation, and we would be remiss if we failed to address it."

"Due diligence and all," Diaz added. She laid out all of the evidence that clearly showed Shultz guilty of fraud, and the Attorney barely blinked. He must have known they had it as soon as they said it because you don't drag a Jimmy Shultz into the stationhouse after an all-night bender unless you have him dead to rights. She started laying out photos from the altercation at the Marriot and the lawyer's interest was piqued.

"Have you been tailing my client, Detective Winters?"

"No. We were tailing a suspect, and Jimmy stumbled onto the scene."

With a predatory smile, he clasped his hands together and said, "What's the question, and what do we get out of it?"

Jackson smiled. He liked that this lawyer wasn't wasting time. "We've got Mr. Shultz on class B felony insurance fraud. Given the policy is in the twenty million range, I doubt a judge would be lenient. Fortunately, your client may have some information that might be useful in establishing motive for our murder suspect."

"And this is a high-profile case, so I'm sure the D.A. would be in a most generous mood if my client's information were to lead to an arrest."

"I'm sure she would," Jackson said. "Because this case is time sensitive, she's on her way in as we speak."

"I look forward to speaking with Mrs. Thomas again," the attorney said with a smile.

A few minutes later D.A. Thomas strode in. An attractive woman in her mid-fifties, she was always impeccably dressed. Today, she wore a navy-blue pinstriped pantsuit.

"Let's cut right to the chase since time is of the essence. Your client is looking at minimum fifteen years for felony insurance fraud, and due to the amount involved, there's not likely to be much leniency. If the information your client provides helps lead to the conviction of Steven Jenkins for the murder of Garrison Williams, I'm willing to bump that to a class D felony and I'd be willing to push for no more than three years with the possibility of parole."

"May I have a moment to confer with my client?"

"Yes. Of course." D.A, Thomas, Jackson, and Diaz left the room. After a few moments, the lawyer knocked on the window and they returned.

"We agree to those terms as long as nothing my client says is used to incriminate himself in any other crimes."

"As long as his testimony stays on track for this case, that won't be a problem." The lawyer nodded his agreement, and the D.A. turned and said, "Detectives, ask your questions."

Jackson's eyes were practically watering the cologne was so thick. He had to hand it to the lawyer and the D.A., if they were having any discomfort, they were masking it well. "Mr. Shultz, what was the nature of your disagreement with Steve Jenkins last night?"

"Steve was working on a movie deal for his video game character Grimwolf. Garrison Williams had initially signed on with the project which brought in a lot of investors including HERO TV. We saw it as a way to dip our toes in the movie pool, and possibly draw Grimwolf into the Bad Cow family of characters. Our brand is growing by leaps and bounds, but we're still playing catch up with the two big boys."

"And when Garrison pulled out, you pulled your support," Jackson said with a nod.

"At first yes, but after a couple weeks, I thought I could attach Colin Stone to the project and lure back the other investors. Colin would have required a much bigger payday than Garrison, so Jenkins would have been required to sign on with Bad Cow giving us the rights to the character, but not the video game. He refused because he believed he could get Garrison to change his mind, and we went our separate ways."

Jackson saw his confused look mirrored on Diaz' face and he asked, "So what happened last night then?"

"Last night, I was riding high on the success of our announcement. HERO TV was getting a ton of good press, and I was in a great mood. I didn't know Jenkins was going to be there, but when I saw him, I went up to talk to him. I thought I could add to the good press by bringing him into the fold. We would have dominated pop culture news for weeks if I could have pulled it off."

"What was the fight about?" Diaz said.

"He accused me of trying to kick him when he was down and he wasn't too happy."

"Do you remember his exact words?" Jackson was hoping he said something incriminating in the heat of the moment.

"Yeah, he said them twice. Once when he shoved me, and once when he punched me. He said, and I quote: 'I've given up far too much of my life and soul for this movie. Garrison Williams' betrayal took everything from me, and now you're trying to steal my character.'"

"What did he mean by everything?"

"He was leveraged in over his eyeballs on his movie. If it doesn't happen, Steve Jenkins won't have a penny to his name. Even if he gets someone to finance a sequel to his video game, he'll get peanuts compared to what he got for the first one. If the movie doesn't go through, he's screwed financially. That's why I couldn't understand why he was unwilling to work with me. I was offering him full retention of his video game rights and a fair split on the character rights."

Jackson chewed on Jimmy's words for a couple minutes before turning to Diaz. "Far too much of his heart and soul, that's a pretty interesting choice of words don't you think?"

"Yes. I do." She packed up her case folder and they both stood.

"Thank you for your testimony, Mr. Shultz," Jackson said as they turned to leave. The D.A. gave a slight nod of her head. Jimmy's chances for a short incarceration looked pretty good.

Chapter 44

"Julia, check out Jimmy's claims about Jenkins' finances. I want to know for sure before we bring it to Wilson."

"This is solid motive if it's true," she replied as she sat down at her desk and started typing on her keyboard.

Jackson started to feel that excitement of closing out a case and catching a killer. His first case back after almost three months of recovery, and it was a big one. After Hodges, this was probably going to wind up being the biggest case of his career. There had been a few bumps along the way, and Chief Alvarez didn't make it easy for him, but he was confident they had their guy. Now it was just a matter of proving it. Jenkins was smart, but if this was his first foray into violent crime. There would be evidence. Average people committing crimes for the first time weren't usually good at covering their tracks.

Looking up at his unit hard at work, he stared at the murder board and put Jenkins photo front and center among suspects. Taking a moment, he cleared all of the information from the board having to do with Karen Matthews and Edgar Ramirez. With less information on the board, it made it easier to focus on the case they were still working on. After staring at the board for a couple minutes, he went back to his desk.

He tucked the Matthews file under the Williams file and said, "Looch, what are you working on?"

"Rivera called. He thinks his guy is close to cracking the second phone from the Collingsworth. I'm trying to get Williams' phone records, but I'm having the same problem I've been having all weekend."

"What's that?"

"That it's the weekend. We'll have more luck waiting on Rivera's team to crack it."

"Okay, why don't you get back down to the convention and keep an eye on Jenkins, but stay incognito."

"Yeah, wear the Batman costume again. I still need to see that bat ass," Diaz said with a playful gleam in her eyes.

"Why don't you go put on your Wonder Woman costume and come with me?"

"Why don't both of you take a few moments to go over the department harassment guidelines," Jackson said with a laugh. "A hoodie and a pair of sunglasses should do the trick, Looch. There's tens of thousands of people there."

"On my way," he said as he turned and hurried from the room.

"I got it," Chang yelled drawing everyone's attention. He pumped his fist in the air in celebration. Noting everyone looking at him, he elaborated. "Serial number for the replica sword. Now I just need to get in touch with the manufacturer and see who they sold it to." Before anyone could reply he was already checking out the website that sold the sword.

Diaz caught Jackson's attention and waved him over to her desk. "I'm getting nowhere with the financials because it's a Sunday, but I did come across this article about how badly Jenkins was leveraged for the Grimwolf movie. The author thought it was too risky a proposition, and he was thorough in his research. Everything he sites has a link to a hard copy. I'm printing out each page, and it looks like Jimmy was spot on."

Standing, she walked over to the printer to get her pages. She had made two copies of each page and was collating them to give Jackson a copy. "Speaking of Jimmy, please don't ever make me go interview him again. That cologne was an instant migraine for me. I can still taste it on my tongue."

"I know what you mean. It's going to take a lot of beer to make me forget that experience."

"Jackson," Chang said without lifting his eyes from the screen. A moment later, he was looking over Chang's shoulder again.

"What am I looking at?"

"The website that sells the Grimwolf broad sword replica."

"I got that, but why am I looking at it?"

Chang chuckled. "Not one for the fine print, huh, boss. I've been unable to get in touch with anyone from the manufacturer, but after a search of the site, I've learned that each sword comes with a matching belt and scabbard."

"Scabbard?"

"Sheath."

"Okay?"

"Each piece of the set has the same number to insure someone is selling you a complete set and not a partial set mixed with less valuable knockoffs. If the sword belongs to Jenkins…"

"He might still have the belt and sheath in his room since we didn't find them in the dumpster. Great work!"

"We're gonna nail this bastard," Diaz said with a wicked grin. Jackson was beginning to figure out that she wasn't the type of person whose bad side you wanted to wind up on.

"Okay, between Jimmy's testimony, Jenkins' finances, and the replica serial number, I think I have enough for a warrant. Pete, why don't you get to the Javits Center and back Looch up. I'm going to bring all of this to Captain Wilson."

"Got it, boss."

"Julia, you're with me."

They stepped into Captain Wilson's office and laid out the case. He assured them that he could get a warrant for Jenkins' room at the Marriot. It was a definite long shot that they could come up with a slam dunk, but an overwhelming amount of circumstantial evidence was beginning to mount. Still, motive doesn't mean murder, even if he lied about it. If the warrant failed to turn up anything useful, they could still get him on assaulting Jimmy, and lying during a police investigation to give them more time to get their ducks in a row because they knew Jenkins was their guy.

"This is good work, Winters. I'm going to send it over to Chief Alvarez now, and try to get the warrant. We should have it in a couple hours."

"Thanks, Cap. We're going to go back to the convention and keep an eye on things."

"You just don't want to be here when the chief gets here to comb through your case."

"He left without yelling at me. Why push my luck?" The captain chuckled as he and Diaz pushed through the door and left for the Javits Center.

Chapter 45

The hum of people in the Javits Center filled the air. Large crowds shuffled along the convention center floor weaving in and out of all of the merchandise booths. He wondered how many of those booths were selling merchandise with his picture on it. A hangover had him reaching for aspirins as memories of the party, the fight with Jimmy, and waking up next to the cute volunteer filled his mind. The convention was lucky he was even able to get out of bed this morning. Maybe that's why they sent the pretty volunteer to seduce him. Not that they had, but after what he had done, he wouldn't put anything past anyone.

Crowds flocked to his autograph table. Life-sized cutouts of him stood at each end of his table and a banner over his head read: Grimwolf. Wearing his full costume, he looked out at the long line of adoring fans, and he wondered if he would be able to get back on his feet financially just by doing these shows for a year or two. Even if he lost his money, maybe he could take advantage of his name while it was still big. Other celebrities seem to be able to do it. Maybe he could give it a shot.

Maybe he would call Jimmy back and think about the offer. He could blame his belligerence on alcohol, sign the contract, and laugh about it over drinks. Jimmy wanted Grimwolf for the Bad Cow comic line. Maybe it would be less money than the movie would have netted him, but at least he wouldn't lose all of his, and he would still make some. A pretty good amount really. Had he been more pragmatic earlier, he might not have to worry about facing murder charges right now. If he let HERO take care of the movie, he would be free to launch a sequel to the first game with new characters Jimmy would want to buy. If he made it through this weekend, he was going to give Jimmy a call.

The cute volunteer he had spent the night with waved to him from Jasmine Connelly's table where she had been assigned. He had already forgotten her name, but he mused that he wouldn't be so quick to forget a night with Jasmine. Returning her smile with a nod, he let his volunteer know he was ready to start signing autographs.

The first customer was a young boy dressed like him. The kid would no doubt want to take a picture with him which would cost extra. Kids were his least favorite part of the conventions, but they were a money-making machine for him, so he plastered a fake smile to his face and said, "Hey, little warrior. What's your name?"

"I am Grimwolf," the kid said in his deepest voice which was still prepubescent high. "But my mom calls me Jake."

The kid handed him an action figure still in the package and he signed it to the kid and handed it back. The mom was handing the money to his agent who only seemed to be around when he was at the autograph table. Several sharp disagreements and the fact that she refused to sleep with him made him sure she didn't like him, but she was a good agent, so he didn't care. As long as she kept the money rolling in, she would never have to jump in his bed to keep her job no matter how much he wished she would.

"Can we get a picture of you and Jake together?" the mom said. The agent nodded that she had paid the extra twenty-five bucks and he stepped around the table. He picked the kid up with one massive arm, and they both gave their best warrior snarls for the camera. The kid gave him a high five and they were gone.

Somewhere around the fortieth or fiftieth customer, he saw a face he recognized. It was one of the detectives. He was dressed in casual attire and trying to look disinterested. His stomach dropped and his gut wrenched. There would only be one reason for the detectives to be watching him after they already caught that moronic Deadpool and that was if they considered him a suspect. His mind began filling with ideas for how he might be able to get away. Leaving early at this point would basically be an admission of guilt, but if he could slip the detectives, he might be able to get to the airport and use his celebrity to get on an earlier flight. Calling ahead to do that would also be a red flag if they were watching him.

His face was a mask even though his heart was doing back flips. What a cruel twist of fate this would be if the NYPD was to suddenly become competent at the very moment he needed them to still be clueless. There had to be a reason they were sniffing around, and his mind wandered. His thoughts threatened to spin out of control even as he kept his smile and signed autographs for adoring fans. *What am I going to do? How am I going to get out of here?*

None of the other detectives were around, so it was possible they had split up to keep an eye on all of the suspects after they figured out the man they had arrested was not responsible for Garrison Williams death. Why had that happened so fast? A quick scan of the autograph area revealed a second detective over by Jasmine's table. Also, incognito and also feigning disinterest. He let out a breath he forgot he was holding. Maybe they were watching all of the suspects. They had nothing. Colin wasn't at the autograph tables yet, so the other two detectives were probably skulking around the photo op area where this whole nightmare had begun.

There was really no reason for him to be worried. He had made sure there would be no evidence leading to him. There was no murder weapon, no motive, and he had a solid alibi. No, these Keystone Cops were merely sniffing around. The convention would be over in six hours, and he would go home. A simple phone call would clear the air between him and Jimmy, and he would be back on track. It just might take him a little longer than he originally thought to join the ranks of the super-rich. No reason to panic.

"And what's your name, beautiful princess?" he said with a real smile to the little girl wearing pink fairy wings and a gold tiara.

Chapter 46

Jackson pulled up to the Javits Center and exited the car. He needed to have a quick chat with Sergeant McGinnis before he joined the other detectives inside. Several costumed young ladies held up what looked like protest signs in front of the convention center that read: **Cosplay Is Not Consent!** Once again, he shook his head at the thought that people needed to be told not to touch or harass someone just because they wore a revealing costume. Glancing around, he saw every kind of person he could think of. Every age, every ethnicity, every religion, every body shape and size, they were all represented in this celebration of pop culture and he got the appeal. Everyone belonged. Even if it didn't necessarily appeal to him. He knew this was a yearly highlight for a lot of people.

Through the crowd in front of the Javits Center, Raina, Jacob, and Amanda ambled towards him. Reflex had him reaching for his wallet. At this point, he might not be joking when he asked Diaz to buy his lunch. She wore a huge grin as the kids approached.

"You guys look so good, and I love Jacob's costume. That's a Green Lantern Wolverine mash up, right?" An enthusiastic shake of their heads told her she was right. "Maybe next year you guys could help me make a costume for Hector"

Raina's smile was so big he wanted to kiss his partner for putting it there. "We would love to. We could even help you out for Halloween if you don't have anything yet."

"I would love that, girls. If it's okay with your dad, I'll bring Hector by next weekend."

Jackson smiled at his daughter and niece. Their enthusiasm was contagious as they waited for his answer. He thought they were about to revert back to their "please, daddy" phase at any second, so he nodded his head and said, "If you girls are up for it, that would be fantastic." A smile floated through his mind as he remembered the thank you gift he ordered for her. He was sure she would want to start using that immediately.

"Thanks, dad," Raina said as she hugged him. Looking up at him with big hopeful eyes, she added, "I have a big favor to ask."

Pulling out his getting-lighter-by-the-second wallet, he said, "How much do you need?"

With her hands on her hips, she frowned at him. "Why do you always assume it's about money, dad?"

His eyes lit up in delight as he put his wallet away in a theatrical fashion. "Oh, it's not?"

She frowned again and Amanda started laughing. "Actually, it is, but that's not the point."

"So how much?"

With pleading hands and hopeful eyes, she said, "Fifty? I'll clean the kitchen every night for the next two weeks. It's a great deal."

Opening his wallet, all he had was four twenties. Handing her three of them, he said, "This is still part of your Sweet Sixteen present, sweetie. You don't have to do any extra chores." Holding up his last twenty, he laughed and said, "And I still have money for lunch, so it's a win-win."

Wrapping her arms around his waist, she squeezed tight and said, "Thank you, Dad."

He kissed her head and sent the kids on their way. Calling after them, he said, "You can pay me back by having a ton of fun today. I want to see pictures. Lots and lots of pictures."

"You spoil them a lot, don't you?" Diaz said with a grin tugging at her lips.

"She doesn't usually treat me like an ATM, I swear. I just think that she had no frame of reference to prepare for how expensive everything was going to be this weekend. Now that she knows, she'll have it down next year. She's a very good planner for this sort of thing. Plus, this is all she wanted for her Sweet Sixteen, even with all of the money I've forked over in the last three days. I'm coming out thousands ahead for not having the big party."

"Whatever you have to tell yourself," she replied with a chuckle as Sergeant McGinnis approached them.

"Julia, can you give us a minute?"

"Yeah, I'll go find Pete and Looch."

"Thanks." As he watched her go, McGinnis smiled at her and continued on towards him.

"How's the case going, Jackson?"

Whoever wrote about Irish eyes smiling must have had Molly McGinnis in mind. There wasn't a happier pair of eyes in the entire city. They both started walking towards the building, and the chill in the air was staring to border on cold. Digging his hands in his pockets, he quickened his pace. She was wearing a department issued uniform jacket, and looked to be warm.

"Case is just about wrapped up. We're only waiting on a warrant and some forensics before we make an arrest."

"That's great. Maybe Alvarez will cut you a break after this."

Stopping, he mustered up his serious face as he looked into her eyes and said, "About that. I wanted to say thank you for taking the blame for the Deadpool fiasco yesterday, Molly."

"It was my fault. Those were my guys and I couldn't get them under control. You sorted the whole mess with one growl into the radio. I wasn't about to let you get in trouble for it," she replied as her hand hit his arm.

"I get it, but please don't do that again." Seeing the wary look on her face he put his hands up and added, "I'm thankful you did. I'm not trying to be a macho jerk I swear. It's just that I already know Alvarez hates me, and he'll always find something to ream me a new one for, but I would hate to see you wind up on his radar. It's not a good place to be, and I like you enough that I don't want you to end up in his dog house. Do you know what I mean?"

"I get it, Jackson. And I appreciate the sentiment, but you don't have to try and protect me. My captain loves me, and she wouldn't put up with any of Alvarez' crap." With a wink she leaned in and whispered, "And for the record, you don't come off as a macho jerk."

"Point taken. I'd just hate to see you end up as a casualty in our never-ending battle. Anyway, I owe you a huge thank you and some drinks for taking care of Raina yesterday. D'Agostino, too. If I didn't love you enough already, you now have my undying gratitude and loyalty for taking such good care of my little girl."

Stepping closer to him, she rested her hand on his elbow and gazed into his eyes. "You know I'll always look out for Raina and Jacob and you'll never need to ask, but I won't say no to free drinks, and I don't think D'Agostino will either."

They reached the building and he held the door open for her. "Great! As long as no more famous people get murdered in our jurisdiction this week, let's plan for Friday at Murphy's."

"I'll be there, and I'll let D'Agostino know. I'm challenging you to a game of darts as well. No trying to get out of it," she said as she stepped into the Javits center with Jackson on her heels. As they continued towards the autograph area, she said, "Hey, do you mind if I bring Kari? Paul's done something that's got her all worked up. I think a night out with friends would be good for her."

"The more the merrier." He wondered if she knew what Kari suspected. Seeing her would be fine as long as they didn't end up back at his place. They had gone down that road a couple times too many, and it usually started with drinks.

"This is where I sign off. I have to check in with the lieutenant at the security office." With a shy wave, she was on her way.

Hoisting a wave, he said, "See you later, and thanks again. Knowing you're watching out for my kids really means a lot to me."

Diaz strolled up to him with a coy smile on her face. "That looked cozy."

Her comment floored him. He and Molly were friends, but cozy was not a word anyone had ever used to describe them. "That was normal."

"Please, I almost had to call the fire department there were so many sparks coming off that conversation."

"I think you're imagining things. You just need to get to know McGinnis better. What you saw was my gratitude for her keeping Raina safe yesterday."

"If you say so."

"Can we talk about something else? I don't know, maybe case related?"

"Fine, Peter thinks Jenkins is on to him, but Looch took up position near Connelly's table hoping to lull Jenkins into thinking we're keeping an eye on all suspects. When Colin Stone makes his way over to the Autograph area, one of us should probably position ourselves near his table." Her eyes said she wanted to do it, and he was fine with that.

"Okay, you can take that assignment. That'll free me up to..."

"Go talk to Sergeant McGinnis some more?"

"To get Rivera set up to move on Jenkins' room when the warrant comes through," he corrected with a frown.

"Right." She drew the length of the word out with a sneaky grin.

"Let it go, Julia."

Chapter 47

They shuffled through the convention center at a snail's pace. How anyone found this to be fun was beyond Jackson's ability to understand. Overall, he had warmed to the whole sci-fi convention idea, especially after seeing how much Raina and Amanda were enjoying themselves, but it would most definitely never be his cup of tea. A glance at Diaz made him smile. Her head was on a swivel, and he knew she would rather be attending this event than policing it. Maybe next year if they were still partners, she would want to go with the girls. At least then, he wouldn't have to worry about anyone messing with Raina or Amanda.

On their way to pretend to be staking out Colin Stone, Jackson knew he stuck out like a sore thumb among this crowd, although there had to be some sci-fi character somewhere who wore a regular suit. Maybe he'd grab some sunglasses from a vendor and go for a terminator vibe. He decided against it as most people would still smell cop on him from a mile away. It would be good for Jenkins to see him and Diaz staking out someone else anyway.

Diaz broke into his thoughts when she said, "Wait up a minute. I'm going to get a selfie in front of the Star Destroyer. Do you want to come?"

The last thing he needed was for the News or the Post or the Times to see him taking pictures with a twenty-foot toy, not to mention that he was against selfies on principle. "No. Thanks. I'm gonna stay here and try not to do anything that will give Alvarez a reason to chew me out again."

Snorting a laugh, she made sure no reporters were following them and made a dash for the giant decoration. Handing her phone out to a Rebel Pilot in his orange jumpsuit, she posed and the man took a few pictures. She flashed him a smile that probably made the guy's day and walked back over to him.

"I couldn't go the whole weekend without getting at least a couple pictures. You should have seen the pictures Peter and Richie scored from the after party. I'm not gonna lie, I was totally jealous. And don't tell Looch I said this, but he was rocking that Batman suit."

Laughing at her enthusiasm, he pointed to her camera. "You know it's not a selfie if someone else takes the photo, right?"

With an elbow to his gut, she said, "It's an expression, Jackson. Get with the times."

His phone buzzed and he answered, "What's up Pete?"

"We lost Jenkins. He disappeared behind the curtain of his booth. It's pretty common for the celebs to duck out for a minute or two, but he didn't come back. I think he knows we're on to him."

Casting a worried glance at his partner, he said, "You sure he's not just taking a lunch break?"

"Yeah. He still had almost a hundred people in line waiting to see him, and they're starting to get a little rowdy. I talked to his agent, and she told me he grabbed the folder full of money from the autographs before he ducked out. She said she turned her head and he was gone with the money and his backpack which held a change of clothes."

"Damn it! I was hoping the warrant would come through before we had to confront him. Okay, get Looch and start looking. I'll have McGinnis get all her guys looking as well. I'll make sure they know he's likely in street clothes at this point. We cannot allow Jenkins to leave the convention center and get back to his hotel."

"I'll ask the captain to send a couple officers over to the hotel. At this point, they are to detain Jenkins on sight for the murder of Garrison Williams," Diaz said as she pulled out her phone.

"Keep me posted, Pete."

"Sure thing, boss."

After ending the call, he glanced around the convention center floor and said, "Julia, you're more familiar with this event than I am. Where might Jenkins be able to go if he wasn't ready to leave the building?"

"There are usually a number of greenrooms for the celebrities to relax when they're not signing autographs, doing photo ops, or in a panel. We should try those first."

"Lead the way."

As they were hustling past the autograph area, he saw his daughter at Lisa Saranna's table again. They were both laughing and talking like they were old friends, and he wondered what they were up to.

192

Nudging his partner, he pointed to them and said, "What do you think that's about?"

A smile slid into place and she said, "I think Raina's playing matchmaker."

"That's what I was afraid of."

They stepped behind the curtain and had one of the convention volunteers lead them to the closest greenroom. Jenkins had enough cash to get out of the city, and he probably wasn't stupid enough to go back to his hotel. They had to catch him here. While they rushed through the much less crowded staff only areas of the center, his phone buzzed again.

"What's up, Cap?"

"Warrant came through and Rivera has found some plastic toys that match the serial number on the toy sword. Go make your arrest."

"We're trying. He gave Chang the slip. We believe he's still in the convention center, and McGinnis has her guys looking for him as well."

"Don't let him get out of that building, Winters."

"Doing our best, Cap."

After he ended the call, Diaz looked at him and said, "What's that smile for?"

"Captain Wilson called the replicas, *toys*, too."

"You're a mess."

Chapter 48

In the furthest greenroom from his autograph table, Jenkins stripped out of his Grimwolf costume and pulled a pair of faded blue skinny jeans out of his backpack. After donning a plain black tee, he laced up his shamrock green Nikes. With a grimace, he tugged out a shamrock green Grimwolf hoodie realizing it might not be the best choice for him to make a quick getaway in. Still, a lot of people at the convention would be sporting his merchandise, so he should still fit in. The cops were looking for a Nordic warrior, not jeans and a sweatshirt. A Fighting Irish hat completed the makeover. Placing the folder full of his autograph money into his backpack, he was ready to pay one last visit to his gaming booth and get out of Dodge.

Tossing his costume into a corner, he made his way to the door of the greenroom and peeked out into the corridor. No one seemed to notice him, and he slipped out into the light foot traffic. Slipping a pair of Ray Bans over his eyes, he made his way to the convention floor where he could blend in with thousands of convention goers. His gaming booth would have a few thousand dollars in cash, and he was going to need the extra money to avoid law enforcement and make it out of the city.

Right up until the point where the pretty Hispanic detective showed up in the autograph area, he had convinced himself that they had nothing, but even though she seemed to be watching Colin Stone, her gaze drifted to him often enough to make him wary. After the way she had reacted to his invitation for drinks, he knew she wasn't checking him out which meant that she had her eye on him because the cops must have something on him. He couldn't imagine what because he had been very careful, but the bottom line is, he's not a criminal and must have overlooked something important. As soon as she left the area, he had decided to make his move.

When he reached the Grimwolf gaming booth, his heart sank. Two of New York's finest had taken up residence right outside his corner booth. He had rented four spots to set up his store and could probably sneak in through the canvas wall behind the register, but he would need a diversion. Glancing around, thousands of people were walking in every direction. Maybe since he was in street clothes, he could just slip on in. No, that would be too risky. He needed to draw the police away. After another minute of searching, he figured out what he needed to do.

Jenkins strolled over to the Lego Star Destroyer located diagonally across from his booth. The placard boasted that the ship had been made with 2,112,037 Lego bricks and had taken close to twenty-eight days for three dozen people to assemble. Standing over twelve feet tall and twenty-one feet long, it was a masterful recreation of the dreaded Imperial ship. The sculpture lit up to make a fantastic centerpiece for the convention. Even the stands holding the ship in place were made from Lego bricks. The whole thing had to weigh a couple thousand pounds. He was sure that if he could somehow tip this thing over, several thousand bricks would break free and cause a big enough mess for him to be able to sneak into his booth.

It was now or never. The NYPD may not have had their best weekend here, but they had well over thirty thousand officers that would be on the lookout for him, so he had to get out of the city fast. Hopping the stanchion meant to keep convention goers from touching the ship, he heard several people yelling as he kicked out one of the Lego supports holding the sculpture in place. With his third powerful kick, he heard the support crack. By this time, a large crowd had formed and the cops outside his booth were on their way over to have a look. Another loud crack sounded as he took off and circled behind the back of his booth.

By the time he reached his register and flashed a smile at his cashier, a loud crash was followed by the clatter of thousands of Lego bricks bouncing across the Javits Center floor. While the cashier was distracted, he reached in and collected all his money and slipped out the back of the booth. Hundreds of people were trying to figure out what happened and the commotion reached uproar status. Glancing back, he saw that the ship had fallen at an angle reminiscent of the downed Star Destroyer on Jakku in one of the newer *Star Wars* movies.

The clamor spread throughout the building, and everyone was wondering what happened as the police were now trying to keep people away from what was left of the Lego sculpture. People scrambled to pick up the tiny bricks and pocket them as more police arrived to push the crowd further back. In his wildest dreams he couldn't have hoped for a better diversion. If only he could figure out a way to skirt the crowd and head out one of the unmanned doors. More police arrived as some people in the crowd began fighting over the plastic bricks. The mayhem was almost worth staying around to observe. If nothing else, this convention would go down in history thanks to him.

With his head down, he fought through the crowds. Everyone wanted to know what was going on by the Star Destroyer, but he was a pretty big guy, and the determination etched on his face moved some of the people out of his way. An unmanned door fifty meters away caught his attention. The police had left their post no doubt to deal with the mess he had made. Another minute or two and he would breathe the sweet air of freedom. A cab would get him to Grand Central within minutes, and he would be home free.

His hopes were dashed when he heard the words shouted, "There he is."

"NYPD, put the backpack down and get down on your knees!" another voice commanded.

People were now starting to look away from the Lego fiasco and turning their eyes on him. The cops weren't close enough to grab him so he took off. A man his size running full speed made people rush to get out of his way. One teen wasn't quick enough, so he lowered his shoulder and sent the kid flying. The cops were behind him, but he was getting closer to the door. He could still do this. Somehow, he was back over in the autograph area, but the only thing that mattered was that unmanned door.

Chapter 49

Jenkins had caused quite a mess, and it was time to take him down. Jackson was sure Alvarez would find a way to blame the demise of the Star Destroyer on him, but he didn't care. All that mattered was catching the killer. Jenkins was running past the autograph booths towards an unmanned door with several police on his heels, but he was starting to gain some distance on them. With the amount of people around, even tasers were off limits. He and Diaz were coming from another direction, and Jenkins didn't appear to see them. Crowds were gathered at the spectacle, and he needed to be careful.

A lane opened up and Jackson shot through it and blindsided Jenkins with a hard shoulder block. They both went flying into Lisa Saranna's autograph table, and the starlet was quick to jump out of the way. Phones were out, and he knew every second of this was going to be on the internet, so he had to be careful.

He scrambled to his feet and shouted, "Stay down, Jenkins. You're under arrest for the murder of Garrison Williams."

A gasp rose up through the crowd as they realized what was going on. Jenkins was back on his feet with the quickness of an athlete stalking towards Winters.

"Down on your knees," Diaz yelled as she pulled her taser.

Jenkins wasn't having it. "I'm gonna kick your ass, Winters," he growled as he took two quick steps and swung a hard over hand right.

Jackson dodged the punch and caught the outstretched arm between his shoulder and head as he picked up the celebrity and body slammed him to the floor. Jenkins scrambled to his feet and tackled Jackson trying to punch him as they rolled on the floor. Jackson sprang to his feet in time to avoid a sidekick from Jenkins. The celebrity launched into a series of martial arts moves complete with cries and grunts that were probably meant to intimidate him, and he wondered why none of the other cops were helping him out. With one look at all the phones filming the event, he had his answer.

By this time, the crowd had given them a wide berth creating a ring around the combatants. Even Diaz was no longer by his side, but she still had her taser out. Jenkins was still showing the crowd how much karate he knew, and Jackson waited until he landed from one of his ridiculous spin kicks before he speared the man. They hit the ground, and Jenkins took a swing at him that he blocked. He dropped a hard knee into Jenkins' gut and followed with two stiff right crosses to his eye that stunned him. Flipping him over onto his stomach, Jackson buried his knee into the small of Jenkins back and hurried to cuff him before he caused any more trouble.

"Stick to video games, tough guy. In real life we hit back."

Jenkins growled, but Jackson dragged him to his feet. "Steve Jenkins," he said far louder than was necessary, but he couldn't resist the dig on the unlikable suspect. "You are under arrest for the murder of Garrison Williams. You have the right to remain Silent…"

The crowd was starting to grow restless, and they were torn. On one hand, one of their heroes was being arrested, but on the other hand he might have killed another one of their heroes. A smattering of boos started working its way through the crowd, and Jackson thought he was going to have a situation on his hand. Things could go bad quick in New York.

Lisa Saranna stood on her table looked out over the crowd and yelled, "Thank you, Detective. Garrison Williams was a good man, and I hope you put this monster away for a long time." He nodded his thanks, and she returned a smoldering smile that almost made him forget where he was.

Just like that the crowd turned and began jeering Jenkins.

"Suck it, Grimwolf!" one teen yelled to the delight of the crowd.

"Your game blows!" another teen yelled.

Jenkins growled and lunged at the duo causing them to yelp and jump back, but Winters had a hold on his cuffs and yanked him back. Several people started laughing at the embarrassed teens, but the rest continued to pepper Jenkins with insults as the police cleared a path to the exit.

"Best con ever!" someone shouted from the crowd to a loud roar of applause.

"Have fun in prison, Jackass!" a Star Trek officer yelled.

"Don't drop the soap, Grimwolf," a robot jeered. At that comment, he could see the realization hit Jenkins face, and the man's head went down.

"Good job, Detective Winters!" an elderly man wearing an Old Guys Rule tee shirt yelled.

"You can cuff me anytime, Detective," a sultry Catwoman purred.

Diaz smiled at that last comment and stepped up next to him as he put Jenkins in the back of McGinnis squad car. She flashed him a wry grin and said, "Nice work, Winters."

"Thanks, Sergeant," he replied. He shut the door and banged on the roof. A moment later, she was on her way to the precinct.

As he stopped for a minute to stretch his back, Diaz said, "You okay, Jackson?"

He knew he was going to be sore, but his bravado got the best of him. "Yeah, that clown wasn't half as tough as he looks."

"I had no idea you could fight, especially after you got your ass kicked by a ninety-pound girl on Friday."

"Couldn't let me just have this moment, could you?" he said feigning annoyance.

Nudging him as they walked to their car, she said, "Wouldn't want your head to get too big, partner. As it is, you've got sparks flying with McGinnis, Lisa Saranna wants to make little Jacksons with you, and that Catwoman we just passed was ready to pounce on you NYPD takedown style."

There was nothing in that statement he agreed with except possibly the Catwoman part, but he let out a laugh and said, "Julia Diaz, I think I'm going to enjoy having you as a partner."

As they approached the Challenger, Bethany Hernandez stepped out in front of them with her cameraman on her heels. She was wearing a low-cut white blouse with a black pencil skirt and a red blazer that highlighted her black hair perfectly. "Detective Winters, how did you know Steve Jenkins was the murderer?"

"No comment."

"Does the D.A. plan to seek the death penalty?"

"Miss Hernandez," he said with his most sincere fake smile. "You know the NYPD is not at liberty to discuss ongoing investigations."

Batting thick dark eyelashes at him, she motioned for the cameraman to stop the recording. Leaning in so close, her breath tickled his neck as she whispered, "Isn't there anything you can tell me, Jackson?"

Pulling back just enough so it was no longer awkward, he smiled and said, "After all the trouble I got in over that Action Jackson headline? Seriously?"

Somehow, she managed to look penitent as she smiled. "I'm sorry about that. The movie reference was just too good to pass up."

A genuine laugh escaped his lips. He hadn't expected that reasoning. Smiling at the pretty reporter, he said, "I'll tell you what, and this is off the record. If the brass allows me to comment on the case, you'll get the exclusive."

The olive branch seemed to satisfy her. "That's all I ask. See you later, Jackson." With that she sauntered away.

As he started the car, his partner looked at him and said, "And don't even get me started on that one."

"Diaz!"

Chapter 50

Jackson was riding high as he stepped into the squad room with Diaz in stride. Even Chief Alvarez would have trouble finding enough cold water to ruin his good mood. There was no feeling in the world like catching a suspect, and a public takedown in front of the lovely Lisa Saranna didn't hurt either. He was pretty sure he still had her card. Maybe he would pull a move out of Lucco's playbook and give her a call.

"Ooh, you're trending," Diaz said with a laugh. "#ActionJackson. #NYPDtakedown. #Grimwolfgetsowned. The first video posted of you taking down Jenkins already has a couple hundred thousand hits."

She watched the video of the fight with an appraising nod. "Nice moves, Jackson. I feel safer just walking next to you"

"As well you should," he replied trying to keep a straight face.

Chang looked pensive as he sat down at his desk. Diaz was still watching video on her phone.

"Jackson, sorry I lost sight of Jenkins. I know that whole Star Destroyer mess could have been avoided if I'd been able to keep eyes on him," Chang said.

"Not your fault. There were too many places he could slip off to where we didn't have eyes. Besides, apparently #BestConEver is trending, so at the very least, this will be an unforgettable experience for the masses."

It looked as though a weight had been lifted from the diligent detective's shoulders. His phone rang and he picked it up. "Really? That's awesome... Yeah, Jackson's going to be elated... Okay, Rivera... Ooh, that's even better... Thanks, Rivera."

Looking at Chang he said, "So, what am I going to be elated about?"

Chang's smile told him it was going to be good. "Rivera's guy got into the phone. It is Williams' phone, and there is a string of angry texts and voicemails from none other than our good friend Steve Jenkins."

"I think I am elated."

"Please, you don't even know what elated means," Lucco said with a laugh.

Shaking his head, he said, "It means thrilled." Looking back to Chang, he asked, "So what's even better?"

"I told Rivera about that idea we had about possible plastic shavings before he processed Jenkins' room, and he found some in the carpet. Tests aren't back yet, but he's pretty sure they'll be a match because the belt and scabbard are part of the same set as the sword. And best of all," he said with a triumphant smile. "I have footage and pictures of the sword on display at Jenkins' booth on Thursday afternoon, and it had yet to be filed down."

Jackson's eyes lit up in anticipation. "I can't wait to interrogate this clown."

"You won't have to wait," Captain Wilson said. "His lawyer just got here, and you've got enough to put him away for a long time. Now why don't you go ruin his day?"

"That is an excellent suggestion, Captain. Julia, you ready?"

"Lead the way, Action Jackson."

He groaned and he heard a few chuckles. Looking over his partner was all smiles.

After holding the door for his partner, he stepped into the room holding a thick manila folder.

"Is that folder supposed to scare me? You got nothing and you know it."

Jenkins' lawyer, Jackson thought the man's name was Don Prescott reminded him to keep his mouth shut. The man was no Calvin Dodd, but no slouch either. He came with a reputation as a competent bulldog of a lawyer.

"Mr. Jenkins, not the ending to the weekend you were hoping for, huh?" Jackson said as he sat across from the suspect and his lawyer. He could feel eyes on him from the one-way window behind him, and wondered if it was just the captain or if Chief Alvarez had arrived.

"Do you have a question for my client or are you just here to gloat?" Prescott said with a hint of annoyance in his voice.

Jackson wondered if they actually had a course on how to talk down to people at law school. Not to be dissuaded, he replied, "Why can't it be both?"

Diaz snorted a laugh.

Prescott frowned and made like he was going to leave.

"Why did you kill Garrison Williams?" Jackson said as he leaned back in his metal chair. The florescent lights cast Jenkins' already troubled face further into gloom.

"I didn't kill Garrison Williams, and you can't prove that I did," Jenkins replied with as much indignation in his voice as possible.

"Do you have any evidence to back up your inquiry, or is this another pathetic NYPD fishing expedition?" Prescott said with an air of invulnerability.

"Evidence? I've got enough evidence to put Mr. Jenkins away twice."

"Maybe three times," Diaz said.

"Let's see it." The challenge was implied in the lawyer's eyes.

Taking out the top photo, he slid it across the desk and watched Jenkins' eye widen the slightest of fractions. He had to hand it to the man, he played it well. "We found the murder weapon— a replica Grimwolf broadsword— in a dumpster on Thirty-Eighth."

"And that implicates my client how?"

Jackson had to admit that Prescott had smarmy down to a science. He'd hate to go up against this guy in court if he didn't have a slam dunk. Setting out the next couple photos he waited for the lawyer to have a look at them.

"It implicates your client because there was a matching belt and scabbard in his room, and the serial numbers indicate they were all part of the same set of toys." He had to throw in the word toys just to rile Jenkins. "And I'm sure when the manufacturer opens up tomorrow morning; he will confirm the sale of the toys to a Mr. Steven Jenkins."

"Circumstantial. Someone could have stolen the murder weapon. Mr. Jenkins had it on display in his booth Thursday. Anyone with motive had access to that replica sword."

Jackson had been waiting for that argument, so he could stick the final nail in the coffin, although he doubted Prescott would give up that easily.

"It is possible someone could have stolen the toy sword, and I guess it's also possible that after they stole it from the Grimwolf gaming booth in the Jacob Javits Center, they then found out what hotel Mr. Jenkins was staying in, broke into his room, and filed the toy sword until the edge was far sharper than it was supposed to be as the plastic shavings in Mr. Jenkins room would suggest."

Hey laid the photo of the shavings along with before and after pictures of the sword down next to the others. "What do you have to say about that?"

"Now you're just wasting my time with wild theories. You don't have enough to hold my client on. Let's go, Steve."

Blocking the door, he flashed a knowing grin at the attorney, pointed to the chairs and said, "That's more than enough, and you know it. Your client isn't going anywhere for a long time. I know you're a busy guy, Mr. Prescott, but you're going to want to hear this."

Taking out another piece of paper from the folder, he started to read. "You're going to find out real soon that ignoring me is not in your best interest. If you don't call me back, I'm going to kick your ass into a coma. No one betrays me and gets away with it, Garrison. Do you hear me?"

"What is this?" Prescott said as Jenkins eyes were growing wider by the minute.

"This? Oh, this is a string of messages your client left on Mr. Williams' phone the night before he killed him. Here's my favorite. You better hope you don't run into me this weekend, you rat bastard. I promise it will not end well for you." Pausing for effect, he looked up and said, "Should I keep going?"

"No. We get the idea." Even in defeat, Prescott managed to sound superior.

"We also have evidence that Mr. Jenkins was leveraged past the point of no return and that Williams pulling out of the movie would ruin him financially, but we could not find any evidence of Garrison Williams ever signing a contract concerning the movie."

"Whoops, looks like someone got ahead of himself," Diaz said in a sing song voice.

"And, we have testimony from Jimmy Shultz after a fight they had in the Marriot last night. Diaz, what did Jimmy say again?"

"He said, and I quote: 'I've given up far too much of my life and soul for this movie. Garrison Williams' betrayal took everything from me, and now you're trying to steal my character. And according to Jimmy, he said it twice.'"

"His alibi is paper thin. No one at the gym remembers seeing him after seven-thirty which gives him ample time to commit the crime. He also had access to the convention floor while vendors were still setting up. That means he had motive, means, and opportunity, and he left a mountain of evidence."

Diaz jumped in and added, "He tried to flee the convention causing quite the disturbance in the process, so even if we did not have a slam dunk at this point, Mr. Jenkins isn't going anywhere. We've got him on causing a public disturbance, destruction of property, lying during an investigation, Assaulting Mr. Shultz, Assaulting my partner and resisting arrest. And given that he tried to run, I'm sure the D.A. will consider him a flight risk. Mr. Jenkins is not going anywhere for a long... long... time."

"So, I'll return to my original question," Jackson said. He slammed the table so hard with his hand that even Prescott jumped a little. "Why did you kill Garrison Williams?"

"It was an accident," Jenkins said, hanging his head in despair.

"Don't say another word," Prescott said, but he knew it was too late. Those four little words were all the D.A. would need. Twenty-five minutes later, they had a full confession and Prescott's only option was to try and get the best deal possible from D.A. Thomas.

Chapter 51

Jackson and Diaz were comparing case notes as they breezed towards the squad room. They were still riding high on getting a confession out of the unlikable Jenkins in spite of the smarmy lawyer's objections. The walk through the well-lit corridors was fairly short from interrogation, and they had a lot of notes to compare. Might as well keep all the ducks in a row and turn over the full picture in chronological order to D.A. Thomas. He was so into the moment and his conversation he almost missed the dark cloud getting ready to rain on his parade.

"What the hell is the matter with you, Winters?"

Chief Alvarez, voice rang out like a church bell in the middle of the night. People stopped short and turned away not wanting to be anywhere near the tongue-lashing Winters was about to receive. Diaz squirmed a little by his side, and he hoped she remained quiet to keep the chief's ire focused on him.

"You're a bull in a china shop without a lick of tact. At every point in this investigation you've either been insubordinate, negligent or just plain stupid. You'll be lucky if you can work security at the mall after I'm through with you. Do you have any idea how expensive that sculpture was? How could you let Jenkins destroy it?"

Winters was unsure it was his turn to speak yet. He usually waited for some prodding.

"Well? What do you have to say for yourself?"

There it is. "Sir, there were too many curtains the general public were not allowed behind that Jenkins could duck through. We didn't know he knew we were on to him."

"Oh, what you didn't know about this case could fill a book, Winters."

"That's not fair, sir. Conventions have a somewhat chaotic atmosphere to begin with. You can't possibly expect Detective Winters to have been able to contain every variable," Diaz said.

Glaring at her with contempt, he said, "You'll keep your mouth shut, Detective Diaz, or you'll be watching meters by seven in the morning. Do you understand me?"

That gave Jackson's hackles a rise. Alvarez was a bully and he needed to be knocked down a few pegs, but he kept his cool, almost. "You're right, sir. There was a lot we didn't know about, and since you apparently know everything, a heads up that Grimwolf was about to destroy the spaceship might have been nice."

Was it possible for smoke to shoot out of someone's ears? Jackson didn't think so until that moment. Diaz' eyes widened, and she looked like she wanted to be anywhere on planet earth besides right there because she was standing next to a sputtering volcano about to blow.

"What did you just say to me? You just got yourself busted down to patrol, Winters."

"Give it a rest, Alvarez. If you didn't piss on him every chance you got, you might realize he's actually a nice guy and a great detective," Commissioner Hansen said as he strolled up with Captain Wilson and Mayor Stetson in tow. Dressing down a chief in public was almost as hardcore as what Chief Alvarez did to him on a daily basis.

"Sir, he's insubordinate and needs to be reminded of the chain of command!"

"Enough. Maybe you need to be reminded of the chain of command. I heard the whole exchange. You were wrong from the start. He did great work this weekend, and instead of an attaboy, you're giving him grief in public with your outdoor voice. I'm surprised it took Winters as long to mouth off as it did. And to threaten Detective Diaz for no reason is just bad leadership. You should probably go cool down before you say anything else you'll regret tonight."

Jackson kept the smile off his face as they watched Chief Alvarez storm off. It might not be a good idea to gloat in front of the commissioner and the mayor. Fortunately, they were all smiles.

"That was some great work, Jackson," Mayor Stetson said. "Two high profile murders solved in two days, and a hug from Lisa Saranna," he said with a chuckle. "I'm glad you're back on duty."

"Thank you, Mr. Mayor. Captain Wilson has given me a stellar team."

Mayor Stetson smiled and said, "Good to see you're still a team guy and not a glory hound."

"It's not just lip service, sir. I couldn't have solved either case without them."

"And the hiccups?"

"All on me, sir."

His eyes lit up with mirth as he clapped his shoulder. "Ha, right answer. How are things? Mom and dad are still doing well down in Florida?"

"Yes, sir. Dad's been working on his golf game. His ultimate goal is to eventually beat you."

"Even with all year to practice, it's never gonna happen," Mayor Stetson said with a smile. "Tell Jacob he still owes me a bottle of Johnnie Walker Blue."

"I will, sir."

"Good to see you again, Jackson." He pulled him in for an embrace followed by a hard pat on the back. "We've got to figure out what we're going to tell the press. This is a big one. Commissioner Hansen is going to give the announcement, and Captain Wilson will be up there with him. There's room on the podium for one more."

"No. Thank you, sir. I'd rather go home and have dinner with my kids."

"Give Jacob and Raina my best as well. And do me a favor. Give Alvarez some space. He's been under a lot of pressure since the Hodges case, and Detective Boyd was his protégé."

"Yes, sir."

With that, they were off to tell the world they had caught Garrison Williams' killer. The commissioner, the mayor, and even Chief Alvarez could all expect to see their political stock climb as a result of his unit's hard work, and he was okay with that because that was the job.

When the brass was out of earshot, Diaz stood in front of him hands on hips and said, "When were you gonna tell me you were friends with the mayor?"

"He's more of an uncle really."

She smacked his arm.

"Ow. Okay, he and my dad were college roommates and have stayed friends. After school, my pop went into art, and Uncle Joe went into politics. They've had a lifelong golf battle going on which usually ends up with the mayor adding another bottle of Blue to his collection."

"You call the mayor Uncle Joe?"

"Not in public, and no one knows. I didn't even tell Captain Wilson for like the first three years of Stetson's first term. Everyone who knows about my family's friendship with the mayor was in that conversation, so please don't tell anyone."

"How come you never bring it up when Alvarez is all over you?"

"It's not a trump card. I'm hoping to settle things with Alvarez without going over his head. Sooner or later, he's gonna get tired of berating me and realize I'm a decent detective."

"I might need to request that transfer after all," she said with a laugh.

"What? Why?"

"Because when your reckless ass gets killed, I don't want to be the one the mayor blames for the death of his favorite nephew."

"I never said I was his favorite," he replied with a wink.

"Whatever, maybe I'll just send him the video of Harley Quinn kicking your ass," A mischievous smile lit up her tan face. She really was a looker.

"Julia, let it go."

"Yeah, that's not gonna happen."

"I can't wait 'til I have some dirt on you."

Chapter 52

Jackson took the mayor's words to heart, but the childish side of him was still happy the commissioner had reamed Chief Alvarez right in front of him. He had tried so hard to lock it down, but when the chief got on Diaz' case for no reason, he had no option but to use his weapon of choice. Sarcasm. Even as the words left his mouth, he knew he would pay for them in some way, but the universe, or karma, or God was with him, and the commissioner arrived at just the right time. Now he had another reason to be riding high.

After finishing and filing all of his paperwork, he said goodbye to the team. Tomorrow would be a light day since they had all worked long hours on their two days off. Truth be told, with all the extra money he had given Raina, Amanda, and Jacob this weekend, he could use the overtime, but he was tired, so easy day tomorrow and back to the grind on Tuesday.

Wearing a light jacket, it seemed as though the temperature had dropped as much as it was going to. The forecast for the morning was cloudy, but it was supposed to be ten degrees warmer than it was today. The Challenger merged into traffic, and he began his commute home. It was close to seven, and the kids should be home by the time he arrived. He couldn't wait to hear about their day. His musings were interrupted by his buzzing phone. Hitting the answer button on the steering wheel, he was a little tense as he said, "What's up, Martin?"

"Jackson, did you know you've been trending all afternoon? Nice takedown of that Grimwolf clown by the way."

Hitting his indicator to turn towards the bridge, he chuckled. "Thanks, brother."

"I just wanted to give you a call and let you know I think I've got the Koslov situation sorted. I spoke to Vince and demanded to see every document. I've been going through it all day, and all indications are that Koslov is trying to take his business legit."

His gut was roiling over Martin being mixed up with Koslov. "Trust me, he's not."

"Jax, listen. Not everything he does is going to be illegal. As long as I don't do anything illegal for him, or take any money from him, I've got nothing to worry about."

Was his best friend really this naïve? This is exactly how they come in and take over. They appear legit, and then coerce you into doing whatever they want. "Martin, I hope you know what you're doing. I really do, but even if everything they want you to do is on the level, the time will come when it won't be. When that time comes, if you refuse, they are not above threatening or hurting Amanda to ensure your compliance. I promise it's better for you to bow out now even if you lose money."

"Problem is if I do that, they can still use me as a patsy if they do go shady."

Day had turned to night, and the bridge was lit up as he approached, a beacon that could be seen for miles thanks to the lower heights of the buildings in Brooklyn. Jackson felt like he was fighting a losing battle with his friend and that his defeat would come back to haunt them. "Kill the deal then. Tell your boss what you think is going on and have him kill the deal. Do whatever you need to do to untangle yourself from Koslov. Trust me."

"No. That's the thing. I need to take the lead on this so that if Vince is willing to get his hands dirty so to speak, I won't be blindsided. I can keep everything aboveboard and I can have it all shut down if they become unreasonable."

"Martin, the Russian mob is always unreasonable, and Koslov is pretty high up the food chain. He's practically an oligarch. Just trust me on this. Pass it off to Vince. Take him out to dinner and tell him your schedule won't allow you to continue."

"He knows my schedule, Jax."

"Get Amanda into driver's ed. I don't know. I can't stress enough how dangerous the game you're playing is."

"I can handle it. It's all legit, and I wouldn't even have a legal leg to stand on to not do it. This is going to be fine, and I won't have any more contact with Koslov than is absolutely necessary. There will be nothing he sees in me that tells him I'd be willing to work with him on something less than legal. Look, I have to go. I just wanted to let you know that I'm not worried anymore. I stepped up and took care of what I was worried about."

"At least send me a thumb-drive with everything so that I can throw it in my safe for leverage in case things go bad."

"I'll think about it. I have to work through the legalities."

Jackson knew this wasn't the end of this problem, but he also knew his best friend well enough to know his mind was made up. "Okay, I hope it all works out for you."

"It will. And, Jax. Thanks."

The call ended, and he rode the rest of the way home in silence. Maybe he was just overreacting. Martin was right about one thing, not everything the Russian mob does is illegal. Martin seemed to think he was on the right side of it, and Martin knew finances a lot better than he did. If Martin didn't get him the info, he might have to go sniffing around on his own. He would do whatever it took to keep his friend safe.

Chapter 53

He finally pulled up to his Brooklyn Heights Co-op on Henry Street at seven twenty-six. His conversation with Martin had put a small damper on an otherwise incredible day, but it was about to pick up when he sat down to dinner with his excited children to hear all about their adventures at the convention. Raina's present should be here by the time she got home from school tomorrow, and he was really looking forward to seeing her reaction when she opened it, but for now, tales of their day would be enough.

Sitting in his car, he finally had the chance to watch one of the videos of his fight with Jenkins. A smile engulfed his face as he watched the idiot trying to do all of those martial arts moves when he couldn't even block a simple tackle. His favorite part was Jenkins face when someone yelled don't drop the soap. He wasn't usually given to excessive gloating, but something about Jenkins had rankled him from the start, so this was a fun one to go down.

Prostitution, blackmail, insurance fraud, and murder, it seemed like a lot more was happening at the Javits Center this weekend than just a Comic Expo. He hoped it wouldn't deter anyone from attending future events as the mass majority of the people were just there having fun like his kids. One thing was certain, if Diaz couldn't take the girls next year, he was going to make sure he was on site even if he had to binge watch Star Trek for a month before they went.

As he stepped out of his car, he noticed Martin's car pull up to his house. "What's up, dude? Why didn't you mention you were stopping by?"

"I didn't know. After we spoke, I got a call from Amanda to come over and pick her, Raina, and Jacob up. They want to go out to dinner, and they said you spent too much money on them already. By the way, do I owe you anything?"

Waving off the suggestion, he said, "No. It's fine. Amanda's family and I know you do the same for Raina."

He was a little bummed though because he had been looking forward to the stories and the excited faces, and now he was going to be eating leftovers alone. It was only fair, Martin hadn't seen his daughter all weekend, and he probably wanted to hear the stories too.

The front door swung open, and the girls and Jacob all ran out. "Dad, you have to see these pictures."

After nearly fifty pictures, the smile on Raina's face was contagious and he was over his little pity party.

"You're trending by the way," Amanda said. "Nice takedown. You were like totally freakin' beast mode, Uncle Jax."

Chuckling, he said, "Thanks, Amanda."

After a good fifteen minutes, the kids were loading into Martin's car. He said his goodbyes, and as he lumbered towards the house, Raina yelled out the car window, "We left a surprise for you inside dad. Thanks for being so cool with everything all weekend." She gave him a wave and they were on their way.

Smiling at his kids, he had no idea what kind of surprise they had in store for him, but he hoped it included food. Opening the front door, he noticed the lights were dim and he was immediately suspicious. He hung his coat on a hook by the door and stepped into the living room. The first thing that caught his eye was the candle light on the dining room table. The next thing that caught his eye was the woman pouring two glasses of wine. His mind flashed back to seeing his daughter talking with his favorite celebrity, and he did a double take. Lisa Saranna was standing in his dining room waiting to have a candlelight meal with him.

Drifting across the room, he saw her face by the light of the candles. She was stunning. A gentle kiss on the cheek greeted him as she said, "Don't be mad at the kids. I thought it might be a little more fun if we got to know each other alone."

"I suppose I can reconsider sending them to boarding school," he said with a laugh as she handed him a glass of wine.

"The girls ordered your favorite Chinese food from the Jade Monkey, and insisted they pay."

"That's what she needed the extra money for," he said with a shake of the head. "She was planning this all day, wasn't she?"

"I'll never tell," she said with a coy smile.

Jackson dished out a plate for each of them, and they talked over the best Chinese takeout in Brooklyn. A lot of flirting took place as they ate before moving to the couch in the living room. They sat close enough that he had a good idea of what she was thinking, but he was also enjoying the conversation so he thought he would let it happen organically.

"So, tell me about this upcoming role."

"It's a run of the mill crime drama except it will have a female lead. The way I read the script, she's basically a female version of you. Tough as nails, single parent, leads a homicide unit. I think she even has a Hispanic partner." She seemed happy to answer his questions even as she moved a little closer to him while she spoke.

His heart was beating a lot faster than normal. Sitting on a couch with the lights down low and drinking wine with your celebrity crush was not something that ever happened in the history of ever, to anyone. He was going to have to give Raina a really nice Christmas gift this year.

"So, you're going to play your character as if she's me?"

"Sort of. There's still a lot of differences with how a man reacts or a woman reacts to the same situation, but my character's more of a tomboy." She leaned across him to put her wine glass on the coffee table and lingered an extra beat as she smiled at him.

It was getting more and more difficult to continue talking when all he could think about was her lips. "I can't wait to see it. I loved Big Time. I thought the ninth season was really strong, and I was sad to see it go. I haven't watched TV since."

Her eye brows shot up. "Really?"

"I mean I watch sports on occasion, but I haven't watched any scripted shows." For a moment, he thought he had talked just a little too much.

"So, you never saw me in the Ultimate Quest?" she said with an air of disappointment. With a twinkle in her eye, she licked her lips and purred, "I wear very revealing outfits."

Yes, back on track. "I'm going to have to get my daughter's Netflix password and binge the Ultimate Quest then."

"I know you'll enjoy it," she said, resting her hand on his thigh.

Everything in him wanted to kiss her, and she was putting out a pretty strong vibe. A great day was about to get even better. Putting his glass of wine on the coffee table, he leaned closer and put his arm up on the back of the couch. In barely a whisper, he said, "So when would you have to begin spending time with me for your role?"

She was so close her lips tickled his ear. "I thought I should start my research right away. I think we may need to work very, very closely for the next several weeks."

As he tuned to face her, his lips brushed hers. He pulled her closer and tasted the sweet wine on her lips. His last thought before he lost himself to passion was: Best! Con! Ever!

Contact Ron
Email: ronfrancis32@hotmail.com
Facebook: https://www.facebook.com/ronfrancisauthor/
Twitter: @ronfrancis32

www.ingramcontent.com/pod-product-compliance
Lightning Source LLC
Chambersburg PA
CBHW060143130626
46556CB00006B/2478